THE POISON GARDEN

WOLFSBANE

4

JENNIFER ALLIS PROVOST

WOLFSBANE

Jennifer Allis Provost

Bellatrix Press

BELLATRIX PRESS

CONTENTS

Author's Note

Hello dear readers, and thank you for coming with me on Eli and Dan's fourth adventure. This story picks up immediately after the events from Thornapple; in fact, the first line features Eli answering Alex's rather charged question. In case you forgot what that question was, just look at Chapter One's title for a clue.

To recap the story so far, Eli and Dan beat Amir and his bone army, Eli was anointed as Mistress of Seers by her great-great-grandmother, Katherine Moore, and Eli and Dan are now official. They live together in Dan's adorable brick house, though Eli still spends a great deal of time at her grandmother's place on Essex Street. Eli's father, Alex, has also been staying in Gran's house, and has left off traveling the world to see if he can rekindle what he and Tessa once had. As for Tessa, she's sick of surprises, and wishes everyone would just say what they feel instead of being so polite all the time.

Eli became Mistress of Seers on her twenty-ninth birthday, which is exactly what Jemima Beauclaire had predicted. She and Dan have just returned to the present, and things are not as they left them. Flip the page, and you'll see why.

Happy reading!

Tessa Who?

I stared at my father, my heart a lump in my throat. "What do you mean, who? Tessa!"

He smiled and shook his head. "Sorry, Bug, I don't know who you mean."

One of the kids asked for more juice, and my father ushered her into the kitchen so he could refill her cup. We had a houseful of relatives I'd never met, and my father seemed to have forgotten the most important person in his life. I turned to Dan, and said, "We screwed up the time line."

He gave me a look. "Ya think?"

I narrowed my eyes at him. "Not helpful."

"Let's go upstairs and change, then we can try to sort this out," he said. "There. Was that helpful enough?"

I frowned but didn't argue, because for all of his snark it was helpful. I also wanted to get out of the seventeenth century dress I was wearing, and I'm sure Dan wanted to ditch the knee breeches and hose he had on. "Hopefully Dad hasn't given my room away to one of the rug rats," I muttered, and we went back up to the second floor. On the way upstairs evidence of my tiny cousins was everywhere in the form of toys, spilled snacks, and the kids themselves.

"For my entire life I've always been the youngest person in this house," I said as we sidestepped around a tricycle. "Now this place is practically a daycare."

"Where are the parents?" Dan asked. "Alex can't be the only adult here."

"Believe me, I have no answers."

We entered my old room at Gran's, and I breathed a sigh of relief when it was not only free of children, but also had our modern clothes lying right where we'd left them. I reached for my jeans, and spied something next to the bed. It was my old backpack, and sticking out of it was my laptop.

"How is this here?" I grabbed my backpack and withdrew my laptop. It was definitely my computer, with the same gnarly scratch over the back left corner, and faded cat stickers I'd gotten from the card shop. It had also blown up in my apartment a few weeks ago, along with almost everything else I owned.

"We definitely made some changes," I said, as I opened my laptop, and waited for it to power up.

"How much do you think has changed?" Dan asked as he pulled off his shirt.

"Hopefully, not a lot." I began unfastening the front of my dress. We'd just dealt with Amir and his bone army, and the last thing I needed was another crisis. "With any luck we can contain the fallout, and come up with a plan."

"As you say, Mistress of Seers."

I glanced over my shoulder, and tried not to laugh. Dan always changed by methodically removing his clothes from top to bottom, and then putting new clothes on in the same order. Right now he was only wearing his knee high hose, and he looked hilarious. "That's right, use my title."

He stood behind me and slid his arms around my waist. "What about Mrs. Lyons?"

"Big talk from a naked guy," I said, then my laptop beeped. I had a ton of notifications from my social media accounts.

"I guess a lot happened while we were gone." I closed the notifications, and went to the website.

"Probably birthday wishes," Dan said, then he kissed my neck and released me so he could finish getting dressed.

"Probably," I muttered, then I started scrolling through my notifications. He was right, they were mostly people wishing me a happy birthday. I noticed the photo icon was blinking, and clicked on it. There were hundreds of pictures of Dan and me, eating out, on vacation, and doing all sorts of couple things. However, none of those things had ever happened.

"Dan, check these out." I turned my laptop toward him, and watched his brow crease as he saw the pictures. "What is going on here?"

He tapped the screen. "This one says it was taken in Aruba two years ago." He glanced up at me. "I don't know if we can contain this fallout."

"We need backup. Tessa sized backup." As I said her name I realized what was missing from the pictures. Not only did I not remember any of these events, I didn't see any pictures of Tessa.

"Where is Tessa?" I withdrew my phone and opened my camera roll. I was confronted with more pictures of me and Dan, and not a single image of Tessa.

"It's like Tessa and I aren't even friends." I faced Dan. "How can that be?"

"I know how we can find out," he said. "Let's go to Tessa's and figure out what's happening. If anyone can make sense of this magical mumbo jumbo, it's Tess."

"Yeah." I scrolled through the pictures again, confirming I hadn't missed an image of her. There was nothing resembling my black haired best friend. "I just hope she's okay."

"Tessa's tough," Dan said as he pulled his shirt over his head. "If anyone can handle this, it's her."

As soon as Dan and I were dressed in our modern clothes we went back downstairs, dodging discarded toys the entire way. When we got down to the parlor, we found my father resting on the couch. Cousin patrol must have gone outside to play.

"You've gotten some more mail," he said, indicating a pile of envelopes on the coffee table. I picked up a few of them, and noticed the return addresses.

"These are all from the witch elders," I said.

"I'm sure they all want to make a good impression on the Mistress of Seers," my dad said with a smile. "They don't want to end up on your bad side by forgetting your birthday."

"Probably means no Hassan," Dan muttered, and I nodded. Maybe this timeline wasn't all bad. I kept sorting through envelopes, and noticed one from Ned Burroughs.

"How did Ned send me a card?" I wondered, then I spied Melinda Howe's name on a different envelope. I turned to my father, and asked, "Have any clan elders died recently?"

"Not that I know of," he replied.

"Not even Jacob Allwood?" I pressed.

"You would have sensed it if anything happened to them," he said. "When such a powerful spirit moves on it creates many ripples."

"Ripples," I repeated, then I turned to Dan. "People who are supposed to be dead are alive."

Dan stared at me for a moment, then he took out his phone and started typing. Figuring he was searching for more witches, I turned back to my father, and said, "Dad, I think something happened to the timeline. Something big."

"I was afraid of this," he said; he had warned us—several times—to have as little impact on the past as possible, otherwise our time travel could have far-reaching consequences. Seems like we'd failed that mission. "Do you have any memories that seem new, or wrong? As if they were recently placed in your mind?"

I opened my mouth to say no, then I thought about all the pictures of Dan and me that showed we'd been a couple for years, and realized I had a few memories to match. "Kind of? They're like a television show I watched a long time ago. The memories are fuzzy, but they're there."

"The best thing we can do is figure out how far back those memories go, and try to reconstruct the timeline from then on to the present. I'll get something to write with." My dad went to find some pencils, or maybe steal a few crayons from the kids. I turned to Dan, who was sitting in the armchair with tears streaming down his face.

"Hey." I sat on the arm of the chair, and rested the side of my head against his. For all that he'd seen as a police officer, he'd never grown a thick skin. His empathy was one of the things I loved most about him. "Did you find more stuff that's not the same?"

"It's the same. She's still gone." Dan tilted his phone toward me, and I almost choked. He'd looked up Charlotte's obituary, and now he was weeping over his wife who'd died more than five years ago.

"She was who you searched for?" I asked. "After all we've been through, after everything you said and pledged to me, you find out the timeline's different and the first thing you do is check to see if Charlotte is still here?"

"I had to know," he said. "What if she was?"

"Yeah, what if?" I stood up and glared at him. "Would that mean we were over?"

"Eli, I had to know if my wife was alive."

I gasped. "I thought I was your wife." My hands were shaking, so I crossed my arms over my stomach. "What am I, second best? An afterthought?"

"Eli, baby, no." Dan reached for me, but I evaded him. "What if Charlotte was alive? I couldn't bring you home if my wife was in the house!"

That was the second time he called Charlotte his wife, present tense. Add to that the tears streaming down his cheeks, and my heart fell.

At Katherine's house, three hundred years in the past, I'd made the biggest mistake of my life.

"Leave," I ground out. "I don't want to see you."

"Eli," Dan began, then my father reentered the room.

"Is everything all right?" he asked, glancing between us.

"Everything's fine," I said. "Dan was just leaving."

"Eli, we need to talk about this," Dan said, but I shook my head.

"Go home to your wife," I snapped.

"You are my wife," Dan yelled back.

"Did you two get married?" my dad asked.

"No," I replied, glaring at Dan as I challenged him to refute me. We'd gone through with the handfasting, but little Elizabeth had wanted to sleep with me and Dan that night. We'd agreed, since it also meant giving Katherine and Montgomery some much needed alone time before the new baby came. Elizabeth snuggled between Dan and me meant there had been no consummation, and that was the final requirement for a handfasting.

"That's a technicality," Dan said, understanding where my mind was headed.

"It's the truth," I shot back. "I don't want to be your replacement for her."

"You're not," Dan insisted, then my father stepped between us.

"Dan, Eli has asked you to leave," he said quietly. "I don't know what happened between the two of you, but perhaps it's best you go."

"Alex, this is a bunch of magical bullshit screwing with us," Dan said, but my father was unmoved.

"Magic isn't bullshit," Dad said. "Everything happens for a reason. If this timeline is different than it was before you traveled through it, the changes are here to teach us something."

Dan frowned, then his gaze found mine. "Eli," he began.

"No," I said, holding up my hand. "I'm upset, and angry, and I don't want to say something I'll regret and make everything worse." A hot tear rolled down my cheek. "Please. Just go."

Dan watched me for a moment, then he turned on his heel and left. I, a grown woman and the most powerful seer in the world, fell into my father's arms and sobbed like a baby.

Never Lived There... Or There

After I'd gotten myself under control, and promised my father we would talk about what happened with me and Dan as soon as I was ready, I went back up to my room. The urge to pull the covers over my head and cry was strong, but I couldn't wallow just yet. This timeline was wrong, and I had to figure out how to fix it.

I had to figure out if Dan really loved me, or if I was nothing but a placeholder in his heart.

A sob bubbled up from my throat. I gave myself a moment to experience and acknowledge my emotions, then I dragged the back of my hand across my cheek and opened my laptop. I had a case to solve, and my feelings would have to wait.

Speaking of cases, I went to open my Nine Lives Investigations folder... but it wasn't there. I searched through each and every dusty corner of my hard drive, followed by my email, and then my cloud storage, but there wasn't a single document referencing my business. Even worse, I couldn't find any evidence that I'd ever been a licensed private investigator at all.

I grabbed my keychain from my bag, and saw keys for Gran's house and Dan's place. No apartment key. On a hunch, I ran an address history on myself, and learned that I'd lived in exactly two places. There was no record of my downtown apartment.

"Two years of my life is gone," I muttered, then I remembered the apartment Tessa and I had shared in Paris. That place wasn't listed on my address history, either. "Make that four years."

I got up and paced around my room, searching for evidence of my time in Paris, or at my apartment, or anything that would make me feel like I wasn't losing my mind. There wasn't much in my room, which would make sense if this version of me had been living with Dan for the past few years. All of my stuff must be at his place... or was it our place?

What if Charlotte had never lived there?

I banished that thought from my mind. I could not, would not go there, and I made myself a mental rule to not search for any information on Charlotte. Nothing good would come of going down that rabbit hole. After I'd clamped down on my curiosity, my mind wandered toward memories of my grandmother. She'd been the Matriarch of Seers, a title that was a level above mine on account of how long she'd held the position. Witches, seers, and the occasional mortal had crossed countries and oceans to ask for her advice, or beg for her help. She'd been a legend among seers and witches alike, but more than that, she was my Gran. I'd gone to her for everything, and she was my rock. Without her, I don't know what would have become of me.

She'd passed a few years ago, and I'd summoned her spirit a few times since then. Not as many times as my father had, but a few. I could summon her now, and ask her what I could do to fix the timeline.

I closed my eyes and cleared my mind, but instead of the calm that normally accompanies meditation, I was assaulted with memories of Dan and me on vacation. We were hiking up the side of a volcano, and the guide was speaking Italian... Were we hiking up Mount Etna? Was this our first vacation together? If I summoned Gran's spirit, would she be trapped in a timeline that wasn't real?

My eyes snapped open, and I stood and shook out my hands. I had no idea what would happen if I summoned a spirit to this alternate timeline, and I didn't want to risk harming anyone to find out. That meant asking Prudence, my best ghostly friend, for help was also out the window. Add to that my father being busy with babysitting duty, and I was on my own.

Or was I? Those memories had shown me a place in Italy, or at least a place where Italian was spoken. Back when Tessa had gone by her full name, Contessa Isabella della Scala, she'd been born into royalty, and after her second husband had died, she'd overseen a large portion of Italy. Maybe that memory of hiking up Mount Etna had been tinged with foresight, and my instincts were telling me to visit Tessa. Historically, my foresight had never served me well, and I tended to ignore it. Things had changed since I coughed up a cursed thornapple seedpod, and my foresight had become useful more often than not.

I needed answers, and only my foresight was talking. That meant I needed to listen. I grabbed my bag and my keys, told my dad I would be back soon, and headed out.

The first thing I leaned upon exiting Gran's house was that I had the same car. That was good, since I liked my car. Why this timeline chose to keep my car and not my apartment was a mystery, but I could hold off on solving that one for the time being.

The next thing I learned was that the town appeared to be the same old town, which was good, since it meant I knew my way around. If the new timeline only affected those close to me, it would be easier to contain. I hoped. When I pulled up to the luxury condo complex that house Tessa's penthouse, I grinned. If anyone could fix this mess, it was Tessa.

I rode the elevator up to the top floor, and knocked on Tessa's door. A wild-eyed and disheveled Tessa flung it open a few moments later.

"Eli," she said, then she threw her arms around me. "Gods below, I think I'm going mad."

Nothing But A New Case To Crack

Today had gone from amazing to awful at the speed of light.

I'd woken up with sunlight streaming onto my face, in a warm bed with my new wife and Katherine's daughter, Elizabeth, wedged between us. We'd gone through with the handfasting, and after Monty tied our hands together and said a few words, it was done. Eli was mine and I was hers, and nothing would ever change that.

There had been a celebration afterwards, with wine and food and dancing. Elizabeth, trooper that she was, stuck it out until the end, then she begged to stay with me and Eli that night. As I laid in bed while the other two slept I wondered if this was a hint of what our lives would be like in a few years: me and Eli and a houseful of kids. My dream of The Lyons Family Estate was finally coming together.

Then we came home, and everything went to shit.

As soon as we realized that the timeline was affected, we ceased acting like newlyweds and fell into detective mode... And then Eli figured out that people who were supposed to be dead were somehow alive again. Alive and well, as indicated by the pile of birthday cards she'd gotten from witches we knew for a fact were deceased. That meant I had to search for Charlotte sooner rather than later. What if Charlotte was no longer dead, but waiting for me at home? If Eli and I waltzed into our house and got blindsided by Charlotte being there, that would have crushed all of us.

But Charlotte was still dead, and I handled everything so badly I made Eli hate me.

I pulled into my driveway, and laid my forehead against the steering wheel as the tears fell again. Here I am, Danny Lyons, a complete and utter failure.

"It's okay if I fail myself," I muttered. "I can't fail Eli."

I got out of the truck and slammed the door so hard the body shook. That's right, I couldn't fail Eli. She needed me, and while she was pissed right now, she wouldn't stay mad forever. This broken timeline was nothing but a new case for us to crack, and I'm the best detective in the department. I'll start working things from my end, and soon—maybe even later today—I'll have some facts to present to Eli. A plan to fix things, starting with whatever had gone wrong with the timeline. And once she's talking to me again, I would fix our relationship. I owed her nothing less.

Divergent Timelines, Divergent Memories

I brought Tessa inside, and had her sit on the couch. As soon as she was comfortable, I went into the kitchen to get her something to drink, all the while silently freaking out. Tessa was never disheveled or wild-eyed. She always had a handle on the situation, no matter what the situation was, and while she had a temper, she never let herself lose control. For a witch as old and as powerful as Tessa, losing control could be deadly. Just compare a list of earthquake-prone regions of Italy to her former residences, and you'd have all the proof you needed.

I grabbed one of the bottles of fancy mineral water from the fridge and joined Tessa in the living room. She accepted the water, but she didn't drink it. After she stared at the bottle for a few minutes, she said, "Until I opened that door, I wasn't sure if you were real."

"Does that mean you forgot about me?"

"No. It means I remember an Eli that doesn't seem to exist." She leaned back against the couch. "Remember the time we spent in Paris?"

I nodded. "Of course I do."

"I remember it, too—only, I also remember living here during that time," she said. "My memories of Helena seem unchanged, but they diverge once you come along."

"Diverge how?"

"In one set, you grow up to be one of the dearest friends I've ever had. In the other set, I know you as Helena's granddaughter, nothing more."

I swallowed, unprepared for how Tessa's partial forgetting of me squeezed my already bruised heart. "What about my father, Alexander?" I asked; he and Tessa had an epic on-again, off-again love affair, and they'd recently reconciled. "What do you remember about him?"

"About Alex? I—" Tessa covered her face with her hands. "Oh, Alex. We aren't together in this now, are we? We hardly know each other."

I sat next to Tessa, and hugged her. "I don't know what's going on," I said. "Do you remember how Dan and I went through the nexus so Katherine could anoint me? When we came back, everything was different. Well, not everything, but a lot of important things aren't the way we left them. I think whatever we did in the past created a second timeline."

Tessa nodded, then she wiped her face and regarded me. "Which timeline is real?"

"The other one," I said, bewildered because how could she not know that?

"Are you certain?" she pressed. "Both sets of my memories are equally strong."

"But you were happy when you opened the door and saw me," I said. "Doesn't that mean we were friends?"

"I suppose. I have been wondering why I suddenly decided I was close with the Mistress of Seers. It's not like you associate with many witches." Tessa tilted her head to the side. "Or do you?"

"I did," I said, then I realized what she'd said. "Who's the head of the Beauclaire clan?"

"Nathaniel and his wife, Jemima," she replied.

"Jemima's alive?" I picked up the bottle of mineral water and let the sensation of the cool glass against my hands center me. "I watched her die in the seventeenth century. Wait—if she's alive, does that mean I was never kidnapped?"

Tessa's eyes widened. "You weren't, not in this timeline. Eli, we need to know who created this reality."

"Someone created this?" I looked around Tessa's condo, which was identical to the one I'd been in so many times, save for my confused friend. "Why would anyone even attempt making a new reality?"

"Someone or something made this mess, either accidentally or on purpose," she said, with a familiar resolve sparking in her eyes. "The question is why."

"What we need to do is determine who is benefitting from these time changes," Tessa said, after we'd relocated to the kitchen and made a pot of tea. She'd pulled herself together, and was once again the fearless witch I knew and loved.

"Okay," I said, since I was always ready to help. "How do we do that?"

"We could start by making a list."

I pulled my laptop out of my bag, turned it on, and opened up a blank document. "Are we sure that this situation is about making someone's life better? What if this is about revenge?"

Tessa paused. "How so?"

"What if someone was trying to work a revenge spell, for lack of a better term, and us traveling through the nexus inadvertently gave it some extra oomph?" I drummed my fingers on the coffee table. "We could just be seeing the collateral damage."

"That's a very good point. We shouldn't assume that any of this is tied to you or I. What does Dan think about this secondary timeline?" When all I did was stare at my blank screen, Tessa asked, "Eli, you're with Dan in this timeline, correct?"

"If I told you I wasn't, would you believe me?"

"No, I would not." She reached across the table and took my hand. That had always been our safe space—whenever we held hands, we could tell each other anything without embarrassment or judgement.

"You love Dan as much as ever. I can see it in your eyes. Tell me what happened."

I blew out a breath, and began, "When we came back from the past, we figured out pretty quickly that things had changed. Once we realized that some people who are dead in the real timeline are alive in this one—"

"What?" Tessa squeaked. "How many people are living, yet dead?"

"At least four that I know of," I replied. "Anyway, once Dan realized this, he dropped everything and searched for his first wife that died years ago, long before we ever met. When he found out she was still dead, he sat there with tears streaming down his face." I dashed the back of my hand across my cheek. "I get why he searched for her, but after everything that happened with us in the past, and how he's still so obviously not over Charlotte, I wonder if both of us should just move on from each other."

"Eli, it's not like you to give up so easily," Tessa said. "You and Dan share a connection in both timelines. Isn't that worth fighting for?"

"Yeah. I guess. It just hurt so much when she was the first person he thought of. Just once, I'd like to be put first." I grabbed a tissue and blew my nose. "I must sound like a spoiled brat."

"You don't. You're only expressing how you feel. Emotions are never wrong. What happened between you two in the past?" she asked, because of course she'd zeroed in on that fact.

"We, um, we had a handfasting ceremony."

Tessa's brows shot up her head. "Then you've committed yourselves to one another, which is all the more reason for you to not give up on Dan, at least not this quickly."

"It's not that I want to give up on him. I just want some space." I glanced at Tessa. "Is space a bad thing?"

She scoffed. "You're asking the wrong person. I've regularly spent decades away from my loved ones."

"But they always took you back."

"Yes. They've always taken me back." She squeezed my hand, and said, "If you want a witch's advice, here it is. If you need time and space away from Dan, both of those are your right. However, know why you want to be away from him. Don't ignore him out of spite, and don't punish yourself because you think you don't deserve love. Remember that Dan needs you, too. Both of you deserve a fully committed partner."

"You're right. I'll talk to him. Just not today."

Tessa smiled. "I'm sure tomorrow will be fine."

I wasn't so sure I wanted to talk to him tomorrow, either, but I kept that to myself. "Before you started psychoanalyzing me, you said we should make a list of who is benefitting from this alternate timeline."

"Yes, well. The obvious ones benefitting are those who were dead, and are now alive."

I typed out the names Jacob Allwood, Ned Burroughs, Melinda Howe, and Jemima Beauclaire. "Possible coincidence, but the four dead yet not dead souls are all witches."

"That is interesting, and I'm betting it's not a coincidence. We're certain they're actually alive, and not four robust spirits?"

I shrugged. "I haven't been near any of them in this reality, so I don't have first-hand knowledge. You said Jemima is alive, and when I asked Dad, he said the other three are alive." Tessa dropped her gaze, her hands fidgeting in her lap. "You really miss him, don't you?"

"I do," she replied. "Alex not being here was the first anomaly I noticed, but half of my mind couldn't understand why I'd suddenly become fixated on a man I hardly knew. The other half just wants him to hold me."

I understood exactly how she felt, since my own heart ached for Dan, yet I also wanted to smack him. Not that I would ever resort to violence or hurt Dan in any way, but I had imagined it a few times. "You two were pretty close again before all this happened, huh?"

"We were. We were as close as we were when I took that trip to Europe a few years before you were born. I was only supposed to be gone for a month, but my clan's business was a mess, and… and it's easy to lose track of time when you're as old as I am." She sighed. "I never should have been gone for so long. I should have made time for Alex, but I took for granted that he would always be waiting for me. Of course, had I been a better partner to him, he never would have had you."

"In that case, I'm glad you took an extended vacation. However, he needs you, too," I said, and I told her about the legions of children he was watching.

"I don't even know if he's the marksman in this reality," I concluded.

"I'm not sure, either," she replied. "Perhaps Alex not taking on that title is also benefitting someone."

"Maybe." I looked at the four names on my screen, all of them belonging to people who should be dead, but weren't. "What if there are other deceased people who aren't dead anymore, or at least appearing to be not dead?"

"How would we find out such a thing?"

"Let's take a walk around town. I want to find some ghosts to talk to."

WE'RE MISSING SOME DETAILS

Since Tessa's condo was in the center of town, it was a simple affair to go downstairs and begin our walk. I quickly learned that while everything had seemed normal while I was driving from Gran's house to Tessa's place, on closer inspection, many things were different. They were poor facsimiles of the real thing.

"It's like we're on a movie set," I murmured. "All the big pieces are here, but the details are missing." I stopped in front of the newsstand. Whereas it usually carried dozens of different newspapers and magazines for sale, today there were only stacks of the regular town paper.

"This is different," Tessa said. She was standing in front of a restaurant called Valley Burger. I'd never been there, but I didn't eat out very much, so that wasn't unusual.

"What's different about it?" I stepped closer to the restaurant, and read the menu displayed in the front window. It never ceased to amaze me what people would do to the humble burger just to make their establishment stand out. This menu featured a burger that used grilled cheese sandwiches as buns.

"I've worked magic here, but it was closed at the time," she replied. "You were with me."

"I was?" I took another look at the sign, then I spied the alley that led to the parking area around back.

"When we were here, it was a Chinese restaurant called Dim Sum Delight," I said, as the clues fell into place. "We were tracking Nathaniel Beauclaire." My voice caught, so I cleared my throat. The day after Tess and I had been to Dim Sum Delight, Dan had been called here on a case. He'd reached out to me for assistance, which led to Dan taking me back to his place so we could go over a few files he'd put together. He ended up getting possessed, then we found ourselves in the shower together, and I ended up exorcising a demon. That incident was the start of our romantic relationship. No wonder we crashed and burned.

His case at Dim Sum Delight was also how we met the Ghost Guys, a group of lame paranormal investigators that were actually Amir Hassan's lackeys. And we all knew how Amir loved messing with time.

"Does Amir Hassan exist in this timeline?" I asked.

Tessa bit her lip, thought for a minute. "Not in the way he does in the other one," she replied. "As for this reality, I recall hearing about the incident with the Iranian coven, when he opened the forbidden time portal. I haven't heard anything about him since then."

"So, he didn't challenge me for the leadership of the seers?" I pressed.

"No. Why would he?" Tessa asked, then her eyes widened. "Your mother. I'm not sure if anyone in this time knows she's witchborn. I've certainly never heard it mentioned, and no one questioned you when you became Mistress of Seers."

I nodded. "At least I can stop trying to prove I'm worthy to be Mistress. That's one less thing to worry about."

"No one's more worthy than you," Tessa said. "About your mother. Is Alex... Are your parents together, now?"

I opened my mouth to say no, then realized that I really didn't know the answer to that. "She wasn't at the house earlier," I replied. "All these other people were there for my birthday, but not her."

"Then we can assume Christina is one of the few constants between timelines."

"Yeah, she's just as bad a parent as she's always been." I swept my gaze up and down the street, and remembered there were other places that had been scarred by Amir's magic. "Let's take a look at my apartment building."

"You're not thinking of renting a place to avoid Dan, are you?" Tessa asked.

"No." I could avoid him quite well by hiding out at Gran's house. "But in the other timeline, Amir destroyed my apartment. I want to see what it looks like here. Now," I amended.

We walked the few blocks to my old building, but no amount of time or distance could have prepared me for the sight of it. Not only was the building undamaged, it was in perfect condition, and based on the curtains and plants and other items I could see in the windows, people were living in it.

People appeared to be living in my apartment, too.

"How is this possible?" I murmured. A few weeks ago, the entire upper corner of my building had quite literally blown to bits. The explosion had damaged nearby structures and thrown everything within a three-block radius into chaos. Now, it was a regular Thursday.

"Even the coffee shop's intact." I peered into the front window, and took a step back. Inside the shop was Renato Florian, a grad student from Braerton College I'd dated briefly back when I first opened Nine Lives Investigations. Once I found out he majored in paranormal studies and was only interested in me for my seer abilities, I ghosted him. I wonder if he'd ever gotten the joke.

"Not in the mood for coffee?" Tessa asked.

"Not in the mood to deal with certain people," I replied, then something caught my eye. "Look at this." The corner of the building was fading in and out of view. In other words, it was glitching, like an old television set that didn't have a good signal. "This wall was destroyed in the other timeline."

"And in this one, it's not really present." Tessa extended her hand toward the wall, then snatched it away as if she'd been burned. "It feels like static electricity. What does this mean for those who are suddenly alive again? Are they fading in and out of existence as well?"

"I don't know. But I can tell you that I haven't felt a single spirit or other entity since I entered this timeline, and that's just weird."

"None at all? How did the guardians appear to you?"

I blinked, and realized who else had been missing from Gran's house: the Feline Federation. To the supernatural community, they were the guardians of the nexus, but to me they were three cats named Smokey, Pumpkin, and Muffuletta. "I didn't see them," I replied. "I thought maybe the cats were hiding from my cousins, but it's not like them to avoid people. You don't think something happened to them, do you?"

"I don't know of anything that could harm them." Tessa tapped her chin. "In fact, I don't remember ever seeing the cats in this timeline. Perhaps beings such as them cannot be replicated?"

"If that's the case, that's further proof that this is the wrong timeline." I passed my hand through the glitching edge of the building. It felt tingly, like when I sat wrong and my foot fell asleep. "It makes sense why there aren't any spirits here. You can't replicate a soul, either." My foresight sparked, letting me know I was on the right track. "What else can't be replicated?"

"I don't know, diamonds?" Tessa began with a shrug, then she paused. "Bennet Carrington's records. All shepherds magically seal their records, and no one outside of their guild knows the spell to unlock them."

"I think it's time we paid the shepherd a visit."

An Abundance Of Moores

It only took us about ten minutes to walk back to Tessa's condo, where a courier was waiting for her in the lobby. The Beauclaire clan had sent over some work for Tessa to handle, and, since the last thing I wanted to do was interfere in her family's business, I told her I didn't mind waiting until the next day to see Bennet. Besides, it was already late, I'd had a hell of an awful day, and I really needed to gather my thoughts. While Tessa worked, I ordered dinner for us and took her up on her offer to stay in her guest room.

When I woke the next morning, I rolled over and smiled... but Dan wasn't beside me. I squeezed my eyes shut, and resigned myself to the fact I was still in the alternate timeline. Why couldn't everything that happened yesterday been a dream, like in a movie or one of those bad soap operas my mother used to watch? I didn't want to be stuck in this alternate version of my life with no spirits, no long-standing friendship with Tessa, and no Dan. Gods, but I missed him. I wasn't even that mad at him, not any longer, but I was hurt. After everything we'd been through both in the present and the past, when I saw him crying over a woman who'd died years before he met me my heart had shattered, and instead of telling him how I felt I lashed out at him in the worst way possible.

And now he was gone, and I was here with my best friend who was only my friend in half of the timelines I'd visited, and I was the Mistress of Seers in a place with no spirits. What was my purpose, if there were no spirits here for me to help? Seers hold the line between life and death, but in this reality there was no line.

No line, no partner, and no purpose. Maybe I should just go back to sleep.

Since wallowing in my problems would accomplish exactly nothing, I got myself ready and joined Tessa in the kitchen. She was sitting at the table with her laptop open, and still working on that clan business.

"Did you sleep?" I asked.

"I did. However, the courier will return at eight to take this back to the estate, and I wanted to check my work."

I didn't remember Tess ever working on clan business matters, but then again she'd been all but excommunicated after she rescued me from the Beauclaire's torture room slash basement where my kidnappers had stashed me when I was seventeen. Maybe this was the sort of work she would have been doing all along, if my abduction hadn't mucked up her life. "What sort of work is it? Can I help?"

"It's just finances, and it's fairly simple. Thank you for the offer, though." She typed in a few more commands, then the printer whirred to life. "All these witches who are too proud to embrace modern life don't know how to use spreadsheets. Some wonder if I've unlocked a new form of magic."

"Or torment," I said, remembering the first year accounting class I'd taken.

She winked at me. "Perhaps I enjoy tormenting them."

After the courier arrived to collect Tessa's completed work, we drove to Bennet's house. He was our local shepherd, which meant that he was responsible for keeping meticulous records regarding the supernatural community: births, deaths, feuds, alliances, and more fell under his purview. Unfortunately, his position didn't involve herding sheep, which was too bad. Lambs were awfully cute.

While we were driving, I'd asked Tessa to call Bennet and ask if he had time to see us. Tessa practically laughed in my face.

"Eli, you're the Mistress of Seers," she said. "If you go to his house, Bennet has to admit you. In fact, if you go to any house in the supernatural community, no one will deny you entrance."

"Really? Am I like that here? Stomping into people's homes and putting my feet up on the furniture?"

She shook her head. "As far as I know, you're quite beloved, even more so than Helena was. You treat others fairly, and are willing to help anyone who asks it of you."

"Good to know." I thought about the lack of spirits in this time, and the resulting silence in my mind. That part of me felt brittle, as if one of my senses had atrophied. "If there aren't any spirits here, who am I helping? And what am I helping them with?"

"Those are very good questions."

When we arrived at Bennet's house, it was the same cape style home from my timeline, with its pointy dormer windows that had always reminded me of eyes glowering down on the passersby. But the garden, now that was different. Instead of the usual English cottage garden of roses and lavender, this one had a Japanese maple as a focal point, and several well-trimmed dwarf evergreens.

"Interesting vibe in the yard," I said as we approached the house. I knocked on the front door, and a moment later Bennet himself opened it.

"Mistress," he greeted. "Please, come in. I've been meaning to reach out to you."

"Thank you," I said as I stepped inside. "You know Tessa?"

"Yes, of course. Please come in, Signora." The fact that Bennet had addressed Tessa with an Italian term of respect told me they weren't as close and they'd been back in the correct timeline. "What can I do for you today, Mistress?"

I bit the inside of my cheek. "Could you please call me Eli, instead of mistress?"

Bennet removed his glasses and polished the lenses with a handkerchief. "If you'd prefer it, yes. I must say, I haven't referred to you as Eli in some time."

"Speaking of time, we think we're stuck in an alternate timeline."

Bennet grunted, and perched his now sparkling glasses on the bridge of his nose. "Yes, well. That would explain a few things."

"Really?" I asked. "What sort of things?"

"Please, have a seat." Bennet led us into his living room, which was as overflowing with books and ledgers as it always was. "I'll just put the kettle on. While we wait for it to boil, I have a few things to show you."

While Tess and I admired the floral wallpaper and lace curtains, Bennet darted in and out of the room depositing books, piles of loose parchments, a small wooden chest, and a plate of cookies on the coffee and side tables. Thank all the gods, the cookies were his famous shortbread biscuits with caramel centers, my favorite.

Once Bennet had prepared and poured the tea, he opened one of the ledgers. "As you know, Mis... Eli," he amended, "my records are incorruptible. They cannot be damaged by any force, be it natural or manmade, nor can they be altered by hand or magic. I now believe they cannot be altered by time, either."

"What makes you say that?" I glanced at the ledger. It recorded births and deaths from the seventeenth century. "Has someone attempted to change them?"

"Not to my knowledge, but a second set has appeared. Look here." He pointed toward a line that read "Katherine Moore—child stillborn". "Originally, your ancestor Katherine Moore's second child did not survive beyond birth, and Katherine herself never truly recovered. She was essentially an invalid for the rest of her life."

"Oh." My fingers hovered over her name, trembling. "That's very sad."

"Yes, it is. However," Bennet opened a second, identical ledger, "in this ledger—which I have to say, appeared without announcing itself and has sent my organizational system into quite a state—Katherine's child survived. She named him Daniel."

"Daniel," I repeated, imagining a little boy running after his big sister, Elizabeth. "What happened to Katherine?"

"She lived on, and had several more children. Katherine and her partner, Montgomery Fletcher, had long and happy lives."

"That's good." I glanced at Tessa. "That's good, right?"

"Of course it is," Tessa said. "What else has changed?"

"Daniel's birth seems to be the first change, or at least it's the earliest one I've come across," Bennet said. "From there on, each version of the Moore family has wildly divergent paths."

"These changes are all my fault," I said, my gaze darting between the two ledgers. "Dan and I got stuck in some time tunnels, and we ended up in the seventeenth century. We came back to this time, but then we went back for my twenty-ninth birthday so Katherine could anoint me as her successor."

"Twenty-nine, you say?" Bennet opened the chest, and I gasped. Inside, nestled on a bed of silk, were my twenty-ninth birthday candles. They were goofy grocery store versions made of white wax, and painted with blue and yellow edging. I'd brought it with me during our second trip through the nexus, as a talisman to ensure we arrived on the correct day. Elizabeth had loved the candles, so I left them behind with her.

"My birthday candles," I said. "I can't believe they survived this long."

"By all accounts, they were some of Katherine's most prized possessions. They were passed on to Elizabeth, and eventually became part of my collection."

I reached toward the candles, but curled my fingers into my palm at the last moment. They were so old I worried they might not survive if I picked them up. "Katherine was one of the best people I've ever met. Montgomery, too."

"Of that, I have no doubt." Bennet closed the ledgers, and picked up his teacup. "Based on your presence here, I assume other anomalies have presented themselves."

"They have." I wrestled with all the things I could and probably should ask Bennet, and figured I should start with understanding my own place in this new world. "Have the recent lineages changed?"

"A moment," he said, and he disappeared into the record room. He returned with two slim leather-bound books. "For starters, there are many more entries in the lineages, starting with Daniel Moore's birth, and that of his younger siblings."

"It seems we have an abundance of Moores," Tessa said.

"What about me?" I pressed.

Bennet's face betrayed that he thought that was an odd request, but he flipped to my entry. "Ah. You, Eliza Jayne, were born to Alexander Adesh Moore and Christina Louise Lind. The information is identical in both ledgers."

"What about my mother's heritage?" I asked. "When she met my father, she thought she was mortal, but she's really a witch."

"A seer of Alexander's standing taking up with the witchborn? That's highly unusual. No offense, Signora," Bennet demurred.

"None taken," Tessa replied. "In the other timeline, Eli's mother's heritage was kept quiet. Was that not the case here?"

"I have no record of Ms. Lind being witchborn, so that is a possibility."

"But she is still a witch?" I asked. "She couldn't be a witch in one timeline and not the other, right?"

"I suppose not," Bennet said. "Have you spoken to Alexander about this?"

"He's busy babysitting my cousins," I muttered. "Does she still live nearby?"

"As far as I know, she lives a few hours away," Bennet replied. "I will obtain her current address for you."

"Thank you." I looked at the piles of ledgers and record books on the table, and wondered where my ancestors were. "What happened to the spirits?"

Bennet was visibly taken aback. "Have you sensed something?"

"No, and that's the problem. I haven't sensed a single spirit since I arrived in this timeline. Also, Gran's cats? They're gone."

Bennet frowned, and looked toward his record room. "I will have to spend some time with my books to discover a definitive answer, but my theory is that if there are no souls present in this timeline, this version of reality must be a construct."

"That's what Tessa and I have been leaning toward," I said. "Then the question remains, how do we get everyone back to the right one?"

"There may not be a right or wrong timeline," Bennet said. "Perhaps they need to be merged together."

"Or perhaps this is the correct timeline, and we need to find a way to bring the missing spirits here," Tessa said. "Both sets of my memories are equally strong. There must be a reason for that."

I opened my mouth to argue with Tess, and was distracted by blue lights dancing across the wall. Bennet went to the window and drew back the curtain. "Eli, Dan Lyons is parked in front of the house."

"Seems he misses you," Tessa said.

I sighed, and rubbed my eyes. "I'll go talk to him," I said.

I stepped out of Bennet's home and saw Dan leaning against a police cruiser. When he saw me, he killed the blue lights, which was nice of him. He was wearing his usual work outfit of gray pants and a blue dress shirt rolled up at the sleeves and exposing his muscular forearms. I liked that. He also had on a tie, which was unusual.

"How did you know I would be here?" I asked.

"I'm a detective, just like you. We figure shit out for a living."

I crossed my arms over my chest. "Is staking out Bennet's house part of a case?"

"No, but in this circus I'm not just a detective. I'm the chief of police."

I blinked. "What happened to Renault?" I asked. Back in the real world, Renault was the chief, and Dan was his least favorite detective.

"I don't know. No one else knows, either." He straightened, as if he would walk up and join me on the porch. I stood my ground. "Can we talk?"

"We're talking now."

"Can we talk a little closer? I'm not fond of yelling my business across the neighborhood."

I walked down the steps, and joined him on the sidewalk. Up close, I saw the dark circles under his eyes, and the fine lines around his mouth that weren't there yesterday. "Did you sleep last night?"

"No. I was busy going through our house looking for something that would fix all of this." He stepped closer, and took my hands. "Did you stay at Alex's place?"

"I stayed with Tessa. She has two sets of memories, one for each reality, and says they're both equally strong." I saw myself reflected in his dark eyes. "Do you remember anything from this life?"

"I'm flying blind here." He squeezed my fingers. "Eli, this whole town is different. I can't make heads or tails of what's happening."

"You don't need to," I said. "We'll handle it."

"Does that we include me?" When I didn't answer, he pressed, "Will we ever be partners again?"

I regarded him, this man I loved so much I'd brought him into my community and shared all of my secrets with him. Hell, I'd even given him a seer's mark, and that was one of the few things that hadn't changed in this wonky timeline. But I still didn't know if he really loved me, or if I was only in his life to paper over the hole in his heart Charlotte had left behind.

"I don't know," I said. "Before I can think about that, I have work to do. I need to fix this timeline."

Dan leaned closer, and said, "We need to fix us. This timeline can wait."

"It can't," I said, then a voice came over the police radio.

"I gotta go," Dan said. "Will you come home tonight?"

"I'll probably be with Tessa," I said. "She needs me. But, you can call me. If you want to, that is."

"I want to." Dan brought my hand to his mouth and kissed my knuckles. "I need you, too, baby."

I nodded, then he got in his cruiser and drove away. As he turned around a corner, I realized I hadn't said goodbye. I took out my phone, and texted him a heart emoji. A moment later, he sent one back.

Eli: No texting and driving.

Dan: What, think someone's gonna arrest me?

I smiled, and slid my phone into my back pocket. We would work this out. We had to. As I thought about me and Dan, I realized that something Bennet had said was wrong. I reentered the house, and said, "Daniel Moore's birth wasn't the first anomaly. In the other timeline, Jemima Beauclaire died before he was born."

"But she remains alive today," Bennet said.

"So I'm told. But, back in the other version of all this, Dan and I watched Amir Hassan brew up some foxglove tea, and I saw her drink it. I felt her spirit leave her body."

"Interesting," Bennet said, as he consulted his ledgers. "This Amir Hassan you mention, is that the same individual who was censured by the Iranian coven?"

"Yes," I replied, surprised that event remained constant. "That was when my dad and I went to Iran."

Bennet shook his head. "Alexander was not present for Hassan's reckoning. After he breached a time portal the coven leader, Mehrded, bound Hassan's abilities for a hundred years. He's remained in Iran ever since, under a type of house arrest with the coven."

I remembered Mehrded, the kindly man who grew flowers in the desert, and who was so powerful he was feared across all of Asia. "Then, Amir and I never met."

"Yet another reason why this timeline isn't so bad," Tessa said. "But, it does make me wonder what the price is for all these good turns."

I linked my hands behind my neck and stared at the ceiling. Tessa had a point in that all magic had a price. If things had changed for the better for me, they had likely ended up worse for someone else. Multiply all these fortuitous instances, and it seemed like someone had ended up with the short end of the stick.

I thought about the dark circles under Dan's eyes, and wondered if that someone was me. Or, gods forbid, him.

"I guess the next question is, who is worse off?" I said to the ceiling. "If we figure that out, we can backtrack to an origin point."

"A sound plan," Bennet said. "I shall consult my records, and see if I can identify a person or group who may be worse off than before."

Tessa and I said our goodbyes, and left Bennet to his research. As we drove away, Tessa asked, "Now what?"

"I think I'd like to have a look at Jemima Beauclaire."

Danny The Fixer

I drove away from Bennet's place with my head spinning. Despite the brave face I'd put on in front of Eli, I hadn't known she would be at his house. I'd planned on asking Bennet a few questions, and seeing what if any insights the old shepherd could offer about this new, worse reality. Then my Eliza walked out onto the porch, and yet again she took my breath away.

Eli was so incredibly beautiful I still had a hard time believing she wanted anything to do with me. I've been around plenty of attractive people in my life, but there was something about Eli's dark hair and almost black eyes that squeezed the air out of my lungs every time I looked at her. Maybe I only reacted that way because I loved her so much.

Based on the way she'd looked at me, with her wide eyes wary and arms crossed over her chest, she was still hurt. No surprise there, since I'd royally screwed up. But she let me take her hands, and tonight I was going to call her. So yeah, I'd screwed up, but I was on track to fix things. That's me, Danny the fixer.

My phone beeped. I glanced at it, and saw the heart Eli texted me. Not gonna lie, I almost teared up , all over a few pixels on my phone screen. Me and my girl, we would be all right.

After my shift ended, I went straight home and plunged into the basement. After I'd been possessed, and we realized the demon riding my body had been staring at some of Charlotte's photographs, I'd hauled out all of the old albums and Eli and me had combed through them for clues. I'd been worried doing that going through my deceased wife's things would drive a rift between us, but Eli hadn't shown the least bit of jealously toward the happy memories I'd shared with Charlotte. In fact, she'd appreciated me letting her into that part of my life.

I stopped dead in the middle of the cellar stairs. While I'd been getting married back in New York, Eli had been getting kidnapped and held hostage by the Beauclaire witches.

Unwilling to confront that mass of emotions, I resumed walking and went toward the shelves on the far side of the cellar. I'd gone through the first and second floors of the house yesterday, but I avoided coming down here. The basement was where I kept the stuff I didn't want to be reminded of on a daily basis, but I felt too attached to get rid of. Since I hadn't found any clues upstairs, I was hoping I could find something—anything—down here. Then I got to the back shelves, and stopped dead in my tracks.

The photo albums were gone. None of the boxes that held Charlotte's stuff were there, not on the shelves or the floor or anywhere else in the basement. Assuming they had been moved, I scoured the place all the way up to the attic crawl space.

Nothing. It was like my time with Charlotte had never happened.

I sat in the middle of the second floor hallway and held my head in my hands. How was this happening? How were so many years of my life gone? I remembered the pictures of me and Eli that had appeared on her computer, and wondered if I'd ever been married. I wondered if I was still a cop from Queens, or if I'd grown up in this country town. And if I'd grown up here, what did that mean for the rest of my family?

Shit. We needed to fix this mess, yesterday.

I got up and shook off my bad attitude, then I stalked into the bathroom and turned on the shower. Eli's shampoo was in there, right beside her ridiculously expensive conditioner. My plan was to shower, have something to eat, and then call Eli. With any luck, by the time we hung up I would be on my way to pick her up, and bring her home. Once we were together again, everything else would fall into place.

My Whole Heart

As it turned out, even though I was the mighty Mistress of Seers, I couldn't just waltz into the Beauclaire house without an appointment. While Tessa sat in the passenger seat making call after call as she attempted to secure me an invitation, I drove toward the estate, but I didn't want to see the house. I wanted to hang out in the Beauclaire cemetery.

Back in the real version of reality, Jacob Allwood and I had driven out to the remote and desolate remains of the Beauclaire Estate in an attempt to gain insight into the situation with Amir. The property itself hadn't been too helpful, since my father had destroyed the house as retribution for them kidnapping me. During our trip, Jacob had mentioned that the Beauclaire burial ground was a few miles west of the house, and even though I hadn't sensed a single spirit in this new world, I was hopeful I could learn something there.

Our trip to the remains of the estate was also the first time I'd spoken to Jemima Beauclaire. That couldn't be a coincidence.

"They'll contact me with your appointment details in the morning," Tessa announced, after she'd dealt with a barrage of texts and calls. She looked up from her phone, and realized where we were going. "What do you think you'll find in the cemetery?"

"Maybe nothing, maybe something," I replied, quoting Dan's oft-said plan. I parked near the gates, and Tess and I entered the cemetery on foot. "Have you been here before?"

"I have, but not for a long time," she replied. "As you know, most of my ancestors are in Europe." She indicated a large mausoleum. "That's where the clan elders rest."

"Let's pay our respects, shall we?"

We approached the pale marble edifice, which for all its rich materials was a rather bland four walled design. I stepped inside the mausoleum, and dragged my fingertips across the names etched onto the shiny brass plates. "Is Sarah Allwood buried here?"

"I'm not sure," Tessa replied. "At one time, we thought we found her bones in the old apple orchard, but doubt has been cast across that discovery."

"I wonder who those bones belong to." Sarah was sneaky, and I wouldn't put it past her to have a secret burial plot with a cult dedicated to worshipping her spirit. Or, maybe in this reality things had gone differently for her, and she was still alive, too.

At the end of the corridor was a set of large bronze doors which were propped open. Beyond them was a stone coffin set on a pedestal. There was no name or inscription on the tomb, but whomever they interred there must have been of great importance to this family.

"How long has Nathaniel been the clan leader?" I asked.

"Centuries," Tessa replied. "He arrived in the New World long before I did. As far as I know, he's led the clan without interruption ever since the sixteenth century."

"Then who is this?" I asked, jerking my chin toward the rich burial. "The previous leader?"

"No one knows," Tessa replied. "It was someone dear to Nathaniel, but he's refused to speak their name since their passing. I don't know if even Bennet knows."

Someone dear to Nathaniel. I reached out with my seer abilities, but no one was nearby. Just in case someone was out there, but too timid to approach me, I left a spark of power behind. If a spirit decided they wanted to talk to me, all they had to do was follow the spark back to me.

"Let's go," I said. "There's nothing happening here. Not yet."

When we got back to Tessa's condo, another courier was waiting for her with a new packet of paperwork. I thought it was a waste of her talents to be the Beauclaire's glorified secretary, but kept my opinions to myself. It wasn't my place to comment on how Tessa lived her life, and she seemed to be happy. Maybe she was right, and this wasn't the wrong timeline.

Maybe Bennet was right, and we needed to merge the timelines back together.

Maybe the gods just loved screwing with me.

Since Tessa had work to do, I made myself a sandwich and headed into the guestroom so I wouldn't disturb her. After I ate, I messed around with my phone for a bit, then a text came through.

Dan: You awake?

Eli: Yeah.

Dan: Can I call?

Eli: Yeah.

I picked up on the first ring. "Hey."

"Hey."

"How was work?" I asked, smiling. Until he spoke, I hadn't realized how much I needed to hear his voice.

"It was work. Turns out that being the chief is a lot of administrative bullshit."

I laughed, picturing a frazzled Dan sitting at a desk behind mounds of paperwork. "You can handle it. Is Jill still there?"

"She is. She's still married to Angel, too, so that's two good things." He paused, and asked, "Anything interesting happen after Bennet's?"

"Tess and I went to the Beauclaire cemetery. There's a big ostentatious burial in the mausoleum, but no one knows who's in there. Big secret."

Dan grunted. "If we've learned anything, it's that these secrets are never good."

"Dan, Jemima Beauclaire is alive."

"That's... that's crazy. There's no rhyme or reason to all of these changes, is there?"

"Bennet thinks we have two timelines that need to be merged back together. Tessa isn't sure which timeline is the correct one."

"What do you think?"

"I think we need to figure out who is benefitting from this new timeline. Follow the money—or in this case, follow the good fortune—and we'll find whoever's responsible for these changes."

"That's my girl, figuring shit out." I heard Dan moving around, and what might have been the fridge door closing. "You do realize if this timeline is the right one, we never had our first kiss at the Allwood house."

I giggled, remembering how a half-naked and filthy Dan had grabbed me and kissed me so hard I forgot my name. "I still can't believe you did that. What made you think that was a good idea?"

"Thought it might be my only chance, so I took it."

"That's what you said about our second kiss," I said, remembering how we'd fallen asleep together on his couch. When we woke, I'd been lying on Dan's chest, and he pulled me up for the sweetest, softest kiss I'd ever experienced.

"Are you saying you liked the second one better?"

"They were both good," I replied, and they were.

"Good enough for you to come home tonight?"

I bit the inside of my cheek. "I don't feel like I belong there."

"Eli. Eliza. This house is yours and mine. You're everywhere here. If you want to come see for yourself, you can do it without me here. Come by while I'm at work. I won't get in the way."

"You're not in the way. Everything's just so wrong here."

"You saying we're wrong?"

"No, but... Dan, I haven't sensed a single spirit since we came through the nexus."

He grunted. "Not even in the cemetery?"

"No. Not a single glimmer. And I'm this all-powerful Mistress of Seers, but if there aren't any spirits for me to help, why am I here?"

"Why are any of us here?" he countered. "Eli, I know I'm new to all of this, but Tess and Bennet are wrong. This timeline is wrong, and I think it's designed to push you and me apart."

"Why would anyone want to do that?"

"To destroy our focus. They want us wrapped up in our heads and not paying attention to whatever they're really after with all this."

"Whoever's doing this has access to a shit ton of power," I muttered. "Tessa's trying to get me in to see the Beauclaires. They're the most powerful clan in the area, right now. There's something off about their cemetery, and I bet it's connected to the bigger issue."

"Want me to go with you?"

"I don't know if I can bring a mortal."

"That's all I am to you? A mortal?"

"Dan—"

"It's fine. Don't worry about it. But know this: every single thing I said to you in our vows I meant with my whole heart."

"I meant what I said, too."

"Then why are you at Tessa's and not here with me?"

"Because you hurt me," I snapped, then I clapped my hand across my mouth. "I'm sorry. I didn't mean to lash out like that."

"It's all right. I get it. But if you loved me, I'd like to think you'd give me the opportunity to fix this. Aren't we worth fixing?"

"We are," I said in a rush. "Dan, I love you."

"Love you too, baby. I'll call you tomorrow."

After Dan and I hung up, I laid in that guest bed staring at the ceiling while my mind replayed our second trip to Katherine's. The moment Montgomery had brought out the red and gold cords, I'd known exactly what they were for. When he asked if we were still interested in going through with the handfasting ceremony, I hadn't hesitated before saying yes. Neither had Dan, and it only took us a few minutes to take our places in front of the hearth.

"Normally, I begin with a speech, but since this is a more intimate ceremony, we can go directly to the declaration of intent," Montgomery said. "Please, join hands."

I grabbed Dan's hands so fast he smiled, and squeezed my fingers. As Montgomery began winding the cords around our hands and wrists, I felt Dan tremble. He was nervous, just like me.

"A handfasting is different from a marriage in that the couple determines how long they wish to keep the bond alive," Montgomery continued. "You may choose to extend this bond for a year, or a decade, or even forever."

"I'd like forever," Dan said.

"Yeah," I agreed, nodding. "We'll both take forever."

Montgomery smiled. "Very well. Forever it is. Daniel and Eliza, the vows you make today will mean that your souls are bound for eternity, through this life and into the next. These vows that you make now, in front of three witnesses, will not be easily broken. Knowing this, do you still wish to commit yourselves to one another?"

"Yes," Dan and I said in concert. We glanced at each other and smiled, then we returned our attention to Montgomery.

"I am glad to hear it. Daniel, will you share in Eliza's pain, seek to protect her from it, and ease her from it? Will you share in her joy, rejoice in her happiness, and always look for the best in her? And will you share in her hardships and toil, so that you may grow together?"

Dan squeezed my fingers. "I will."

Montgomery nodded, and turned to me. "Eliza, will you share in Daniel's pain, seek to protect him from it, and ease him from it? Will you share in his joy, rejoice in his happiness, and always look for the best in him? And will you share in his hardships and toil, so that you may grow together?"

"I will."

"I ask you both, will you share in each other's dreams and work to fulfill them, use the heat of your tempers to strengthen the bond between you, and will you honor and respect each other and always treat each other as equals?"

"We will," we replied.

"Daniel, is there anything you would like to say to Eliza?"

Dan cleared his throat. "Eli—Eliza—I don't know if I can ever describe how much I love you. You're everything to me, have been since the first moment I saw you. All I want to do is live the rest of my life with you."

Montgomery inclined his head toward Dan, then he turned to me. "Eliza, is there anything you wish to say to Daniel?"

I looked up at Dan, my handsome, kind, intelligent partner. "I'm an idiot, you know that? I resisted being with you for so long, all because I was afraid of admitting how much I truly love you. All that resisting accomplished was two years we weren't together, when we could have been laughing and smiling and slow dancing in the kitchen every night. I can't get those two years back, but I can give you the rest of my years, if you want them."

"I want them," Dan said. "I want all of them."

"Daniel and Eliza," Montgomery continued, "you have proclaimed the bond between your souls before these witnesses, and whatever gods deem us worthy of their notice. I proclaim your bond to be both strong and true. Please, seal your bond with a kiss."

Dan tugged me close and kissed me. "I'm gonna love you forever, baby."

"I'm going to hold you to that."

Butterflies

The next morning, I went into the kitchen and found the same scene from the day before: Tessa seated at the kitchen table working on her clan's financial statements. "Let me guess, the courier will be here soon?" I asked.

"He always returns at eight sharp," she replied without looking up from her work. Today she was working on paper, instead of her laptop. "Honestly, some of these witches are so foolish when it comes to money, it's a wonder they aren't in the poorhouse."

"Are you their only accountant?" I asked, as I poured myself some orange juice. Tessa grew her own oranges on her magical climate controlled deck, which meant she had the best juice in town.

"I wouldn't classify myself as an accountant," she replied. "I'm more of an overseer, and I make sure the accountants are correct."

"Do you catch a lot of errors?"

"I don't, but numbers of this magnitude always warrant a second look." She closed her notebook, then she handed me an envelope. "Bennet sent over your mother's address and contact information."

I accepted the envelope, and set it on the counter. "Have you ever met her? My mother?"

Tessa tilted her head to the side, and thought for a moment. "In this reality, no, I don't believe so. In the other reality, I recall meeting her once when she was pregnant, and once when you were a baby."

"Really." Since I'd never heard either of those stories, I sat across from her. "What was she like while she was pregnant?"

"Happy," Tessa replied. "Both she and Alex were very happy that you were coming, which was hard for me." She frowned, and added, "While I've never held Alex's choices against him, it was difficult for me to watch him start a family without me. I distanced myself from him, and your grandmother. In hindsight, I wonder if that was the correct action."

"Did you want to have a family with Dad?"

"I thought we were one," she said softly. "But I got called back to Europe, and while I dealt with one calamity after another, I ended up being apart from Alex for two—no, three—years. I couldn't fault him for moving on, and I never have." She sighed. "Perhaps it was never meant to be with Alex and I."

"Can I tell you a secret?"

"Absolutely."

"A while ago, I thought my mother had cursed my dad. Turns out I was wrong, which is great, but while Dad and I talked about it, he told me that he'd always wanted children. That was one of the reasons he was so happy with my mom. He thought he would finally get his big family."

"Really," Tessa said. "Alex never said as much to me."

"He didn't want to burden you. He said that if you wanted to have a child with him, it should be your choice, not his."

Tessa nodded, and looked away. "Your father is a very good man."

I pulled out my phone so I could give Tessa a moment to compose herself. A text from Dan was waiting for me.

Dan: Headed to work. Call if you need me.

Eli: I'm here if you need me, too. Have a good day.

A waited a moment for a response, or to see the little bubble that meant he was typing. Nothing. He was obviously still mad at me from our conversation the night before, and I could hardly blame him. I'd made it seem like our relationship wasn't important, when nothing could be further from the truth. I only hoped I hadn't ruined things between us.

"Are you all right?" Tessa asked.

"Just wondering how to fix things with Dan," I replied, as I slid my phone in my pocket.

"It's really quite simple. Go to him, and tell him how you feel. Then, when he responds, listen to him." Tessa stood, and went to the cabinets. "Nearly every problem that surfaces in a relationship can be fixed by speaking honestly, and listening without judgement."

"I don't know if I'd call this a problem."

"If you're sleeping here and not with him, it's a problem." Tessa set a skillet on the stove. "Eggs for breakfast?"

While Tessa made breakfast, I opened the envelope Bennet had sent over. My mother lived in Oak Grove, which, according to the internet, was a two-hour drive from Tessa's place. I wondered why she lived farther away in this reality, since in the correct timeline she only lived twenty minutes away from me. But if her address was different, maybe she was different, too. Maybe she actually wanted to be my mother.

"Can I borrow a dress?" I asked.

"My closet is yours," Tessa replied. "Are we going somewhere?"

"I'm going to visit my mother."

After we ate breakfast, I showered and raided Tessa's closet for something appropriate to wear to see my mother. We hadn't seen each other for twenty years, at least in the real timeline. Who knows how long it had been in this one. Regardless, I wanted to look nice.

Spending time in Tessa's massive closet was like having an exclusive store all to yourself for the day. Like many witches, Tessa had accumulated a great deal of wealth during her long life, but the fact that she'd been born into royalty meant she had started out rich. All of that wealth meant her clothes were of the best quality, and cut in timeless designs that would look good today, or ten years from now. I only needed to look good for a few hours, then it would be back to jeans and tee shirts for me.

After trying on multiple outfits, I ended up choosing a blue wrap dress. It had short sleeves and a modest neckline, and, since Tessa was close to my height, the skirt was the perfect length and hit just below my knees. I paired the dress with some black heels, and felt like I was fit to meet with my estranged parent.

If only the butterflies in my stomach would calm down.

"Want me to go with you?" Tessa asked when I finally emerged from the guest room.

"I think it's better if I go alone." I didn't know if my mother remembered Tessa, but she didn't trust any form of magic. If she saw me approach her with a witch beside me, she might take that as an act of aggression. "Thanks for the offer, though."

"Anytime." Tessa hugged me, and said, "And before you ask, yes, you may stay here tonight if you need to. My door is always open to you, Eli."

"Thanks, Tess," I said, then I went down to my car and began the drive to Oak Grove.

The drive was long but uneventful, and just under two hours after leaving Tessa's condo, I parked in the street across from my mother's house. It was a nice house, with white shutters and a neatly trimmed hedge. I wondered how long she had lived here. I wondered if she would remember me.

I struck down that thought, because how could anyone forget having a kid? Even my mother wasn't that anti-parental. Since ruminating in the car would get me exactly nowhere, I got out and headed up the walk. There was a doorbell camera next to the front door. She probably already knew I was here.

I rang the bell, and waited. A few moments later, my mother opened the door, and I gasped.

"Mom," I said, as all of my composure and carefully rehearsed speeches flew out the window. "It's me, Eliza!"

Her brow pinched, then she stepped outside and shut the door. "What are you doing here?"

"What are *you* doing here?" I demanded. "Have you been living here since you left me in the hospital? Which was awful, by the way."

She crossed her arms over her stomach. "You were better off there. I couldn't help you."

"You never tried," I shot back. My hands were shaking, and I took a breath to calm myself. "Sorry. I came here to talk to you, not start a fight."

She pursed her lips and pushed her hair behind her ear, which was something she did whenever she had to deal with things she'd rather ignore. Even after all this time, she looked exactly the same as the day she'd left me, which wasn't really a surprise. Witches hardly aged, after all. "What would you like to talk about?" she asked.

"Why did you curse me?" When she didn't respond, I continued, "We found surveillance footage of the last time you went to see me in the hospital. You had a thornapple blossom in your hair, and somehow you cursed me with one of the seedpods. I need to know why you did that."

My mother blew out a breath. "That wasn't a curse," she began. "My intent was to contain your witchcraft, to protect you from all of this." She gestured vaguely, as if she'd meant to protect me from the mailbox and the flower beds.

"All of what? You can't run from what you are. You, of all people, should know that."

"Well, I didn't know that, did I?" she countered. "I had no idea I was a... was different until you brought it out of me."

"Is that it? You abandoned me because I made you realize you're a witch?" I shook my head. "That's a lame reason, Mom. Even you can do better than that."

"I did not abandon you," she snapped. "I left you with people who could handle you."

"Then why the curse?"

"It was not a curse!"

Her eyes flashed as the back of my neck went hot; I'd definitely gotten my temper from her. Before I could say or do anything else, I heard children yelling inside the house.

"There are kids here?" I asked, then I made a connection. "Do I have siblings?"

"You probably have hundreds, what with Alex gallivanting all across the world," she replied.

"I'm an only child," I said, resentful that she dragged my dad into this. "Or am I? Mom, do I have sisters? Brothers?"

She swallowed, then she said, "Eliza, I was not expecting you, and I am not prepared to do this right now. I'd like you to leave."

"When will you be prepared to talk to me?" I asked. "Mom, I need answers!"

"I'm sorry, Eliza. I created this life to give myself answers. I don't have any for you."

My mother, the woman who'd brought me into this world, refused to meet my eyes as she darted back inside the house. A second later, I heard the door's lock slide into place. Mom had locked me out of her life. Again.

THINGS I THOUGHT I'D LOST

I got in my car and drove away from my mother's quaint little house in her quaint little town. I hadn't expected our reunion to be all hugs and weepy tears, but I hadn't expected it to go that badly, either.

Two hours later I was back in my hometown, but I didn't go to Tessa's or Gran's house. I drove aimlessly, wasting gas and wishing I could turn back time and talk myself out of this ill-advised visit with my mother. Maybe I should have called first, or written her a letter; then again, she probably would have hung up on me, and letters are easy to ignore. Just like she had always ignored me.

How can she not want me?

I took a left and realized I was on Dan's street. Our street. My driving hadn't been so aimless, after all. I pulled into the driveway behind Dan's SUV, and through my haze of tears I stared at the house. It looked just the same as it always had, with its crisp brick façade and big, welcoming windows. Right then, I needed something familiar and welcoming.

I needed Dan.

I got out of the car and knocked, which was weird. Who knocks on the door to their own house? But I'd left things with Dan on a bad note, and the last thing he needed was me barging into his space. So I knocked, and stood on the front step, half-terrified he too would send me away. Then he opened the door, and my heart was in my throat.

"Eli," he said, then he noticed my tear-streaked face. "What happened?"

"I went to see my mother."

He cupped the side of my face with his hand, and wiped my cheek with his thumb. "Do you want to come inside?"

I nodded. He stepped aside, and I entered the house. The living room was just the same, with its brown leather couch and coffee table strewn with paperwork and empty cups. I sorely needed this sameness. I faced Dan, and realized he was different.

"I've never seen you wear a uniform before." He was wearing his black police uniform, though he'd unbuttoned his shirt and removed his belt and holster. "I thought the police chief wore regular clothes."

"There was a thing at the station," he said. "Everyone asked about you."

"Do I often attend these things with you?"

"Seems so." He put his hands in his pockets. "I take it this visit with your mother didn't go well."

"She didn't even ask how I am." I wrapped my arms around my stomach. "She didn't even say hello."

My voice caught, and Dan reached for me. I fell into his arms and pressed my face against his soft tee shirt. He smelled like fabric softener, and his chest was warm and solid and safe. As he wrapped his arms around me, I remembered what Jacob Allwood had once called us: a circle unbroken. It was a witch term for soulmates.

"I'm sorry, baby," he said, his lips against my forehead. "Do you want to talk about it?"

I nodded. "Yeah. I do."

We parted, and he tilted his head toward the kitchen. I followed him into the room, and stopped short once I was in there. Whereas before, the only plants in the house were four potted herbs that lived on the kitchen windowsill, now there were at least a dozen plants of varying sizes hanging from the ceiling and sitting on the counter. "Where did all these plants come from?"

"I'm guessing they're yours." Dan took two bottles of water out of the fridge and set them on the table. "I'd offer to make you some coffee, but you're already pretty shaky."

"This is fine. Thank you." I stared at the plants crowded around the window, and wondered when I'd bought them. Did Dan and I go to the greenhouse together, did I buy them on my own, or were some of them gifts? I may never know.

"Eli?" Dan prompted. "Why did you go see her today? Did something happen?"

I scoffed. "What hasn't happened?" His shoulders slumped, and I felt even worse. "I thought, what with all the things that are different now, that she might be different, too. That she was finally ready to be my mother."

"But she wasn't."

Willing away tears, I bit the inside of my cheek. "No, she wasn't." I cleared my throat. "She did say that the thornapple was never a curse.

She was trying to protect me, like you thought. She wanted to suppress my witchcraft, and in her mind that must have been the right thing to do."

"How did you leave things with her?"

"After two minutes of speaking with me, she decided she had enough. She went inside, locked the door, and that was it." I twisted open the bottle, and closed it again. "I waited twenty years to talk to her again, and that was all I got. Two minutes! What I did learn was that while everything else seems different, she's exactly the same."

"Everything's not different," Dan said. "I still feel the same about you."

A hundred rude comebacks fought for release, and letting any of them out wouldn't be fair. It would just be me lashing out, and Dan didn't deserve my misplaced anger. Instead of saying something I might regret, I drank some water. While I was deliberately not looking at Dan, I noticed something behind him on the counter.

"You have an espresso machine?"

"Pretty sure that's yours, too," he replied. "Those whole milk lattes you like aren't cheap."

I blinked, and a memory that wasn't mine flashed before my eyes: Dan, giving me the espresso machine so we could make lattes at home and stay in bed longer in the morning. "Yeah, I guess they aren't," I mumbled. "I should go."

"Go where? This is your house just as much as it's mine." When I didn't answer, he asked, "Before you leave, can I show you something? It's upstairs," he added.

I nodded, then I followed Dan up to the second floor. On the way, I noticed all the little things that were different; there was a potted palm on the landing, and a beaded curtain hung on the window. The hall carpet was different, and there was colorful artwork on the walls.

"What's in there?" I asked, since the spare bedroom doors were closed.

"Later," he said. "Check this out first." He opened the master bedroom door, and I gasped.

"You painted," I said, as I stepped into the room. The walls were my exact favorite shade of lavender. Above the bed were two framed child's drawings.

"Are those the pictures Abby drew of us?" I asked. One of my first big cases had been when I found Abigail Stevens, a young girl who'd been kidnapped. The police didn't have any leads, then a ghost had told me where to find her. I rescued Abby and brought her home.

"They sure are," he replied. "You always said it was a good likeness of me."

"Is the bathroom still all white?"

"Go look."

I ducked into the bathroom, and saw that the white tile walls and floors were the same, but there was a new blue and yellow rug on the floor, and matching curtains. Scattered around the bathtub were an assortment of bubble baths and a few half-burned candles. I opened the shower door, and saw my favorite shampoo and conditioner sitting on the shelf.

"I really do live here." I faced Dan. "Have I lived here for a long time?"

"I only know what you know." He held out his hand. "Come see the closet."

I accepted his hand, my fascination over all the little details that were clear evidence of me overriding the fact that technically I was still mad at him. Dan squeezed my fingers, then he led me to my side of the closet.

"What's so interesting about clothes?" I asked.

"Eli, look. They're your clothes."

"Well, of course they are," I began, then I spied a familiar black sleeve. Hardly believing my eyes, I pulled out my leather jacket, my favorite item of clothing I'd had for over ten years. Only, it shouldn't be here.

"This blew up in my apartment." I stuck my hands into the pockets; the left had some loose change and a pen. In the right pocket, I found my lock picks. "My picks! But, how?"

"That's what I've been trying to tell you," Dan said. "This isn't just an accumulation of stuff. These are your clothes. Look." Dan picked up my boots. "I've seen you wear these at least a dozen times, and here they are. And this." He grabbed a white shirt off a hanger. It was my favorite gauzy peasant top. "You wear this all the time, too."

I ran my hands over the clothes, and he was right. Except for a few odd shirts, these were my clothes. Things I'd assumed I would never see again, things I was certain had been destroyed, were all cleaned and pressed and waiting for me to wear them.

"I don't understand any of this," I whispered.

"One more thing." Dan beckoned me to his side of the closet. He opened the top drawer of his dresser, and paused. "I found something."

"Something bad?"

"You tell me."

He handed me a black velvet box. I opened it, and broke into a cold sweat. Inside the box was the most beautiful ring I'd ever seen. It was an oval sapphire—which was my birthstone—set in white gold. Filigree details surrounded the central gem, and the setting was studded with tiny flashing diamonds. Next to the sapphire ring were two plain white gold bands, one sized for my finger, and a larger ring for a man's hand.

Dan's hand.

"Did I know about this?" I asked. "Or were you planning on... on something?"

"I don't know," he said softly. "All I know is that I came in here looking for socks, and I found that." He watched me for a moment. "You don't seem very happy about this."

"I feel like my head's going to explode." I looked at the jewelry box in my hand. "Can I have a minute?"

"Take all the time you need. I'll be downstairs." Dan left me alone in the closet, then I heard him shut the bedroom door. I drifted back toward my side of the closet, and sat on the floor in front of my clothes.

My clothes.

I'd never thought of myself as particularly sentimental, but being reunited with my leather jacket and boots and all my jeans that had been washed so many times they were as soft as silk was tying me up in knots. And it wasn't just clothing taking me down memory lane. When I opened the drawers, I found other bits of my life, old thumb drives and concert tickets, pretty rocks I'd picked up on walks and dried flowers and toys I'd held onto for decades. Everything I'd thought I'd lost was right here, waiting for me to find it.

Speaking of things I thought I'd lost, I still clutched the velvet box. I took out the sapphire ring and slid it onto the appropriate finger. It fit perfectly.

Did we go for fittings, or was Dan going to surprise me? It was like Dan to engineer a surprise, and he knew sapphire was my favorite gem. I set the box with the other two rings aside, then I stood in front of the full length mirror. My eyes were still red and puffy, so I ducked into the bathroom and washed my face. That done, I went back into the closet and put on my jacket and boots. When I stood in front of the mirror again, I looked like myself.

I felt like myself.

I raised my left hand, so it was over my heart, and watched the sapphire catch the light. My anger with Dan had fizzled down to almost nothing long before he'd presented me with this perfect ring. Of course, he had to check if Charlotte was alive. He's a caretaker, and if she'd been here he wouldn't have turned her out on the street just to move me in. Dan was just trying to do what was right in this confusing, fucked up timeline, and he was downstairs dealing with all of this alone while I hid in the closet and played dress up.

I didn't want him to be alone.

I went downstairs and found Dan fast asleep on the couch. I saw a half empty beer on the table next to him, and laughed softly; he was such a lightweight. I kicked off my boots and laid down next to him, my head on his shoulder and my left hand over his heart. I kissed the corner of his jaw, then I let my eyes close.

When I woke, we were still on the couch, but Dan was awake. He'd also moved me so I was lying on top of him. One of his hands rested underneath my jacket on the small of my back, while the other stroked my hair.

"There you are," he said, when I opened my eyes. "Why'd you put the coat on? Were you cold?"

"I missed it." I propped myself up on my elbow so I could see him a bit better. "I missed you."

"I missed you, too." He took my left hand and rubbed his thumb across the sapphire. "I see it fits."

"It does." He brought my hand to his mouth and kissed my knuckles. "I'm sorry I freaked out."

"I'm sorry, too." He tightened his arms around me. "I was so scared I'd lost you."

"After everything that happened back at Katherine's house, and then when I saw you check if Charlotte was alive…" I squeezed my eyes shut, willing myself to not feel that pain and despair again. "What would you have done if she was alive?"

"I honestly don't know," he replied. "And you want to know the worst part? When I saw her obituary, I was relieved. Not in a way that I was happy she was gone," he added.

"I know you'd never be happy over someone's death," I said. "When we went back in time, I wasn't expecting the handfasting. I thought we'd make sure everyone was all right, then Katherine would anoint me, and that would be it. Then Montgomery brought out the cords, and…"

"And?" Dan prompted.

"And I never realized just how much I wanted to be your wife," I finished. "Then we came back, and everything was wrong, and I got so swept up in the wrongness I thought I'd made the wrong decision with you, too."

Dan smoothed back my hair, and kissed my forehead. "I'm so sorry, baby," he murmured, his lips against my skin. "I never meant to hurt you."

"I'm sorry, too. I never should have run from you."

"It's okay. We're back together now. Just like we said in our vows, we use our tempers to strengthen what's between us."

"Why are you so understanding?"

"Because I love you."

I pressed my face against his throat, drinking in the scent of him, and slid my hand underneath his shirt so it rested over his heart. "Lying with you on this couch might be my favorite thing in the world."

"Not bubble baths?"

I smiled. "Those are nice, too."

Now that I was thinking about warm baths, I realized the leather jacket was too much. I pushed myself upright so I could remove it, which left me straddling Dan's waist. He watched me take off the jacket, then he raked his gaze across my body.

"You look great in that."

"I borrowed it from Tess." I felt his cock harden beneath me, and rocked my hips. "What is it with you and dresses? Every time I wear one, you act like I'm the only woman you've ever seen."

"You just don't understand how beautiful you are." He set his hands on my hips and pushed himself against me. "And you are the only woman I see."

I slid back and unfastened his pants, then I paused, my hand hovering over his cock. "Not gonna stop me?"

"Why would I?"

Thus emboldened, I freed his cock and stroked it once, twice. It was hot and hard and wrapped in the softest skin I'd ever felt. Dan's eyelids went heavy, and he arched his back. While he was distracted, I bent forward and took him into my mouth. He was surprised at first, then he lay back and sank his hands into my hair. I dragged my tongue along the underside of his cock, smiled when he moaned.

He fisted his hands in my hair. "I want more of you."

"How much?"

"Everything."

I released him, then I stood and slipped off my panties. Before Dan could say yes or no or even take his shirt off I got back on the couch and fit his cock against me. I paused, my gaze locked with his, then I slid down onto him. I gasped as a shudder rolled across my skin; somehow I'd forgotten over these last few days apart just how much he filled me.

Dan slid his hand underneath my dress and squeezed my hip. "You fit me like a glove, baby."

I smiled, because who doesn't like it when their partner's mind is in the same place as theirs, then I unfastened my dress and let it fall to the floor. My bra joined it a moment later, then I pitched myself forward until my elbows bracketed his head and my lips hovered above his.

"Show me how much you missed me."

A Wolf in The Flower Bed

Hours later, I woke up in our bed wearing nothing but the sapphire ring. Dan was on me like cling wrap, and I took a moment to feel like everything was fine, and that this was where I belonged.

Only, things were far from fine, I didn't belong here, and neither did Dan.

I rolled over, and kissed Dan until he woke up. He smiled, but my face must have betrayed my feelings. "What's wrong?"

"Nothing. This room is perfect, as is the house, your job, and everything else."

"But, it's not right," he finished. "And everything isn't perfect. Some things are definitely not right."

I propped myself up on an elbow, and asked, "What have you noticed?"

"You don't have your business," he replied. "Remember the sign I got you? It's not here."

"I never got my private investigator's license," I said. "I never had my apartment, either. Not for one day."

"Then the changes go back at least two, maybe three years."

"Longer than that. My dad doesn't remember Tessa," I said. "Well, he knows of her, but he doesn't remember having a relationship with her. And there's Tessa's two sets of memories, and Bennet's got two sets of records."

Dan grunted. "How far back do the double records go?"

"Three hundred and seventy-two years. The first anomaly is when Katherine had her second child. She named him Daniel."

"Really," Dan said, flush with pride. "He must have been the start of your cousins."

"Not only that, seers never left this area. Remember how I wanted to recreate the community Katherine had? In this timeline, it never left." I paused, and busied myself with tracing little circles on Dan's chest. "I think I created this timeline."

Dan frowned. "Is that even possible?"

"When I went to see my mother, she told me that she'd created a life she wanted," I began, deliberately not looking at him while I remembered my mother's annoyance at having to deal with me. "We know she's insanely powerful, and she's manifested stuff before."

"Like changing the weather when she was pregnant with you," he said, and I nodded.

"Not only that, she confirmed she gave me the thornapple to dampen my witchcraft, but even before the seed pod came out of me, I manifested stuff, too. Remember all the bleeding hearts?"

"How could I forget?" He grinned, because the morning after our first night together we'd woken up to bleeding hearts carpeting the entire town. "And now that you don't have that dampener, you think your natural ability was boosted by the nexus and you created a new timeline."

"Accidentally," I added. "I accidentally created a new timeline. Not that I don't love what we have here, but it's not right."

"Not only that, we don't know how others have been affected," he said. "So, Mistress, how do we put things back?"

"Somehow, we need to make the people stuck in this timeline remember the correct one." I flopped onto my back, and sorted out my thoughts. "Remember when Ned Burroughs was on City Hall's steps, and he was stuck behind a time slip?"

"I had to ring the clock tower's bell to snap everything back to the present."

"Exactly. We need to make a bridge between the two timelines, so the real events stick and everything else falls away." I remembered something, and said, "The cats aren't at Gran's."

"That can't be good," he said. "Think someone catnapped them?"

"I don't think anyone could," I replied, remembering the massive felines they became when threatened. "But I have a theory."

Dan kissed me between my breasts. "Lay it on me."

"Stop trying to distract me," I said, while making absolutely no effort to get away from him. "There aren't any spirits here, and a soul is the one thing that cannot be replicated. I don't think the cats can be replicated, either."

"Further proof that this is the wrong timeline," Dan said, as he nuzzled my neck. "Then what happened is that someone basically made a photocopy of the correct timeline, but some important parts got lost in translation."

"Kind of," I said, then he grazed his teeth across my earlobe and I moaned. "What are you doing to me?"

"Reminding you that you're mine, and that I get to kiss you whenever I want."

I turned into his arms. "Just kissing?"

"Whatever you want, babe."

Later still, we showered and went downstairs. Being that I'd shown up a few minutes after Dan got home from work, and I hadn't eaten since breakfast and neither of us had dinner, we were starved. Unfortunately, there was very little food in the kitchen.

"I guess we don't cook," Dan said as he closed the fridge.

"Who needs to cook? I got this," I said as I grabbed a box of cereal. "Is there any milk in there?"

"No."

I set the box down and frowned. "This is serious. We might starve."

Dan laughed, and grabbed a menu from the drawer. "I'll order pizza. Pepperoni mushroom?"

"Perfect." I glanced out of the kitchen window. The setting sun was putting on quite the light show in the backyard. "I'm going to visit the plants."

"Are you going to put anything else on?" he asked, since I was only wearing one of his oversized tee shirts.

"Nah. It's warm out."

Dan shook his head, and went back to ordering dinner. I stepped outside, and sunk my toes into the thick green grass. Going barefoot was one of the best ways to learn about a place, and I wanted to soak up as much information from the earth as possible. Then I got to the raised beds, and stopped dead in my tracks.

Almost every poisonous plant had been replaced by something innocuous.

"Pizza is on its way," Dan announced as he joined me in the yard. He stood behind me and slid his arms around my waist, and noticed my rigid frame. "You cold? Told you to put more clothes on. Lucky I'm here to warm you up."

"Dan. What happened to the plants?"

"Hmm?" He raised his head from my neck. "Everything's blooming. Does that mean they're more poisonous?"

"These are different plants." I crouched down, and examined the petunias and impatiens. "The belladonnas and foxgloves aren't here, and even the snakeroot's gone. The only baneful herb remaining is the aconite."

"Aconite?" Dan crouched beside me. "Which one is that?"

I pointed at the indigo blue flower stalks. "That one. One of its common names is wolfsbane. It's also called queen of poisons."

"Based on that name I'm guessing I shouldn't touch it?"

"Handling it with your bare hands is a bad idea. Back in the day, it was used for poisoned arrows."

Dan grunted. "Nothing else here is poisonous?"

"Well, you wouldn't want to eat most of this stuff, but only the wolfsbane will outright kill you."

"Then why is it still here, when the rest of the poisons are gone?" He stood, and offered me a hand. "One thing's becoming very clear in this timeline. All of these changes are happening for a reason, and I don't think you manifested everything. There's a lot going on here."

"You're right. It's not like I would make my father forget Tessa, or make Tessa into the Beauclaire's glorified secretary."

"Think any of this is a vendetta against Tess?"

Before I could respond, a man peeked over the side gate, and said, "Hello? Pizza delivery for Lyons?"

"Hey, that was fast," Dan said as he went to pay for the pizza. The delivery guy craned his neck to get a look at me, so I foiled his plans and went inside. Dan joined me in the kitchen a moment later.

"Didn't I just order this like five, ten minutes ago?" He opened the box, and the pizza was hot and steaming. "Weird."

"Like you said, this timeline isn't all bad." I opened the fridge to grab something to drink, and remembered our lack of milk. "How will I have coffee in the morning?"

"I will get you some milk," Dan said, as he set two plates on the table. "I should have added something about coffee to our vows. 'I, Dan, promise to always have your coffee perfectly prepared and waiting for you.'"

I stood on my toes and kissed his cheek. "Careful. With talk like that I'll have you making lattes every day."

"I can handle that." We sat, and started on the pizza. It was delicious.

"You know what else is weird," Dan began. "That delivery guy looked familiar."

"Has he delivered here before?"

"No. I must be remembering from somewhere else."

"Did the cameras catch him?" I asked, since Dan had several strategically placed surveillance cameras set up around the house and yard. "I might recognize him."

"Let's see." Dan wolfed down his slice of pizza, then he got up and left the room. He returned carrying his tablet, to which he'd linked the cameras. "Here's our guy."

Dan set the tablet in front of me. On it was a still shot of the delivery guy's face. "He does look familiar," I said, then I spied the name on his jacket: Gary.

In a rush, I remembered the Ghost Guys.

"Remember when Amir first came to town, and he had those lame ghost hunters working for him?"

"Those losers? What about them?"

"Gary was their tech guy."

While we ate, we rehashed everything that had happened with the Ghost Guys. They had worked for Amir, who mainly used them to distract and occasionally stalk me. As far as I knew, the three of them had been arrested for breaking and entering on Dan's property, and were still in jail. Of course, this had all happened back in the real timeline.

"If Hassan never met you, then he probably never hired those ghost clowns, either," Dan concluded. "Bennet's certain Hassan in still in Iran?"

"He is. What's more, my dad and I never went to Iran. In this world, Amir has never been to this country." I tapped the notebook with my pencil. "I was never kidnapped by the Beauclaires, either."

"That's why you think you manifested this world. You skipped over most of the bad stuff." Dan took my hand, and rubbed his thumb across my knuckles. "I wish I knew you back then, or had been nearby when they grabbed you off the street. I wouldn't have let those assholes near you."

I squeezed his fingers. "I wonder how we met in this world. If I was never a private investigator, then you never would have taken my statement after the Forge Heights case."

"But we have Abigail Stevens' drawing of us, so you must have rescued her."

"I could have just run into her at the truck stop," I said. "You don't have to be an official detective to help someone."

"True, very true. We could have met when you brought Abby home. Or maybe we were high school sweethearts."

I giggled. "We're too far apart in age to have been in high school at the same time. Besides, you went to school in Queens. I've never been to New York."

"Never? Now there's the real crime. As soon as this is behind us, I'm taking you to the city. But, based on this house, and all the pictures and other mementos, we've been in a serious relationship for years. In fact, two years ago we went on that trip to Aruba, which means we had to have been together for a while before that."

"I guess it would be weird to just meet someone and go to an island together."

Dan dropped his gaze to our hands. "There's nothing here from my life before I met you. I don't think I was ever married before."

I stood and circled the table, and embraced him. "I'm sorry. I wish I knew how to undo all this."

"We'll figure it out." He scooped me onto his lap. "We always do."

"What if whoever did this didn't know you'd been married?" I asked. "The major changes in my life are all public knowledge. Everyone in the supernatural community knows I was kidnapped, knows I dated Amir, and they all know I was a private detective."

"But they probably wouldn't have taken the time to look too deep into my life," Dan said, proving yet again that our minds worked the same way. "And they probably never knew about Alex and Tess, so that got left out, too."

"When you get to work tomorrow, can you do some research on the Ghost Guys? I don't think it was a coincidence that Gary delivered our pizza."

"I agree, and I can start files on all three of them. What was the third guy's name?"

"Um, I don't know if I ever knew his name. No matter how involved or not involved the Ghost Guys are, I really think some of these changes were caused when we passed through the nexus."

"We'll figure it all out, but first I have a question. Since you think us going through the nexus influenced events to a certain degree, any I idea how I ended up as the chief of police?"

I paused, and thought about how I felt about Dan's job. "When you got suspended, I felt awful. Making you the chief might be my convoluted way of apologizing."

He wrapped his arm around my shoulders and kissed my temple. "You're always looking out for me," he said. With his other hand, he grasped my ring. "You do realize that based on your theory, you also probably manifested this."

"At least now you know what I like."

Another kiss. "Yeah. I do. What are you going to do tomorrow while I'm at work?"

"I'm going to make my dad remember Tessa."

Isa And The Marksman

The next morning, Dan put on a suit and went to work, and I put on some jeans, a tee, my leather jacket, and my old black boots, and went to see my father. I hadn't even called him since I'd left him alone with the all those kids, although he'd seemed to have a handle on the situation. He'd always wanted a house full of children, and it looked like he finally got his wish.

I bet he hadn't wanted to be the only adult in the house, though.

When I pulled into Gran's driveway, I took a moment to appreciate the familiar sights and sounds: the wrought iron fence, the crunch of the gravel driveway under my tires, the hillside behind the house covered in roses and brambles. Then I got out of my car and opened the mudroom door, steeling myself for the onslaught of many young cousins... and heard nothing. Not only was the house devoid of children and therefore silent, there was no sound of twelve tiny paws running to greet me. The cats had been present for my entire life, and now they were gone. I hoped they were okay, and that I would see them again.

"Dad?" I called. "Are you home?"

"In here."

I followed his voicetold and found him in the solarium, pruning the oleanders. "I see the cousins have departed," I observed.

"They went home shortly after you left the other day." He put down his shears and took off his gloves. "How are things with you and Dan?"

"Better. Pretty good, actually," I added, as my face warmed.

"Good. You're happy when you're with him, and I like it when you're happy. Come on, I'll make us some coffee."

I followed him into the kitchen. "I went to see Mom yesterday."

My father, the refined man who regularly mingled with the witch equivalent of royalty, snorted. "And how was Christina?"

"Same as always," I replied. "She accused you of fathering children all over the world."

Another snort. "Don't you think I'd tell you if you had siblings?"

"Of course you would. She's just nuts."

"Is she still out in Oak Grove?" he asked, and I nodded. "What made you drive all that way?"

"Remember how I told you that me and Dan thought we changed the timeline? Well, we definitely did, and part of me hoped she was different. That maybe she could finally be a mother to me."

Dad faced me. "But she wasn't."

I shook my head. "She sure wasn't. If anything, she was pissed I went to see her."

Dad smiled sadly. "I'm sorry, Bug. I wish I could explain your mother's behavior, but I'm as baffled as you are."

"I know. Anyway, about the changes in the timeline... Back in the other one, you were different."

"Oh?" He turned back to the coffeemaker. "Different how?"

"Do you remember Gran's friend Tessa? Actually, do you remember Gran's cats?"

"Ma's cats? You mean the three she had when she was a kid? They're not around anymore."

"They were, in the other timeline."

"That's..." He paused. "They were here, weren't they? They were... important?"

"Yes." I stood next to him at the counter. "What else do you remember?"

"About the cats?"

"About anything." Now that I'd gotten Dad to make a connection to his real memories, I wracked my brain to figure out how I could open the floodgates, and recalled one event he could never forget. "When I was seventeen, I was kidnapped."

"No, you weren't."

"Yes, I was. I was taken by two witches and they stuck me in a basement, where they tortured me for three weeks. I almost died."

Dad's hands trembled, and he gripped his coffee mug to steady them. "After you got out, I burned down the house."

"You did," I said. "Do you remember who you were with? Who brought you to the house, and helped you rescue me?"

"Tessa." Dad set down his mug and faced me. "Tessa."

"Yes! I astral projected to Tessa, because she's a witch and witches were holding me. Tessa found you and brought you home, then the two of you rescued me. I will never forget when that basement door opened, and you and Tessa were standing there. That was the moment I realized I was going to get out of there."

Dad pulled me into his arms. "I wanted to kill them," he whispered. "I wanted to murder every last one of them, but not quickly. I wanted to stretch out their deaths over days or weeks. Months. I wanted them to suffer, because they made you suffer."

"But you didn't," I said. "You handed them over to the clan elders. You did the right thing."

There was wetness on my neck; man, I hadn't wanted to make Dad cry. "I should have been here for you."

"Dad, you've always been here for me," I said, and it was the truth. My father had been the best parent in the history of parents, full stop, but I wanted him to think about someone other than me. "You've always been there for Tessa, too. You two met a while ago, huh?"

"I was twenty-two when Tessa and I met," he began. "Ma told me one of her dearest friends was coming by for a visit. I couldn't fathom how they were such dear friends if they hadn't seen each other since before I was born, then Tessa was here and I understood. How could anyone forget her?"

"She is pretty unforgettable."

"She is," Dad said, then he drew back and regarded me. "Where is she? Why isn't she here, with me?"

"She's at her place. I can take you to her."

Dad nodded. "Let's go."

During the short drive to Tessa's condo, I explained to my father that she had two sets of memories, and was having a hard time reconciling them. By the time I pulled into the parking lot, I'd given him all the bad news.

"The Beauclaires are using her as a secretary?" Dad shook his head. "That's not right."

"Tell me about it." We got out of the car, and headed toward the elevator. "Tessa is so far above those fools."

Dad pressed the elevator's call button, and frowned. "I hope she wants to see me."

"She does. Trust me, Dad, she needs you."

"I hope you're right."

We exited the elevator and knocked on Tessa's door. When she opened it, Dad fell to his knees and wrapped his arms around Tessa's waist.

"Isa, my Isa, will you ever forgive me?" he implored. "I'm so sorry I forgot you."

"You didn't forget me. It was a spell." Tessa sank her fingers into Dad's hair. "Alex, get up." He did, then Tessa grabbed his face and kissed him as if her life depended on it. For all I knew, it did.

"I see you two are good," I said. "I'll just get out of your hair."

"Eli, wait," Tessa said over Dad's shoulder. "The Beauclaires will see you tonight at eight."

"Thanks, Tess. Call if you need me." I watched my father and Tessa go inside and shut the door, and understood they wouldn't call me for anything less than the end of the world. Maybe not even for that, and that was as it should be.

COUNTRY ROADS

After I kissed Eli goodbye—and kissed her a second time, just for good measure—I hopped into my truck and headed toward the station. When I was a block away from work, I veered off course and headed north on Route Nine. Now that Eli and I were good, I needed some time alone with my thoughts, and these country roads were great for thinking.

There was plenty I didn't like about living out in the suburbs, and a big chunk of this area was downright rural. Where I'd grown up, the average lawn was the size of a postage stamp, and backyards were either nonexistent, or concrete pads reserved for family get togethers. My nonna's house was an exception, since she had a small greenhouse to grow tomatoes and other vegetables. At one time I thought Charlotte got the idea for us having a greenhouse from Nonna's place, but it turned out I was wrong about that. Let's face it, I was wrong about a lot of things.

For one thing, I was wrong about what my life would end up like. I'd never wanted to be cop, but my dream profession—teaching—didn't come with good pay or benefits. Thanks to my then-partner's chronic health issues, I couldn't rely on her to contribute to the household income, and I needed the best insurance plan I could get to keep her as healthy as possible. So I talked to one of my older brothers, and he talked to a few of his buddies on the police force, and I applied to the academy. I got accepted, and two weeks after I graduated with my history degree, I started my career as a police officer.

Being a cop in Queens was all right. It wasn't great, but I loved the neighborhood and I did a good job. Then the time came for us to buy a bigger place, and we ended up moving a state away to live near a bunch of liberal art colleges and dairy farms. I remained a cop, but my usual calls went from writing up traffic violations and investigating break-ins to capturing escaped livestock and overseeing property line disputes. Still, not a bad life, but not what I wanted my life to be. But me and Char, we had each other, so it was all good.

Then she died, and I was all alone out here.

I pulled off Route Nine and followed a few back roads to an old yellow farmhouse. When we'd first moved, we rented this place while we looked for a place to buy, and let me tell you, it was a fiasco. We were every bad movie about city slickers on a farm come to life, and we experienced every catastrophe you could imagine. But we figured everything out, one problem at a time. After a few months of frozen pipes and a crash course in yard and septic system maintenance, I knew we could handle anything.

As I watched the farmhouse from my spot on the main road, I wondered who lived there now. Were they newlyweds like Char and I were? Were they an old married couple settling into their golden years, or did they want to work the land? From what I recalled, this place came with acres and acres of fields. The amount of work to maintain this place blew my mind back then, and I hadn't attempted planting anything. But maybe I should have.

Maybe the key was to put down strong roots, and nurture them as best you could.

Nowadays, I had some serious roots. I had my brick house, which thankfully hadn't come with acres waiting to be plowed or a septic system; believe me, town water is the way to go. And I had my Eliza, and she had her own roots. Now that we were together, I finally felt like I belonged out here... and that was when it hit me. For the first time since I'd left New York, I didn't feel like a New Yorker. My home was here now, and it was up to me to help Eli fix this timeline so we could get back where we belong.

Our home was here in the country, but I finally understood that home isn't a place, so much as a feeling. My home was with Eli, and it always will be.

I started up the truck and swung a u-turn without looking. It's not like these country roads are heavily traveled. Even if it had been rush hour, I needed to get moving. I had work to do and a case to crack, then me and Eli were going home.

VALLEY BURGER

Eli: Dad and Tess are together again!

    Dan: Good job, Cupid.

Dan: What are you up to? Can I take you to lunch?

Eli: I like lunch. On my way!

Even though it was only ten in the morning, and therefore way too early for lunch, I went straight to the police station. Now that Dan and I had worked through our rough patch, I couldn't get enough of him, and I liked it that way. I liked being happy and in love and wanting to see Dan's face more than anything else in the world. Hopefully, these warm fuzzy feelings would remain strong when and if we fixed this broken timeline. Although, this reality was turning out to not be as bad as I'd feared.

When I stepped inside the police station, the desk sergeant, Mahoney, grinned at me. "Hey, Eli. Chief's in his office," he said as he waved me through. "We've missed you around here lately."

"Sorry! I'll come by more often," I said, because I couldn't really mention how we were living in a false reality. Then I was at Dan's office door, and took a moment to watch him work. He was writing on a legal pad, and was concentrating so hard on his work a little line had formed between his brows. At least, I assumed he was concentrating on work. For all I knew he was finishing up a crossword puzzle.

"I know you're there," he said without looking up from his notepad.

"I know you know."

Dan looked up and smiled at me, then he stood and came around to the front of his desk. "I have to warn you, there's a running bet around here that centers on what happens when you come to see me."

"What sort of bet?"

"How long it takes me to close the blinds once you're in my office." Dan took me into his arms as he pushed the office door closed behind me. "There's also a bit of speculation about what we get up to in here."

"Is there?" I asked, as I wound my arms around his neck. "Don't they have anyone else to gossip about?"

"Guess not." Dan kissed my forehead, then he led me to his desk.

"You're leaving them open?" I asked, glancing at the blinds.

"I like messing with the odds. Here, I did some digging on the Ghost Guys." He slid the legal pad toward me. Scrawled across the top were three names: Mike Delacorte, Gary Williams, and James Roberts.

"Just three regular guys," I muttered. "Are they paranormal investigators here, too?"

"Not sure, but the pizza guy was definitely Gary Williams." Dan swiveled his monitor around, and I saw Gary's driver's license picture on the screen. "He appears to only deliver pizza, but it's him. All three of them work at the same shop."

"Weird." Before I could delve further into the weirdness, there was a knock at the door.

"Chief?" Mahoney asked as he cracked open the door. "Everyone decent in here?"

"Funny, Mahoney," Dan said. "What's up?"

"There's a Jacob Allwood asking to see you."

"Jacob's here now?" I asked.

"Eli, you know him?" Mahoney asked.

"He's my uncle," I replied, then I faced Dan. "Why would he be here?"

"Probably looking for you," Dan replied. "Send him over, Mahoney. Thanks, buddy."

"Will do," Mahoney said as he ducked out of the office. A few moments later, Jacob stood in the doorway. Yet again, I marveled that he was such a robust spirit that others regularly mistook him for being a living man... And realized I was wrong. Jacob wasn't a spirit at all.

"Mr. Allwood," Dan greeted. "What can I do for you?"

"We seem to have a problem," Jacob began. "It centers on me being alive."

The three of us relocated to one of the interrogation rooms. According to Dan, the one he chose was free of surveillance equipment, so whatever we said would remain confidential. Once we were inside, Dan locked the door and faced Jacob with his arms crossed over his chest.

"Let's cut to the chase," Dan began. "How long have you been alive?"

"Unsure," Jacob replied. "By all accounts, I've been living my life in the same manner for years. Decades, even. However, a few days ago I woke up, and for the briefest moment I marveled that even though I'm a ghost I still needed to sleep." Jacob sat, and set his hands on the table palms down. "But that makes no sense. It's plain that I'm not a ghost, and I'm certainly not dead. And yet..."

"Have you had any other out-of-place thoughts?" I asked.

"Oh, yes. Several. As is my practice, I meditated on these odd thoughts, and I found a cache of memories buried deep within my mind." Jacob paused, tracing the wood grain on the table. "I've been dead for some time, haven't I?"

"Since last March," I replied. "Your spirit was trapped in a barrel of apple seeds. Dan and I freed you," I added.

"Thank you. The addition of apples means Sarah's involved, yes?"

"Like a fairy tale gone bad, she's all over this story," Dan said. "What made you come here today?"

"I seek Eliza Moore's help because she's the Mistress of Seers, and therefore the best person to handle anything of a spiritual nature," Jacob replied. "Also, there has been recent activity at the nexus. I assumed that the nexus's involvement is what started all of this."

"Wait, how do you know what happened in the nexus?" I asked.

"Whenever anyone passes through it a blue pattern appears in the sky above the Moore house," Jacob replied. "The pattern has appeared three times in recent weeks."

I looked at Dan. "There's something we didn't know."

"But why did you come here looking for Eli?" Dan pressed. "She's not on the force."

"No, but she lives with the chief of police," Jacob replied. "When neither of you were at your home, I assumed at least one of you would be here. It seems I was correct."

"Great detective work," I said. "Our current theory is we're living in a false timeline that was somehow created when we used the nexus to travel through time. A few people who died in the real timeline are alive here. Some people have memories from both timelines, while others seem wholly unaware of what's going on. No mortals appear to be affected, except for Dan."

Jacob snorted. "Mortals constantly ignore what's happening right in front of them. I believe their indifference toward the supernatural community is what's kept their race alive for so long. No offense," he added, with a nod toward Dan.

"None taken," Dan said, "but that's an interesting concept. I have no memories from this timeline, and I'm mortal. Maybe the mortals aren't in on it?"

"It's possible this timeline was set up to benefit mortals." I tapped my chin with my forefinger. "Or maybe to control them."

"Who wants to control mortals?" Dan asked. "Oh, right. You people."

Jacob's eyes flashed. "Have a care, or you may not like the consequences of your actions."

"Have a care how you speak to Dan or you definitely won't like the consequences," I snapped, glaring at both of them for good measure. "We need to work together, not snipe at each other."

Jacob dipped his chin. "You're right. Apologies to both of you."

"And to you, Jacob," Dan said. "I'm not sure what memories you have of me, but we've always gotten along well. I appreciate that."

"As do I," Jacob said.

"Now that we're all friends again," I began, "what I find the oddest aspect of this reality is that there aren't any ghosts. We're in a spiritual dead zone."

"Interesting," Jacob said. "Do you think that's why I'm alive again?"

"That's a possibility," I said. "We're still not really sure how much this new timeline encompasses, but we do know that the shepherd, Bennet Carrington, also has duplicate records. The earliest anomaly happened three hundred and seventy-two years ago."

"And what was that anomaly?"

"Jemima Beauclaire's passing."

Jacob blew out a breath. "She remains alive today."

"I have an appointment to see the Beauclaires tonight at eight," I continued. "I'm hoping if I see Jemima, I might gain some insight into what's happening here. If nothing else, I'll find out if she remembers me."

"You're not going to the Beauclaires alone, are you?" Jacob asked. "I can accompany you."

"I'll be with her," Dan said, his forceful tone surprising me. "Where Eli goes, I go."

"If you have time, could I ask you to look in on Ned Burroughs and Melinda Howe?" I asked Jacob. "They shouldn't be alive, either."

"I can certainly look in on Ned," he replied. "As for Melinda, she's prickly on her best days, but I will see what I can learn."

"I understand. I appreciate anything you can do to help us."

"Of course. We of the clans are beholden to the Mistress of Seers."

Soon after Jacob left to visit the clan elders who may or may not be alive, Dan made good on his promise and took me to lunch. While we drove to the restaurant, I teased him about his protective nature.

"Now you're my bodyguard?" I pitched my voice lower, and said, "Where Eli goes, I go."

"That's right. There is no way I'm letting you set foot on Beauclaire land alone. I will be there every step of the way, and if anything looks off, we're leaving."

"What if I'm not ready to leave?"

He gave me a look that said discussion was off the table. "If things get weird, I'm getting you out of there. End of story."

"Yes, Officer Lyons. Wait, should I call you Chief Lyons? Mr. Chief?"

I got some side eye, but he was suppressing a smile. "I solved the mystery of what happened to Renault. Turns out he never got divorced, and he's an officer down in West Haven."

"Good for him. Exactly where are you taking me for lunch?" I asked, as we passed restaurant after restaurant.

"I thought we'd grab some pizza."

"We had pizza last night. Oh, you want to see what the Ghost Guys are up to."

Dan grinned at me. "You got it, babe."

We turned onto Elm Street, and headed toward a plaza. As Dan turned into the parking lot, he frowned. "This is the address, but that's a hardware store," he said, jerking his chin toward the business.

"Weird," I said. "The other day, Tessa and I went by Dim Sum Delight. It's a burger joint now. Maybe something's up with all the restaurants."

"Even if there is, that doesn't explain where our pizza came from last night. And I still don't understand how they delivered it so fast."

"Magic pizza?" I suggested with a shrug. "Honestly, I've got nothing here."

"We've also got nothing to eat. Want to hit up that burger place?"

"Sure."

We turned around and went back to the center of the city, and Dan parked in the municipal lot. As we walked toward Valley Burgers, we passed by my old apartment building.

"Speaking of weird, this building might be the weirdest of all," Dan said. "The last time we were on this sidewalk, we were surrounded by firemen."

"It was awful," I said, remembering the dust and ash and how my ears had rung from the explosion. I shielded my eyes from the sun and looked toward what used to be my office window. The curtains snapped shut. Curious, I glanced at the balcony. I could see the outline of a person leaning against the sliding door, watching the sidewalk. I turned my back to the building, and said, "We're being observed."

Dan dipped his head, asked, "Where?"

"My apartment."

Dan slipped his arm around my waist, and also turned his back to the building. A moment later, I realized he was watching the building's reflection in the restaurant's wide plate glass windows.

"Thoughts?" he asked.

"None so far," I replied. "Let's get lunch and see what happens."

We went inside and got a table far from the front windows, and looked over the menu. It featured beef, beef, and more beef, and side dishes of meatballs and mini meatloaves. "I realize this is a burger place, but this has to be the most meat-centric menu I've ever seen."

Dan flipped the menu over. "I've never wanted a salad so much in my entire life."

"The French fries come with dipping gravy," I said, then I recognized the man behind the counter. I grabbed my phone and started typing.

"Who are you calling?"

"My mom," I replied, and hit send on my text.

Eli: Check out the cook. Mike Delacorte.

Dan: Isn't that convenient? Want to bet who's watching us from your apartment?

The server arrived to take our order. Dan set his phone on the table with the screen down, which the server noted. I wondered if he was the third Ghost Guy, the least memorable of them all. Then again, the server might have just recognized Dan as the police chief, and I was reading into the situation.

After we ordered, Dan grabbed his phone and set a few more texts. "Work," he explained, when he was done.

"Okay." I didn't want to pry into any of his cases, so I asked, "Have you talked to your family back in New York lately?"

"No," he said; from his tone, I understood that when he told me there was no evidence of his life before we met, he worried that his family had been wiped away, too. I reached across the table and squeezed his hand.

"Tell me about them. What's your mom like?"

"She's great," he replied. "Ma runs a pretty tight ship. She had to, what with all the stuff we got up to. There's seven of us, and we're all close in age, so there was regular chaos."

"I bet. Do they all have families, too?"

"Most of them. Around the holidays we all descend on our nonna's house. She cooks for days, and the food is amazing." He took my hand in both of his. "I want to bring you out there."

"Then we'll go," I said. "Think they'll like me?"

"Of course they will. They'll love you, just like I do." He straightened the ring on my finger. "Maybe we'll have something to tell them."

"Think they'll be all right with the handfasting? It's pretty unconventional."

"Oh, you haven't seen the spare bedrooms," he began, then the server arrived with our food. We'd each gotten a cheeseburger and fries.

"What's so interesting about those spare rooms?" I asked, then I took a bite of my burger. It was pretty dry, and it could definitely use some ketchup.

"One's pink, and one's blue."

"Who picked that color scheme? The second floor's painted like a basket of Easter eggs." Wondering if we'd gone to the paint store drunk I took another bite of my burger. Dan raised an eyebrow, and I realized one very common reason why someone would paint a room in those colors.

And I started choking on my burger.

"Eli? Baby, drink some water." Dan moved around the table to help me, but the server ran to our table and planted himself between us.

"Are you all right, ma'am?" the server asked. "Is this man bothering you?"

I swallowed the offending lump of food, and glared at the server. "No, he is not bothering me," I snapped. "I choked on your dry burger."

"I can bring you a side of gravy," the server said, then he sidestepped to keep himself between me and Dan.

"Why don't you bring her some water, instead?" Dan suggested. "And stop trying to keep me away from my wife."

The server backed away from Dan, who finally made his way to me. "You okay?" he asked, as he patted my back.

"I'm fine," I said. "I was just shocked about, um, the room colors."

"Imagine how I felt." Dan reclaimed his seat, and lifted the bun off his burger. He frowned at the patty, and said, "I'm all set with this place."

"Me, too. Should we get a box?"

"Only if you want to burn these in effigy." Dan went to the counter, and paid for our food. When he returned he dropped some cash on the table for a tip, because he was polite, not because the food warranted anything extra. "Ready?"

"Definitely."

We left our barely eaten lunch behind, and got out of the restaurant as fast as possible. When we stepped out onto the sidewalk, the curtains in my apartment window once again snapped closed.

"These guys are not subtle," I muttered. "Also, I'm still hungry."

"Me too, babe." Dan draped his arm around my shoulders, and we walked toward the car. "What we really need to do is go grocery shopping so I can come home for lunch."

"Do you even know how to cook? Because you know my specialty is cereal."

"I make great sandwiches." We leisurely walked back to the parking lot, as if we weren't being watched the entire time. Once we were in the car, Dan cupped my face with his hands.

"You're sure you're all right?" he asked. "The burger wasn't poisoned?"

"I can handle poisons," I reminded him. "Sudden insinuations that we're having kids, not so much."

"Hey, I didn't paint those rooms. At least, I don't think I did." Dan swept his thumbs across my cheeks, then he kissed my forehead. "Why was the server trying to make you coughing into me somehow bothering you?"

"I don't know, but I'm starting to think you're right. This timeline is set up to drive us apart." I gripped his hand. "But that's not going to happen, right?"

"Never." Dan tilted up my chin and kissed my lips, then he released me and started the car. "We should probably act like we aren't on to them," he said, as he pulled out of the parking lot. "What are you going to do while I pretend to work?"

"The police chief pretends to work? What a waste of tax dollars." Dan narrowed his eyes at me, and I laughed. "I'll probably just go home. I need to find something to wear to meet the Beauclaires tonight."

"That a formal event?"

"Technically, I can wear whatever I want, but I want to look strong. Powerful." I thought about our earlier interaction with Jacob, and said, "Did you notice when Jacob said that the witch clans are beholden to me?"

"I did. Why?"

"I've never heard that before. No witch has ever said that to me, and I'm pretty sure no one ever said it to Gran."

"Then why did Jacob say it to you?"

"I don't know, but I mean to find out."

MR. AND MRS. BEAUCLAIRE

Dan drove us back to the station, where I got in my car and he went back to work to raid the vending machine. Since my own stomach was still mostly empty after our trip to Valley Burgers, I stopped by the grocery store. In less than an hour, we were stocked up on bread, cheese, cold cuts, bananas, and the best foods, cereal and milk. Even though all I'd done was acquire food for the house, I felt like a homemaker.

Finally, I felt like Dan's partner.

After everything had been put away, I went upstairs and stood in the hall in front of the freshly painted spare bedrooms. I stared at the closed doors for a good five minutes, then I shook out my hands and flung open the closest door. The walls were pale blue, and the room was empty save for that suggestive paint color. I gave the room a once over, then I opened the other room's door. It was pink, just like Dan had said, and it was also empty. I sat on the floor in the middle of the pink room, and wondered what the hell was going on.

It wasn't a secret that Dan wanted kids. He hadn't named this house the Lyons Family Estate for nothing. However, while we'd had superficial discussions about children, we'd never gotten as far as pre-decorating a room—make that *rooms*—for our potential offspring. What's more, I was certain I never would have manifested baby rooms, which made me wonder if Dan had also influenced reality when we came through the nexus. Then again, Dan thought this timeline was designed to shatter our focus. These rooms could be meant to keep me with Dan in anticipation of a baby, or make me freak out and leave him for good.

Since the pink walls weren't offering up any answers, I took a shower, and spent time in my closet picking out something to wear. As I considered outfit after outfit, I thought about what Gran would have worn to such a meeting. She always believed in dressing well, both to show and command respect. Tessa had much the same opinion, but I didn't want to waltz into the Beauclaire house wearing a modest dress and sensible shoes. I wanted to look like me.

Which was why Dan found me wearing yet another combination of jeans, boots, and a fitted tee when he came home from work. "Looks like I'm overdressed," he said, gesturing at his tie.

"You look great. I went shopping," I said, then I set a sandwich in front of him. "And look. Dinner!"

"You really are perfect," Dan said, then he took a huge bite of his sandwich. "Better than Valley Burger, too. Speaking of which, remember those texts I sent while we were at lunch?"

"I do," I replied, since he'd sent those texts shortly before I'd choked on my burger. "Let me guess, it was about that place?"

"Close. I ran an occupancy history on your old address. Seems that one Gary Williams has leased your apartment. The other two ghost clowns run the burger place."

"So the Ghost Guys transformed from the weird ass podcast guys Amir sent to irritate me into entrepreneurs, and have set up shop in my apartment, and in the restaurant where Amir possessed the cook." I poured milk onto my cereal. "Are we sure Amir is still in Asia?"

"I can't really run an international search without cause," Dan said. "Bennet's certain he's in Iran?"

"That's what he said, but this nonsense reeks of Amir."

"It does." Dan glanced at the clock. "We should get going soon. It'll take about two hours to get to the Beauclaire house."

We finished eating and left our plates and bowls in the sink, then we hopped into Dan's SUV to go to a house built of literal nightmares.

"I can't believe I'm going back there again," I said, as Dan backed down the driveway.

He stopped the car and faced me. "You don't have to go there. We can arrange a meeting with them someplace else."

"We really can't." I smiled tightly. Based on Dan's worried face, it was more of a grimace. "I was never kidnapped in this reality, so I have no reason not to go their house."

"The fact that you don't want to go there is reason enough."

"I'll be okay. Promise. Besides, Tessa did all that work getting me this appointment."

His frown didn't let up, but he put the car in drive. "If anything seems the least bit off, we're leaving."

"You're really taking this protection thing seriously."

"Yes, I am." He glanced at me, and continued, "That piece of shit never bothered you in this timeline?"

"Not that I know of," I replied, understanding that the piece of shit in question was Nathaniel Beauclaire. "If Jemima is still alive, then he wouldn't have had any reason to."

Dan grunted. "Think Sarah Allwood's alive, too?"

My mind spun with the possible implications of Sarah being alive and well and causing all sorts of trouble. "If she is, let's hope she isn't there tonight."

"Agreed."

By the time we reached the Beauclaire Estate the sun had long since set. The house, which was large and painted a dark gray, loomed over the darkened landscape like a horror movie set. I half expected a colony of bats to swoop down from the gables and transform into a vampire.

"Alex destroyed this place?" Dan leaned closer to the windshield, craning his neck to see as much of the house as possible. "The house is huge."

"He incinerated it down to the ground," I replied, remembering the charred cellar hole that was all that remained in our timeline. "Even the landscape and the outbuildings were destroyed right down to the soil."

"Remind me not to piss off your dad." We got out of the car, and walked to the front door. "Notice the lack of security?" Dan asked, since there were no guards or fences present.

"Oh, there's plenty of security. You just can't see it."

"I am really starting to hate magic. It's so sneaky."

"Why do you think I wanted to be a private investigator instead of the Mistress of Seers?" I asked. "All I ever wanted was to leave the supernatural community behind, but I can't." I faced Dan, and smiled sadly. "Can't run from what you are."

"No, but maybe we can run away together." Dan put his arm around my shoulders and kissed my hair. "Say the word, baby, and we're outta here."

"You'd do that? What about your house, and your job?"

"There's other houses and jobs, but I've only got one Eli."

I pressed myself against him. "You say the best things."

Dan kissed my hair again, then he knocked on the door. A moment later, a liveried servant opened the entrance and grimaced when he saw us. Nice.

"Mistress, Mr. Lyons," he said, as he greeted us with a shallow bow. "Mr. and Mrs. Beauclaire await you in the drawing room. Shall I take your coat?"

"I'm good, thank you." There was no way I was letting an article of clothing out of my sight at this place. With my luck, it would come back spelled eight ways to Sunday.

"Very well. This way, please."

We followed the servant through the house, which was decorated more like a medieval castle than a mansion. I'd been in the Allwood home plenty of times, and while it was large and showy, it was primarily a home. Here at the Beauclaire house, a suit of armor would have fit right in.

At the end of the corridor was the oak paneled drawing room. A fire blazed away in the hearth, and several upholstered chairs were clustered around it. Nathaniel himself was standing next to the mantle, while a second person, who I assumed was Jemima, sat in the shadows behind him.

"Mistress, thank you for coming," Nathaniel said, as if Tessa hadn't called in a ton of favors to set up this appointment. "Would you or your companion care for any refreshments?"

"We're fine, thanks," I replied. Nathaniel nodded to the servant, who bowed and left the room, shutting the door behind him. "Thank you for seeing us."

"Of course. We of the clans are beholden to the Mistress of Seers," Nathaniel said. Confusion momentarily skated across his face, but he recovered quickly. "Please, have a seat. What can we do for you?"

"I have a question I need answered. It's of a rather sensitive nature, which is why I wanted to meet with you in person." I paused, glancing between Nathaniel and Jemima. I could barely see her, thanks to the deep shadows on that side of the room. "In your family cemetery, there's a rather interesting mausoleum. I need to know who's in it."

Nathaniel's face hardened. "That is none of your concern."

"Actually, my concern is all over it," I said. "I hold the line between life and death, and something has happened to our ancestors. I must do a full accounting of their souls, and I cannot do that without knowing who I'm looking for."

"You overstep," Nathaniel growled.

"And you conceal that which should be common knowledge," I countered.

Jemima shifted in her chair, and asked, "What do you believe has befallen our ancestors?"

I faced her, noticing how the firelight reflected on her dull hair and skin. Had she been sick all these centuries? "I can't sense them. It's as if someone took their souls and hid them away from me."

"You can't sense any spirits?" Nathaniel demanded.

"Not a one."

Nathaniel leaned toward Jemima, and asked, "Do you feel any different?"

"No," she replied, "but as you know I hardly feel anything at all." Slowly, creakily, Jemima rose from her chair and came into the light.

I felt magic pop, much like your ears do when coming down from a great height, then Jemima's thin glamour fell away and I saw her for what she really was. Up close, she looked more like a mannequin than a person. "The body in the mausoleum is my own."

"How," I began, then Jemima stepped further into the light. Her skin was smooth and opaque, like plastic, but it was cracked and flaking where her mouth had moved. Her makeup was garish, with bright pink lipstick and thick black eyeliner that looked like it was applied with a paintbrush. I noted how she avoided the heat of the fireplace, and understood.

"You're... you're made of wax?" I reached toward Jemima, only to curl my fingers inward. I turned to Nathaniel, and said, "You kept your promise, and didn't put her in someone else's body."

"It took me years to fashion a wax form for my beloved," he said. "Once it was done, I freed her spirit from the bottle she'd been trapped in, and was finally able to hold her again."

"Hang on," Dan said, the first time he'd spoken since we entered the room. "Are you referring to the glass bottle Hassan trapped you in a few hundred years ago? The day we met you?"

"Yes." Jemima nodded, and little flakes of wax fell from the seams of her neck and chin onto her shoulders. "I remember well how you helped me that day, and how you convinced Nathaniel not to put me into another's body. Thank you, both of you."

I shuddered, chilled at the thought of being thanked for Jemima ending up as a human candle. "So if it took years to create this form, and your spirit was in the glass bottle the entire time, then you were protected when whatever happened to the rest of the spirits," I concluded. "Nathaniel saved you in more ways than one."

"He did," Jemima said, with a loving glance toward her husband. "He's done nothing but care for me ever since."

"What event occurred to compromise our ancestors?" Nathaniel asked.

"My great-great-grandmother gave birth to a child that shouldn't have lived," I replied. "That, coupled with recent activity in the nexus, has created this situation. We appear to be living in a separate timeline that's been running alongside the original. It's gone on for so long I don't know if there's any way to recover."

"Do we need to recover?" Nathaniel asked. "I am quite content to rule my clan here with my beloved. We do not seek or want change."

"What about everyone else?" Dan asked. "You can't set the world on fire just to save one soul."

Nathaniel fixed Dan in his gaze. "Can't I?"

"I don't think fixing this timeline will affect you at all," I said, with a nod to Jemima. "Your spirit was safe inside the bottle when everything changed. In fact, I'd venture to say you're the only spirit who survived in this new timeline."

"If spirits have been absent for the last few hundred years, exactly what has the legendary Moore family of seers been doing all this time?" Nathaniel asked.

"That's exactly what I'm trying to figure out."

LOVERS LANE

On the ride home from the Beauclaire Estate, I had a lot to think about. Dan, however, couldn't get past Jemima being made of wax.

"So her whole body is made of wax," he said. Again. "She doesn't have a skeleton in there? Like how you first build an armature when you're sculpting?"

"I honestly have no idea," I said. "It's not like I x-rayed her."

"Do you think they have sex?"

"Dan!"

"I'm serious," he continued, undeterred. "Wax melts pretty easily, so unless they do it in a cold room—"

"I'm not talking about this any longer."

"Eli, I have questions!"

"If there's anything I don't have answers to, it's Nathaniel and Jemima's sex life." I barely suppressed a shudder. "I guess we know why they don't have any children."

"That would be tough to pull off. First of all, they'd have to find enough wax that matched the rest of her skin, then they'd have to heat her up and expand her belly a little bit at a time. It would be pretty labor intensive, no pun intended."

"Never mind that you can't exactly grow a baby inside a wax person." I drummed my fingers on my leg. "What's really amazing is that he's kept her animated for all this time. Where is he getting all of this power?"

"Not the ancestors. Think he's siphoning power from his clan?"

"That would explain a few things."

"Such as?"

"Such as how Tessa seems less powerful," I replied. "I mean, she's doing the clan's financial statements."

"I'm surprised she puts up with that." We reached a four-way intersection, and Dan took a right instead of going straight.

"Where are we going?"

"Thought I'd take you someplace special."

"We can't just go home," I began, then I bit my lip. Dan was trying to do something nice for me, and here I was, being ungrateful. "Sorry. I was just daydreaming about bubble baths."

He reached over and squeezed my hand. "I'll run you a bath when we get home, okay?"

"Really?" I asked, perking up.

"Really." He kissed the back of my hand. "Hey, do you think Jemima takes baths? What about waxy buildup in the pipes?"

"I refuse to answer that."

Dan laughed, but left off his speculations about Jemima and her waxy form. As he kept driving, the road's incline revealed he was following the ridge. Eventually, he pulled off the road and parked.

"Come on," he said, as he pocketed the keys. "The view up here is amazing."

"How did you learn about this place?" I asked as we went around to the front of the car. He'd parked in front of a cliff that overhung the valley we lived in.

"Sometimes we get called to check on kids making out up here," he said. "They call this spot Lovers Lane."

"Lovers, huh?" I teased, then I turned and saw the city spread out beneath us. Most of the homes were nestled in the center of the valley, and the illuminated windows and streetlights twinkled in the darkness. Beyond the town was the river, silent and sleek as it curved among the mountains. Dan was right. This view was pretty amazing.

"I can't believe we live here," I said. "From up here, it looks like a fairy tale." My gaze traveled around the edges of the valley, and I spotted three of the six witch clan estates. They were large and imposing, like castles guarding the edge of the village. "Where's our house?"

"Should be over there." Dan pointed with one hand, while his other arm snaked around my shoulders. "I like that you're calling it our house again."

"Me, too." I slid my arms around his waist and pressed my cheek against his chest. "Why did you want to come up here?"

"Being in that house with those two was pretty intense," he replied. "I figured we could both use some time to decompress." He kissed the top of my head, and for a few minutes we stood together and enjoyed the night.

"I learned something in the Beauclaire house," I said.

"Something besides the new, questionably improved state of Jemima?"

"Never in a million years did I expect that," I said. "I also didn't expect to not be afraid of Nathaniel."

Dan smoothed my hair back from my face. "You've been afraid of him for a long time?" he asked, his lips against my forehead. "You've always seemed more annoyed than anything."

"He's plenty annoying," I said, as I burrowed deeper into Dan's arms. "Even though we only met face to face earlier this year, I've always known who he was. When I was a kid, I would hear Gran and my dad whisper about the Beauclaire witches. They were the most powerful clan in the area, and everyone walked on eggshells around them. Then, two Beauclaire witches kidnapped and tortured me."

Dan tightened his arms around me. "Eliza, what happened in that basement?"

"I know what you're thinking, and no. Not that." I leaned back so I could see his eyes. "They were told to keep me a virgin. I heard them talking about it."

"Sick fucks," Dan grumbled.

"They never said Nathaniel or anyone else's name, but he was the head of the clan," I continued. "Some part of me has always worried he would come after me again, that he would send stronger witches, or somehow overpower me. I've been living in fear of them for twelve years."

"And that fear's gone now?"

"It is, and I didn't even realize it until we were all in the same room. I looked into his eyes and felt nothing, not fear or shame or any of the crappy emotions he used to bring out in me. I've never been so happy about feeling nothing."

"I felt a lot of things," Dan said. "Mainly, the urge to punch him in the nose."

I hid my face against his chest as I laughed. "My knight in shining armor."

"You know it." Dan pressed his face against my hair. "I understand why Tess thinks this might be the right timeline. I love being with you like this. I love that many of the people who hurt you in our other life never came near you in this one." He tilted up my chin, and kissed me. "I love everything about you."

"I love you, too." I watched the twinkling lights spread out below us, and thought about all the people going about their lives, oblivious to the secondary timeline. "What if we don't fix the timeline?"

"Shouldn't we fix it?"

"What about all the people who are alive here, but aren't in the other?" I pressed. "Jacob and my cousins, and even Jemima. If we go back to the other timeline, will they just snuff out?"

"Are they really alive here?" Dan countered. "People are missing, too."

I gasped. "Your family," I said, and he nodded. "Can you call your mom, ask her how she is? How everyone is?"

"I can do that."

"Okay. New plan. You call your mom, and once we figure out how they are, then we'll plan further. Agreed?"

"Agreed. I gotta say, as long as they're all right, I wouldn't mind staying here with you. It's like we got our happy ending."

I sighed, imagining a life filled with me and Dan and no spirits. It was what I'd always wanted: a normal life. So why did I have the nagging feeling that something was very, very wrong?

Shine a Light

The next morning, Dan was grinning as he walked into the kitchen. "Why are you so happy?" I asked. I was trying to get some coffee out of the espresso machine, and it was fighting me at every turn.

"I just talked to my mother," he replied, leaning over to kiss my temple. "She and the whole crew are doing fine."

"That's great," I muttered. I pressed a button that I thought would make espresso come out. Nothing happened. "Do you know how to work this thing?"

"That contraption's way above my pay grade. Ma sends her love."

"I've met your mother?" I asked, then a jet of steam shot out from the milk frothing wand. I screamed and jumped back, colliding with Dan.

"Let's unplug this for now," he said, while I glared daggers at the machine that was keeping me from my caffeine fix. "Of course you've met my mother. We've been together in this version of life for years." He reached for the expresso machine's power cord, and paused. "I just realized how weird that sounded."

"Weirder than a kitchen appliance with a grudge?"

"Debatable." He checked his watch. "I've got time. Want to hit the coffee shop?"

I tossed the kitchen towel onto the counter. "Definitely."

I drove to the coffee shop, since it would be silly to take both cars, and I didn't want to walk home. Besides, this meant I got to drop Dan off at work and pick him up later, which was oddly fun. Domestic bliss was a new and welcome sensation.

When we got to the coffee shop, many of the patrons backed away from Dan and whispered behind their hands. "What's with all the hairy eyeballs?" he asked.

"Maybe they recognize you as police, and they've got weed in their pockets?" I suggested. We stepped up to the counter to order, then the barista scribbled something on a piece of paper and slid it across the counter to me. It said, *do you need help?*

"No, I just need coffee," I said. "Thanks, though. A whole milk latte and a medium black, please." The barista nodded and went to make our drinks. I faced Dan, and showed him the note. "Something's going on."

He crumpled the paper in his hand. "Something not good, I'm guessing."

We picked up our coffees and went out to the sidewalk. When we walked past the newsstand, I saw the headline on the local paper and almost dropped my latte.

"What's wrong?" Dan asked, and I pointed at the paper. It read:

Local Police Chief Berates Woman In Burger Joint

"Let me get one of those," Dan said to the seller as he bought a paper. "Keep the change." Dan unfolded it, and swore. "There's a picture."

"A picture of what?" I peeked over his shoulder, and saw a black-and-white photograph of us that was taken yesterday at Valley Burger. The shot was framed so you could only see me from behind, and I was sitting while Dan was standing up, scowling. Conveniently cut out of the picture was the server that had tried to jump between us while I was choking.

"This is bullshit," Dan said. "This paper's slandering me."

"It's libel if it's in print." Dan gave me a look. "Right. Not the point. Why is this even in the paper? One person yelling at another isn't that interesting. And on the front page, too."

"I know why. Those ghost clowns are the ones trying to drive us apart." Dan stalked down the street.

"Where are you going?" I asked, as I jogged to keep up with him.

"I'm going to Valley Burger to give these assholes a piece of my mind."

"Wait," I said, as I grabbed his arm. "Not a good idea. We already know that they have some kind of hidden camera in the restaurant, and if they're selling pictures like this to the paper, they've obviously got no scruples. If you tear in there while you're upset, they might spin it against you and make the whole situation worse."

"Yeah. You're right." Dan wiped a hand down his face. "What should we do instead?"

"First, kiss me." I stood on my toes and pecked his lips. "Now let's walk back to the car, smiling and happy."

"As much as I enjoy kissing you, I don't see what this will accomplish."

"Happy couples are boring. If we go around town smiling and in love, everyone will forget about that stupid picture."

"When I get to the station, I'm going to pull every license Valley Burger has," Dan said. "I am going to get them closed down."

"Or we could redirect that energy into fixing the timeline."

Dan wrapped his arm around my shoulder as we walked. "Now you're talking, babe. I've had enough of this one."

The police station was utter chaos.

The waiting room was packed full of people wanting to make statements against Dan's past behavior toward them, and the phones were ringing off the hook. According to Mahoney, who'd been dealing with the brunt of the complaints, no one had any specific examples of Dan behaving badly. Instead, they all told vague stories about how he'd been rude, or mean, or dismissive of their concerns.

"A few people have retained lawyers," Mahoney continued; beads of sweat formed on his brow, and I wondered just how many people he'd dealt with already. "The department's counsel is preparing a statement."

"A statement about what?" Dan demanded. "This is total bullshit."

"Bullshit or not, it's making the department look bad," Mahoney replied. "And after everything that went down a few years ago, the higher-ups are especially sensitive to negative press."

"What happened a few years ago?" I asked. Mahoney stared at me as if I'd asked him to eat a tarantula.

"You... you of all people must remember, Eli," he said.

"I'm forgetful. Help me out?"

Mahoney glanced warily at Dan. Dan gestured for him to continue. "Around five years ago, Chief's wife—first wife—passed. Shortly thereafter, you two met, and the timing was, ah, awkward."

"Awkward," I repeated. "Exactly how awkward was it?"

"There was a formal inquiry into Mrs. Lyons' death," Mahoney replied. "Chief was never charged with anything, but the public loves a scandal."

"They sure do," I murmured. I turned to Dan, who was white as a sheet. "Let's hide out in your office, for now."

Once we were inside the office, Dan paced back and forth with his hands on his head. "I lied to you."

"You did? About what?"

"About my mother. She didn't send her love." Dan stopped moving, and leaned back with his hands covering his face. "When we talked this morning, she appeared to not like you very much."

"Oh. Well, people don't always get along."

"No, she really does not like you, and now it all makes sense. That, and why there's no evidence of Charlotte left anywhere in the house. People think I killed her and replaced her with you."

"Dan, that's..." I glanced toward the lobby, and the words died in my throat. Dan looked at me, and his face fell.

"You think I did it, don't you?" he asked, his voice quiet and desperate.

"No! I know you'd never hurt anyone, and you would especially never hurt Charlotte."

He sat heavily on the edge of his desk. "What am I going to do?"

I wrapped my arms around him. "You're right. Someone or something is deliberately trying to make our lives awful. Every time something good happens, something bad happens that makes everything so much worse."

"Every step forward is met with two back," he said. "How do we get out of this hell?"

"We are going to leave this godforsaken timeline behind, and live our lives without all this garbage."

"What if the garbage follows us home?"

"It might," I allowed, "but we have to try."

Dan and I snuck out of the back of the station, and went straight to Tessa's condo. I hated intruding upon her time with my dad, especially since they'd just found each other again, but if we were going to attempt something as crazy as leaving this timeline—or merging this reality with the real one—we would need power. The most powerful witch I'd ever known was Tessa.

When we got to her place, I sent her a warning text, so she knew we were on our way up. The last thing Dan or I needed was to catch those two in a compromising situation. A few minutes later, we knocked on Tessa's door, and the lady herself opened it.

"I was wondering when you'd be by," Tessa said, smiling. "Hello, Dan. By your presence at Eli's side, I assume all is forgiven between you two?"

"She loves me again," Dan said. "How are you, Tess?"

"Fantastic. Come out to the deck."

We followed Tessa through her condo, and found my father lounging next to the pool, reading a book.

"Eli, Dan," he greeted. "I'm so happy you're here."

"Believe me, in here is better than out there," I said.

He closed his book. "Tell me what happened."

Dan and I told Tess and my dad everything we could remember, from all the little inconsistencies in our lives to two of the biggest anomalies we'd found to date: Tessa working as the Beauclaire's secretary, and Dan's questionable past.

"I don't know if the paperwork I'm overseeing qualifies as an anomaly," Tessa said, but I shook my head.

"You once ruled half of Italy," I said. "You're more powerful than Nathaniel, which is why he's always stayed away from you. In the past, you were the only one from your clan who stood up to him. Now you're double checking his spreadsheets? That doesn't make sense."

"She's right, Isa," my dad said. "A few decades ago, you were looking into creating your own court similar to what you had in Europe, far away from Nathaniel and his machinations. What happened?"

Tessa blinked. "I'm not sure. In this reality, everything fell through, and eventually when Nathaniel offered me the position as the clan's financial overseer, I accepted. That was a little more than ten years ago."

"And what happened in your other memories?" I asked.

"Everything is similar, but after you were abducted, I cut ties with the Beauclaires and went back to my maiden name," Tessa replied. "Either way, I never established a court."

"But you didn't establish a court for two very different reasons," I said. "It's like whoever glued together this timeline didn't know what had happened between you and the clan, so they shoehorned you in wherever you fit. Not that you belong as someone's secretary," I added.

"Something's definitely off," Dan said, "and I'm starting to think that however this timeline popped into existence, it's being fueled by people with an axe to grind."

"Against me?" Tess asked.

"Against a few people," Dan replied. "Also, what's up with Jemima being made of wax? Did you know about that?"

"I certainly did not." Tessa shuddered. "What an awful existence she must have, being trapped inside a cold, unfeeling lump of wax."

"I think Jemima's the biggest anomaly of all," I said. "She's also the only spirit that exists in this timeline."

"What do you mean?" Dad asked. "Why haven't you..." His voice trailed off as realization dawned on his face. "You're right. There aren't any spirits here. What's more, try as I might, all I can remember doing for the past few years is looking after all of your cousins. I don't remember acting as a marksman, or working as a seer at all."

"Do you know any of my cousins' names?" I asked. "Or who their parents are?"

He shook his head. "I don't."

"I don't think they're real," I said. "Just like my old apartment building isn't real, and Bennet's second set of records, and I don't think Jemima's real either. I think someone with very limited magical knowledge tried to pull off a whopper of a spell, majorly screwed up, and here we are."

"Then we need to strip away the falsehoods and shine a light on the truth," Tessa declared. "I'm still not certain which set of my memories are correct, but once we burn away what's not real, I'll know." She squeezed my dad's hand, then said, "How will we establish which reality is the correct one?"

"I have no idea."

We stayed up half the night debating how we could pull off correcting this reality and returning everyone to the correct timeline. All of those "how" discussions dovetailed into a debate on if we should attempt such a thing. Dan was determined to look at this situation from all angles.

"What do you mean, if?" I asked. He'd debated us into yet another corner. "We have to make things right."

"Making things right means a lot of people will go away," he said. "Jacob, Jemima, all of them will be spirits again."

"And your cousins," my dad added. "I don't think any of them will still exist."

"But we don't think they're real," I protested.

"Are we the ones to make that determination?" he asked. "Don't forget, the cousins all began with Katherine's second child, Daniel."

I swallowed, and turned away. In the real timeline—or, the one I thought was real—my great-great-grandmother's second child had been stillborn, and she'd never recovered from his birth. Katherine had also reached through time to help me, and had anointed me as Mistress of Seers on my twenty-ninth birthday. I didn't want to damn her to a life as an invalid again.

But wouldn't Katherine prefer to live an authentic life, and not this weird facsimile we'd somehow gotten trapped in?

"I can't speak for everyone who's been affected by this… whatever this is," I began. "But I feel like I can speak for Katherine. She valued truth, and integrity, and I don't think she'd want any of the details of her life painted over, no matter how hard the experiences were." I thought about the horrible things that had happened to me, and Dan, and how they'd never happened in this reality. And how this version of our lives, while picture perfect on the outside, felt hollow.

"Without the bad, we cannot appreciate the good," I continued. "It would be great for everyone to live forever in a land filled with puppies and rainbows, but when we hide from the shadows, the light ends up burning us. We need to make things right, no matter the cost."

Dan kissed the back of my hand. "Well said, baby."

"I agree," my father added. "I enjoy having a house full of children to look after, but I need to be the marksman."

"Seers need you," I said. "Without you, who's negotiating on our behalf with the witch clans?"

"We all need you," Tessa added. "And we need a Mistress of Seers who can interact with the dead. Our ancestors need our help, just as much as the living do."

"All right." I looked at each of them in turn, and nodded. "Let's do this."

Queen Of Poisons

The sky was just turning orange as we all piled into my car and drove back to Gran's house. Our reasons for returning to her house were twofold. We needed power, and that house, coupled with the nexus hovering above it, had plenty to spare. I was also hopeful that at some point the cats would return, thus signifying we'd made it back to the correct timeline. Besides that, I missed the little guys. I hoped they were okay.

Once we were at the house, we assembled in the front parlor. Without the Feline Federation there to greet us, the place was as quiet as a tomb.

"So," Dan began, with his natural leadership skills on full display, "how do we begin?"

"We need to concentrate on what's real," I said, then I remembered a story Gran was fond of telling. It involved an event that happened right here in the parlor. "Dad, didn't you and Tessa first meet in this room?"

"We did," he replied. "I'd just come up from the radio room. Ma told me she was having friends over, and I didn't want to intrude, so I spent the afternoon tinkering with some of the new equipment. This was years before I became the marksman, so none of the guests needed to talk to me."

"What made you join the rest?" I asked.

"My stomach," he replied. "I was down there for hours, and I missed lunch. So I came upstairs, sweaty and dusty and starving, and there was a group of people I didn't know in the parlor. They were standing in the foyer, so I assumed they'd just arrived."

"Actually, we'd been here for some time," Tessa said. "Helena and I were so excited to see each other we stood around chattering like fools. She had just been telling me about her son, going on and on about how brilliant he was, when Alex joined us. You weren't that dirty," she added.

Dad smiled, and looked down at the carpet. "I also remember you were wearing a hat with a black beaded veil, and against your hair it sparkled like the night sky. Then you turned and faced me, and I thought Venus was among us." Dad took Tessa's hands. "The sight of you still takes my breath away."

I leaned against Dan's shoulder, so happy that my dad and Tessa had found each other again. "I love their love," I said.

"Me, too." Dan wrapped his arm around my shoulder and kissed my hair. "If Alex and Tess can keep coming together against all the odds they've faced over the years, fixing reality should be a piece of cake."

"If only," I muttered, then I thought about how Dad and Tess had found each other, and how they kept finding each other. In every instance, they latched on to their true memories, and all the falsehoods melted away.

"Maybe this is how we fix things," I began. "We need to focus on what really happened, not on all the memories that appeared in our brains later on. We need to find the actual timeline and pull it back, a piece at a time."

Tessa pursed her lips. "All of my memories seem equally real," she said. "What if I focus on the wrong thing?"

"It's the same for me, Bug," my dad said.

"But not for me," Dan said. "For whatever reason, probably because I'm mortal, I have zero memories from this reality. If you concentrate on something recent and aren't sure if it's real, run it by me. For instance, I know all about how Tessa once referred to me as Officer Muscleman," Dad added, with a pointed look at Tess. As for Tessa, she merely shrugged.

"I still refer to you as Officer Muscleman," she said. "All right, let's begin by concentrating on how else I've tormented Dan."

"Hey, now," Dan said.

"You brought this on yourself," I said. "What did you think teasing Tessa would accomplish?"

"Think she'll turn me into a toad?"

"You better hope not."

Dan and I followed my father and Tess as they went through the first floor room by room, telling stories and sorting through their memories. When we were in the mudroom, we heard about a time she and my father got caught in a downpour out in the rose garden, and in the kitchen they told us about the many meals they'd cooked together. While they were still laughing about a collapsed cake, they left the kitchen and went upstairs. I moved to follow, but Dan held me back.

"Give them a minute," he said. "They don't need an audience up there. They just need each other."

"They're falling in love all over again," I said, watching as they disappeared past the second floor landing. "This is why I always thought my mother cursed Dad to fall in love with her. He's so obviously made to be with Tessa."

"They do make a good pair." He took my hand, and led me into the solarium. "You know, this is my favorite room in the house."

"Why is that?" I asked as I wound my arms around his neck, even though I already knew the answer.

"Here is where I learned not once but twice how much you love me," he replied, as he dipped his head to kiss me. "We belong together, Eliza. In this reality, the one we came from, and whatever place we end up in next." He rested his forehead against mine. "Doesn't matter to me where we are, as long as we're together."

"You're right. Together till the end." I thought about all the times Dan had helped me, even back when we first knew each other, and I was desperately trying to hide the truth about me being a seer from him. He turned up wherever I was, no matter what I was doing, and helped me whether I wanted him to or not. Usually it was a not, but why was that? I'd never distanced myself from mortals in the past; in fact, I'd become a private investigator with the sole purpose of helping them without magic. Then Dan came into my life, and for the longest time, all I did was push him away. In the midst of wondering why I'd behaved that way, it dawned on me.

I never wanted to push him away. I was trying to protect him. Long before I realized how I felt about Dan, I did everything in my power to keep him safe.

I slid my arms around his waist, and rested my cheek against his chest. "Once all of this is over with, I want to go home and spend the next ten years in bed with you."

"You got it, babe." He kissed the top of my head. "Hey, isn't that the same flower that popped up in our garden?"

I turned around, and saw a potted aconite sitting next to the oleanders. "Weird," I murmured, as I walked over to inspect it. "There has never been an aconite in here."

"You called it something else before."

"Its common name is wolfsbane."

"No, you said something more dramatic." He snapped his fingers. "Queen of poisons."

We looked at each other, then at the indigo flower stalks. "We talked about summoning our ancestors for help, but I don't think that's specific enough," I said. "What we need to do is summon the Queen of Poisons."

"Who's that? Sarah Allwood and her nasty apples?"

"No. My grandmother."

My grandmother, Helena Moore, was absolutely legendary, and not just because she was the Matriarch of Seers. She'd come to power at a contentious time, and during the strife a family of seers from the old country, the Monvoisons, had decided they wanted a stake in North America. Gran didn't appreciate them trying to encroach on her territory, and she let them know that they should stay on their side of the ocean. Being that Gran had been young and newly anointed, they laughed at her.

Big mistake.

The Monvoisons had lauded themselves as the greatest poisoners in history, having served royal houses across Europe for centuries. While they were busy bragging, each and every member of their clan took suddenly and violently ill, until they all needed to return home at once. Without saying a word against them, Gran had eliminated her foes and sent them running, never to look back. Ever since, the European witches had referred to Gran as the Queen of Poisons. And now, it seemed we needed her to poison us back to reality.

When my dad and Tessa came back downstairs, I told them about my plan. Neither of them were on board.

"I don't know, Bug," my dad said, as he shook his head. "Even if we could summon Ma to this reality, should we? Maybe there aren't any other spirits here for a reason."

"Then why does aconite keep popping up?" I asked. "Every time a baneful herb tries to get my attention, it means something. The oleander, the thornapple—"

"The bleeding hearts," Dan interjected.

"Exactly," I said, making a mental note to ask Dan to not mention how I manifested a crap ton of bleeding hearts the first time we had sex around my father. Some things parents just didn't need to be reminded of. "Therefore, it stands to reason that this aconite is trying to get my attention for a reason."

"It's a pretty big leap to go from a baneful herb trying to get your attention, to those plants telling you we need to summon Ma," Dad said gently. "Let's talk about this, and make sure we understand what we're getting into. We don't want any harm to come to her spirit."

I looked down at my hands, irritated that he wasn't agreeing with me, but understanding why he wanted to be cautious. I didn't want to risk Gran's spirit, either. While I was struggling to come up with something to say, Tessa spoke.

"Perhaps this is a bit off topic, but I've never known plants to reach out to a seer or a witch," she began. "Any type of plants. Do only the poisonous ones speak to you?"

"I don't know if they speak to me," I began, then I remembered my first case at Forge Heights. "But, belladonna has reached out to me a few times, first when we were at the retirement center, and later when I found the original plant the cuttings were taken from."

"Other plants speak to you, too," Dan said. "Those herbs in the kitchen window? You fuss over them like they're your babies. You always know if they need water, repotting, anything."

"That's not speaking," I said. "I just pay attention."

"You do pay attention," Tessa agreed, "perhaps more than most. What if the aconite is saying that you're the Queen of Poisons?"

"That's nuts," I said. "That was Gran's title. I've never even poisoned anyone."

Tessa shrugged. "Perhaps you don't need to."

"Maybe not," I mumbled, then I got up, went into the solarium and grabbed the potted aconite, then I returned to the kitchen and set it in the middle of the table.

"Let's talk about poisons," I said. "If one were the Queen of Poisons, and one was inclined to speak with the aconite, what would said poisonous plant want one to do?"

"Would a plant ask for help?" Dan ventured. "They're stuck in this new world order, too. Maybe they want you to fix things."

"Interesting. Dad?"

He rubbed his chin, and studied the plant for a moment before he replied. "Aconite is very, very deadly, and one must approach it with caution. It has earned the name queen of poisons many times over."

"Is there a king of poisons?" Dan asked.

"Arsenic," my father replied. "But it's not a plant-based poison. For the purposes of our discussion, I believe the aconite is urging you to move forward with caution. I have to say, I agree."

"Fix things, but be careful while you do it," I said, summarizing both Dan's and my dad's opinions. "Tessa?"

"Aconite is also sacred to Hecate, the witches' goddess," she replied. "Hecate represents many things, but one of her aspects is acting as a guardian to the souls of the dead."

"Huh." I leaned back in my chair, and regarded the blue flowers. "And I feel like it wants me to get something. Maybe instead of guarding the souls of the dead, I should retrieve them, but be careful doing so." As I said the words out loud, resolve settled onto my shoulders. "That's what the aconite wants me to do—not just summon Gran, but everyone."

"Everyone?" Dan repeated. "That's a tall order."

"It is," I agreed; I'd never summoned more than a dozen spirits a once, and even that had drained me pretty fast. "What if we start with our own ancestors, and we branch out from there? That should work, right?"

"Will it be safe?" Dan asked. "For us, and the spirits?"

"If I cast a protection circle, we should all remain safe while we're inside it," Tessa said. "Then if things prove to be too unstable for the spirits, Eli can send them back."

"We can do this," I said, my confidence bolstered by those around me. "We can get our ancestors, keep them safe, and begin fixing the timelines."

"You've convinced me," my dad said. "Let's go out back and cast a circle."

"I'll grab the salt and candles," Tessa said as she got up from the table.

"I'll get the rue and vervain," Dad said. "Can't be too safe."

"Get the belladonna, too," I said.

"What are those other plants for?" Dan asked.

"Vervain and rue will keep negative energy away," I replied. "As for the belladonna, it's my favorite. I like having it nearby."

"All right then, Poison Queen," Dan said as he picked up the aconite. "Where are we setting up?"

Since Gran's house had been occupied by six generations of seers, we stocked fifty-pound sacks of salt in the pantry. Good thing, too, because Tessa emptied out almost two full sacks when she cast the circle.

"That is a pretty big circle," Dan said.

"It needs to be large enough for the four of us, and any spirts that need protecting," she explained.

"What will they need protection from?" Dan asked.

"Anything, really," she replied as she poured out five additional mounds of salt, and set a white candle in each. We also kept cases of candles in the pantry, mostly because our electricity tended to go out in the winter. "For all we know, our ancestors are being held by a nefarious entity, or behind a wall of spells."

Dan stared at Tess for a moment, then he turned to me. "What can I do?"

"Just be here," I replied. "You're my rock. But if you sense any new or sneaky magic, a heads up would be much appreciated."

"Heads up. I can do that."

I shook out my hands, then I pulled off my boots and socks. "I need to be in contact with the earth," I explained, when Dan's brows pinched. "Summoning this many spirits drains a lot of energy. Contact with the earth will help me replenish my stores faster."

"We should all go barefoot," my dad said, then he kicked off his ancient hippie sandals; I often teased him about wearing those monstrosities when he saw the Beatles perform live. He tossed his sandals outside the circle, then he finished arranging the potted plants in the center. "We're ready when you are, Eli."

I flexed my fingers. "Let's do it."

We all entered the circle, then Tessa poured out the last bit of salt and sealed us inside. I snapped my fingers to light the candles, then we joined hands.

"Ancestors," I began. "I can't sense you, but I know you're still out there. You belong here, with us. Moores, I call to you."

Dad squeezed my hand. "All of your ancestors," he whispered.

"Allwoods, and Linds," I added, "I call to you. Find safety in this circle."

"Moores and Guptas," Dad intoned. "I call to you."

"Della Scalas and Lombardos, I call to you," Tessa said.

"Lyons and Matarazzos," Dan said, after I tugged on his hand. "I call to you."

"We call to you all," I continued. "Find safety here, in this circle, with your family."

The wind picked up, but the interior of the circle remained strangely calm. I tightened my grip on Dan and my father's hands, momentarily worried we would blow away to a land filled with lollipops and munchkins. That only happened in children's books, right?

"The sky," Tessa said. We looked up as one, and saw the impossibly fluffy steel gray clouds amassing directly above us. The wind caught the clouds, and the entire mass began spinning.

"Are those the ancestors?" Dan asked.

"I have no idea," I replied, then my foresight sparked at the base of my skull. It was one of the few times I'd felt it since we arrived in this timeline, and it was giving me a warning. "The wind is keeping our ancestors away from us."

"Or is it keeping us from them?" Tessa asked. "I'm going to try something."

"Try what?" I asked, but she'd already closed her eyes and begun chanting. A moment later, a blue glow covered her, then the glow coalesced into sparks that hopped off her skin and dissipated into the wind.

"What are you doing?" I asked.

"Stopping the wind," she replied.

"Magic incoming," Dan said.

"From Tessa?" I asked.

"Not just her," Dan said. "It's in the sky. It's coming down! It's—"

The wind whipped itself into a frenzy, then we were thrown back and out of the circle as if we'd been hit by a sonic boom. Only, nothing hurt and my ears weren't ringing. I crawled to Dan, and felt my heart clench when I saw he wasn't moving.

"Dan? Dan!" I grabbed his shoulder, jolting him awake.

"What the hell was that?" he rasped. Grateful, I collapsed onto his chest.

"Are you all right?"

"I'm okay," he said, wrapping his arm around me. "Just got the wind knocked out of me." He kissed my hair, then we sat up. Dad and Tess were on the far side of the circle. As I watched them check on each other, I noticed the sky.

The clouds were gone, but the sky was gray. A dark, deathly gray.

"I've never seen a gray sky like that before." The sky wasn't just gray, it didn't look like any sort of atmospheric condition I'd ever heard of. It was like someone had welded a sheet of steel over the town and trapped us inside with whatever bad forces were at work. "I hope the ancestors didn't get stuck in that."

Tessa gasped and pointed at something behind me. I turned, and on the ridge where the Allwood Estate should be standing was a craggy black mansion straight out of a horror movie.

"Did I hit my head, or is that an all new house of horrors?" Dan asked.

"Shit," I muttered. "I think we made things worse."

A Grayer Version Of The World

We shook off the aftereffects from the spell, then we got back inside the house as fast as possible. That metallic gray sky wasn't just weird, it was disconcerting. While I closed all the curtains so I wouldn't have to look at it, my father called our go-to information man, Bennet. His objective behind the call was to find out exactly what the four of us were up against in this newer, grayer version of reality.

"This is not good," Dan said as he brought in the potted plants. "Definitely not good."

"We'll be fine as long as we're inside," I said with more confidence than I felt. "Where's Tess?" Dan pointed toward the front parlor. Tessa was at the bay window, peeking through a gap in the curtains at the creepy black mansion.

"What do you think that means?" I asked, as I joined her. "Did the Allwoods go bad?"

"I can't explain why I feel this way, but I don't believe that's the Allwood Compound," she replied. "Not any longer."

"It's not," Dad said as he entered the room. "According to Bennet, that is the Court of della Scala."

"Wait, are we in a third timeline?" I asked. I reached out with my abilities, seeking any sprit that wanted to connect. Nothing. "I still can't feel any spirits."

Dad closed his eyes and bowed his head. After a moment, he sighed. "Neither can I."

"Perhaps that's why the sky is different," Tessa said, then she turned to my dad. "I set up my court? Please tell me my ex-husband didn't create one instead."

"The court is yours," Dad replied. "Apparently, twelve years ago there was a backlash against the supernatural community, which resulted in witches being persecuted again. You declared war on the mortals, and set up your court as a haven for witches and whomever else needed your protection."

"Is a haven really necessary?" Dan asked. "You're all so powerful. What could a mortal do to harm you?"

Tessa, my father, and I turned to Dan as one. "Witches have been persecuted for thousands of years," I said. "In some regions, so-called powerless mortals have hunted them to extinction."

Dan's face crumpled. "I'm sorry. I didn't mean to come off as insensitive. But for things to get this bad in modern times, when most people don't even go to church any longer, never mind believe in witches, something big had to have happened."

"Something big did happen," my father replied. "Eli's kidnapping."

I gasped and covered my mouth. "Mortals knew about it?"

"In this timeline it was a group of mortals rescued you," Dad replied. "A mortal man saw you being abducted, called the police, and followed you to the Beauclaire house. After the police got you out, the house was searched, and the truth was revealed. According to Bennet, the resulting unrest rivaled the Inquisition."

"Then, I never astral projected to you," I said to Tessa. "Are we even friends in this reality?"

"I don't know," she replied. "Unlike the last new timeline, I don't have any memories from this one."

"Nor do I," Dad said. "Perhaps it's because we were protected by the circle, but I will say this. Any doubt I had over which timeline was the correct one is gone. My memories from the timeline we just left are already fading."

"As are mine," Tessa said, then she drew the curtain aside again. "I don't appear to be a very benevolent ruler, do I?"

"Bennet didn't comment on you, other than to confirm that the black manse is your court," Dad replied, quite diplomatically, even for him. "I'm the marksman again, and Dan remains the chief of police."

"And me?" I asked. "What do I do?"

Dad frowned. "You haven't left this house since you came home after your kidnapping."

"Oh," I said. My hands were trembling, so I stuffed them into my pockets. "If I'm a fraidy cat recluse, then I'm actually living in my worst nightmare."

"You're not," Dan said. "This isn't real. None of these alternative timelines are real. They're just someone screwing with us. We got out of the last one, and we'll get out of this one."

I nodded, because I appreciated his unwavering faith in me. I only hoped I could live up to it. "Okay, so what we need to do is research. Tessa, go to your place and scare someone into telling you everything that's happened in the past twelve years. Dan, go to the police station and find out who these mortals were who conveniently foiled the Beauclaires without getting incinerated. Me and Dad will stay here and see what the house and the internet can tell us."

"Shouldn't I go with Tessa?" Dad asked.

"Would you be with her?" I countered. "Are seers under her protection, too? Or would it look too weird if you two were together?"

"If I'm the big bad witch on the hill, I can associate with whomever I like," Tessa said. "Come along, Alex. Let's find out how evil I am."

After my dad and Tessa left, Dan took my hands. "Will you be all right staying here alone? I can always wait here for Alex and Tess to get back, and go to the station tomorrow."

"I'll be fine," I replied. "Besides, I feel like we should learn as much as we can as soon as we can, and get out of here. There's something wrong about this timeline, even more so than the last one."

"No arguments there." Dan withdrew his cell phone and typed something. A moment later, mine pinged.

"You texted me?"

"I wanted to make sure we can contact each other." He pulled me into his arms and kissed me. "I will be back as soon as I can."

I nodded. "I'll be here."

With that, Dan left to go to the mortal police station, and I was all alone in the house. Man, I really missed the cats.

Alone

The first thing I did while alone at Gran's was to check out every room in the house, basement to attic. I even took a flashlight down to the wine cellar, and I peeked into the radio room, too. I didn't find anything too out of the ordinary in the basement, but those wine bottles sure could use a dusting. After I cleared those rooms, I did a circuit of the first floor, and then the second, and finally went through the library and all the way up to the cupola.

While I was in the highest point of the house, I took a moment to gaze over the town. Tessa's black court was the most obvious anomaly in this reality, but from up here, many other changes in this time-line were apparent. The streets and sidewalks were only clean and well-maintained for a few blocks from Gran's house, and only as you moved closer to the witch communities. The farther you went into the mortal neighborhoods, the worse things got. The riverfront in the real timeline, which was a predominately mortal region, had walking trails and public art installations. In this reality, the same area was dotted with abandoned buildings, burnt-out cars, and broken pavement.

That was the direction Dan went in.

I took out my phone, and looked at the text he'd sent me before he left. It was a heart emoji, and the longer I stared at it, the more I became convinced I would never see him again.

That was nuts. I knew it was nuts, and nothing but a stress response to this new, admittedly scary timeline. What's more, my foresight was silent, so it wasn't like I was having premonitions of something bad happening to either of us. Still, I wanted to call him, but I didn't want to be needy. Wasn't I just complaining that this timeline's version of me was a lame recluse? Therefore, I texted him.

Eli: How is it out there?

Dan: Weird. I'm at the station, but stuff here is archaic.

Eli: Archaic? How?

Dan: We only have paper files. It might take me a while to look up stuff from twelve years ago.

Eli: I think we have internet here. I'll see what I can find.

Dan: Sounds good. Talk soon, babe.

Man, nothing reassured me as much as when Dan called me babe.

I slid my phone into my back pocket, and went down to my bedroom. One of the few constants between all of these realities was my room at Gran's, and this timeline was no different. This version was packed with my belongings, which made sense if I'd never had my downtown apartment, or lived in Paris with Tess or here in town with Dan. As I checked out my overflowing wardrobes, I did wonder why I needed all these clothes if I never left the house.

Maybe I sneak out at night. I shut the wardrobe, found my laptop, and plugged it in. Thank the tech gods, we had internet. While I wondered why I had internet access when the police were bumbling around with paper files, I accessed the local newspaper's archive. It didn't take long to find the many, many headlines all about my kidnapping and rescue.

I skipped over the stories purporting to share the sordid details of what had happened to me—I was there, after all—and drilled down to the original reports. One listed the names of the volunteer firemen who'd been first on the scene and gotten me out of the house. The paper had even printed their headshots with their names captioned below, and I nearly choked when I read them. My rescuers were Mike Delacorte, Gary Williams, and James Roberts. The fricken' Ghost Guys were heros.

I took a picture of the article and texted it to Dan. When he didn't write back immediately, I sent him another text. And another.

Nothing.

Frantic, I called him. It went to voice mail. Just as I was about to have a full-blown panic attack, the front doorbell rang. Assuming it was Dan, relief washed over me. I bounded down the stairs and threw open the door.

Standing on the front step, staring at me, was Renato Florian.

Accusations

As soon as I got to the station, I realized that coming here alone was a bad idea.

I already didn't feel good about leaving Eli alone at her grandmother's house. I understood that the house was probably the safest place for her in this timeline, and Eli was far from helpless. Still, I wanted to be the one standing between her and anything that could harm her. As her husband, that was my job.

I laughed to myself. I still couldn't believe we were married.

I also couldn't believe what a mess the station was. It had been sorely lacking in amenities and modern technology in the real world, but this was beyond the pale. The desk sergeant, Mahoney, was taking down information in a spiral notebook, there wasn't a computer in sight, and the floor looked like it hadn't been mopped in a hundred years.

"Dan the man," Mahoney said when he saw me. "What's happening out there, Chief?"

"Nothing yet." At least I was still the chief. That ought to make things easier. "And you know how I like it when things are boring."

"Too bad the good times never last," Mahoney said. "There's been some more sightings. Everything's up on the board in the conference room."

"Thanks," I said, as I crossed the station toward my office. I had no idea what was going on in the conference room, but I found my office in the same place it was in the last timeline. That was good. As soon as I got through the door, my phone buzzed. I checked it, and saw a text from Eli.

Eli: How is it out there?

Wasn't that a loaded question. We sent a few messages back and forth, then we agreed to do some research on our own before talking again. I set my phone down on my desk, and frowned. Damn it, I missed Eli already. I debated sending her a mushy message all about how much I loved her. Or maybe a heart emoji, she liked those.

"Knock, knock."

I looked up, and saw Jill Sanders, the department's forensic scientist, standing in the doorway. Since Jill was one of the few people I trusted from the original timeline, her presence in this one meant things were looking up. "Hey, Jill."

"I didn't know if you'd make it in today." She glanced at my phone. "Texting your girlfriend?"

"Nah. I don't have a girlfriend." I slid my phone into my pocket. Trustworthy or not, everyone in this strange new world was on a need to know basis when it came to Eli. "Mahoney said there's some new stuff up in the conference room?"

"Sure is. Come on, I'll give you the rundown."

I followed Jill from my office and into the bigger conference room, ignoring the stink eye I was getting from almost everyone in the station. Apparently, I was not a beloved leader. When I entered the conference room and saw what was displayed on the walls, I almost did a cartoon style double take.

Pinned up on the walls and the bulletin boards were images of people being abducted, beaten, and tortured in dozens of different ways. One image was of a woman tied to a pole and being set on fire. Like an actual witch hunt. Suddenly, Tessa opening her home as a haven to all witches seemed like a very good idea.

I noticed Jill watching me. After putting on my best poker face, I asked, "Have there been any new developments?"

"Funny you should ask." She grabbed a file folder and dropped it onto the table in front of me. It was labeled Operation: Witch Hammer. Good to know we weren't being subtle about our bigotry. "We have some new evidence against one of the more powerful witches."

"Enough to pick her up?"

"I think so. She's been making regular forays from her base into our side of town. And you know what happens when they break that law." Jill gestured toward the picture of the burning woman.

Cold sweat broke out on my shoulders. "Show me what you've got." I really hoped the witch in question was Tessa. If a group of witch hunters showed up on her doorstep, she would hand them their asses. Then Jill opened the folder, and I almost choked.

Lying on the top was a picture of Eli.

The picture was grainy, and in black and white, but it was definitely her. The images appeared to have been printed off from a surveillance camera, and they showed Eli creeping around behind a building. She'll be glad to know she's not really a recluse.

"Where was this taken?" I asked.

"Behind a paper factory near the canals," Jill replied. "There's more."

Jill began laying out the pictures. They recorded how Eli walked into the camera's field of vision, and then she entered an alley. After this went on for three images, the perspective changed, and I realized this set of pictures was taken by a different camera. These later images clearly showed Eli's face, and how she approached a man who was waiting for her in the alley. His back was toward the camera, but he was about a foot taller than Eli, had broad shoulders and dark hair, and since he wasn't wearing a jacket you could clearly see his police-issued shoulder holster.

Shit.

"Interesting, isn't it?" Jill asked. "I've got some video, too."

"Of this meetup?"

"Yes."

"Let's see it."

Jill went to the video setup, while I tried not to have a heart attack. Eli had obviously been meeting up with me, but the pictures hadn't captured my face. All I had to do was remain calm, and get the hell out of here.

The video started up, and we watched Eli enter the alley. "Is there any sound?"

"Unfortunately not." The man—me—came into the frame, and took Eli's hands. "Don't you remember what you said to her?"

"How can you think that's me?" I countered. "The camera didn't get that guy's face."

"It's you and you know it," Jill said. "Want me to enlarge the image and read the serial number off the sidearm?"

"You're out of line, Sanders."

"You're breaking the law, Lyons," Jill shot back. "Fraternizing with the enemy is prohibited, and this woman is public enemy number one."

"Fraternizing? You've got some balls accusing me of that."

"Fine. You're fucking a witch." Jill paused the video. On the screen was an image of me and Eli, holding each other. "I saw your phone earlier. Who were you texting? You called them babe."

"That's none of your business. We get any actionable information on this witch, or did you only drag me in here to accuse me of random shit?"

"We know who she is and where she lives," Jill replied. "Her name is Eliza Moore, and she lives in the blue house at the end of Essex Street. She's the kid that got abducted by witches around ten years ago. Turns out she's one of them."

"Maybe they converted her," I said, though I had no idea if you could convert to witchcraft if you weren't born to it. Apparently Jill didn't know either, since she kept right on with her report.

"Convert or not, the problem is that she rarely leaves her base, and she's never alone," Jill continued. "These images are the first time we've caught her without protection."

"And instead of her body, you brought me pictures." I moved toward the door. "Keep working your case, and let me know when she might go out again. If Moore sets foot on our side of town, I want to know about it. And Sanders, keep your half-assed speculations to yourself."

I left the conference room before Jill could reply, went into my office, and sat behind my desk. Not only were witches persecuted in this reality, the police were the brute squad. I needed to find whatever useful information I could get my hands on, and get back to Eli.

I knew I shouldn't have left her alone.

Three hours later, all I had was a headache.

No, that's not true. I learned that the station did have computers and internet access, but the signal was notoriously unreliable on the mortal sort of town. Jill said the witches were keeping us offline. I thought witches as a whole had better things to do, but I kept my opinions to myself.

While we didn't have decent internet access, we did have a basement packed full of paper files. I went down there to pull information about the Ghost Guys, but there weren't any records about them. That meant either that information had already been checked out, or they didn't have criminal records in this reality. I figured the former was true. Since that avenue was a bust, I moved on to property records, and started digging up old blueprints from where the Allwood Compound once sat, which was where Tessa's place was currently located. I had made exactly zero headway when my cell rang. Hoping it was Eli, I accepted the call.

"Yeah."

"Dan," came Alex's voice. "Are you with Eli?"

"I'm at the station."

"Have you talked to her?"

"No." I'd tried calling her a few times, but nothing would connect. "What's wrong?"

"Neither Tessa nor I can reach Eli, either." Alex cleared his throat, and added, "We cannot leave the estate right now, and I'm hoping you will check on Eli for me."

I slammed the file cabinet drawer closed. "I'm on my way to her right now."

FRESH HELL AND A PICNIC

Renato Florian, of all people, was standing on my front step, grinning like the Cheshire Cat. "What are you doing here?" I demanded.

"We have a lunch date." Renato held up a basket and smiled. "Picnic, your favorite."

"Yeah. My favorite," I mumbled, as Renato walked inside my house as if he was somehow welcome there. If that was the case in this reality, I needed to get out of here, fast. "I need to grab something from upstairs. One sec."

"Want me to come with you?" he asked, looking at me in a way that told me he'd been to my room before. I was suddenly very glad that this was a false timeline.

"I'll be right back," I said, evading him as I sprinted back up to the second floor. Once I was inside my room, I shut the door and leaned against it, and wondered what fresh hell I'd stumbled into. I'd dated Renato a few times was back when I first opened Nine Lives Investigations, but we had been far from serious. Definitely not serious enough for him to assume an invitation to my bedroom, and after I'd broken it off with him, I never saw him again...

Except for that time Tessa and I walked by the coffee shop in the last reality, and Renato was waiting in line inside it. That coffee shop was in the same building as my old apartment, and down the street from Valley Burger.

The pieces were falling into place.

I went to my laptop and scrolled through the news articles. Sure enough, Renato was the brave mortal who had witnessed the witches stuff me into their car's trunk, and he followed them all the way to the Beauclaire house. The article ended with a quote from me naming Renato as my savior. The pseudo paranormal researcher I'd dumped almost three years ago had engineered a new reality and made himself my boyfriend.

This timeline was getting worse by the moment.

I linked my hands behind my head and blew out a breath, and felt my sapphire ring. That ring hadn't existed until the second reality, but I'd brought it with me to this one, just like I'd brought Dan from the first. I wondered if that had happened because the ring had been with me in the protection circle, but as I gazed around my room, and noted the other things that existed here but were lost in the real time-line—important things, like my laptop—and I realized I could take them with me wherever we traveled next. Which, hopefully, would be home.

Based on that logic, it also meant that my dad and Tessa were their normal selves because they'd come through with me in the protective salt circle. Therefore, we all needed to leave together. No way was I leaving any of them behind. Renato, though, he could go to hell for all I cared.

I grabbed my backpack and moved around the room, stashing my laptop, a few notebooks, and anything else I could fit inside of it. I was already wearing my favorite boots, and my leather jacket was in the kitchen where I'd left it earlier. Once my bag was full, I double checked to make sure I had my power cords, then I went back downstairs to face the creep.

"Hey," Renato said when he saw me on the stairs. He'd spread out a blanket in the center of the parlor floor, and had our picnic lunch spread out on top of it. "Why do you have a backpack?"

"No reason," I said as I breezed past him, and entered the kitchen. I grabbed my leather jacket, and a banana. For all I knew, those sandwiches he'd brought over were drugged. When I went back into the living room, I sat across the room on the red couch, and kept my backpack next to me.

"Why are you all the way over there?" he asked.

"Are we, like, a thing in this reality?" I countered.

"What do you mean, 'this reality'?"

"Haven't you noticed? The timeline keeps changing. Some moron is altering reality."

"If they're altering reality, they can't be a moron," he began, and I smiled to myself. This may be a new reality, but it had the same old arrogant Renato.

"But they are," I insisted. "There aren't any spirits here. Whoever is behind this built a place with seers, but there aren't any spirits for the seers to talk to. Pretty dumb, huh?"

"How do you know there aren't any spirits?"

I gave him a look. "I'm the Mistress of Seers, dumbass. How long did you think you were going to get away with these fantasy lives before I caught on to you?"

Renato withdrew a gun from the back of his waistband and shot me. It happened so fast I didn't even realize I was hit until I saw the redness seeping down my shirt. I reached for my phone, but I got dizzy and fell back against the couch. Moments before I blacked out, Renato stood over me and grinned.

"Who's the dumbass now?"

I wasn't in any pain, which was weird. The way I understood it, getting shot hurt. A lot.

I sat up, and realized that while I was still in the parlor, I wasn't on the red couch. I was on the blue one, which was just weird because I never sat there. It wasn't that it was uncomfortable or out of the way, but it had always been Gran's favorite seat, and even now sitting on the blue couch felt like stealing her spot. She apparently still loved it after death, because her spirit was beside me.

"There's my girl," Gran said. "I've been waiting for you to wake up."

"How did you get here?" I asked. "I haven't felt a single spirit in this reality."

"We're here, but hidden from you," Gran replied. "The people who created this new reality are mortals, and since they don't have a connection with the dead, they couldn't account for us in their ritual. I've been trying to get you to notice me for days."

"Sorry," I said. "What changed? Why can I see you now?"

Gran nodded toward the far side of the room, and I gasped. Lying on the red couch was my body, motionless and covered in blood.

"Am I dead?"

"You're very close," she replied. "It's going to take a great deal of energy to heal you, and the fool that shot you can't get out of his own way long enough to get you any help."

"Yeah, Renato is a moron," I said, surprisingly calm in the face of my imminent death. I'd no sooner spoken than Renato ran in from the kitchen with a handful of towels, and pressed them against my shoulder.

"Why did he shoot me?" I wondered.

"From what I've gathered, he didn't mean to," Gran replied. "Apparently he only wanted to scare you, but he's such a bad shot he hit your shoulder when he was aiming for the wall."

"Has he at least called an ambulance?"

Gran's face darkened. "He can't. In this reality, ambulances won't serve supernaturals."

I faced her. "Am I going to die?"

"No." Gran held my face, and repeated, "No. Not if I have anything to say about it."

I nodded, feeling like a scared little girl, but this was Gran. I trusted her implicitly. If she said I was going to make it, I believed her. "How do I get help?"

"I'm already helping you," she replied. "Normally, we would call on the ancestors for healing energy, but your path to them has been blocked. Therefore, I am acting as a conduit. It will take some doing, but we will heal you." Gran patted my hand. "I do miss you, Eli, but I don't want you to join me. Not just yet."

I leaned against her shoulder, and she wrapped her arm around me. "I don't want to go, either. And Dan…" I snuffled, and wiped my cheek. "I don't want to leave Dan."

"That detective's a fine man."

"He is. Wait, have you been watching us?"

"Not like that," Gran said, "but I do watch over you. Good thing, too. As soon as I realized something was off about the house, I came by to investigate."

"Is this mess all because we went through the nexus?" I asked. "Dad warned us we might alter the timeline."

"Yes and no," she replied. "This Renato has been trying to access the spiritual plane for some time, but with very little success. Things changed for him when that scoundrel Amir Hassan sustained a brain injury. For some reason—as you know, legal matters were never my strong suit—once Amir was hospitalized, the three men he associated with were released from jail. Apparently, there was no longer a reason to hold them?"

"Then, those three met up with Renato, and they made a new reality?"

"In short, yes," Gran replied. "While Renato appears to be holding a grudge against you, one of the others is irritated with Tessa."

"I bet it's Mike," I said, remembering how Tessa had been thoroughly unimpressed with him when he'd come by the office. "But there must be someone else involved, someone powerful. These four couldn't conjure a puddle in a rainstorm."

"You're right. A singularly powerful witch must have assisted them, but I haven't figured out who that might be yet," Gran replied. "Good thing you're a detective."

I smiled, and watched myself across the room. The energy Gran was funneling from our ancestors into my body hummed like a weak electrical current traveling across my skin. "Think I'll be able to wake up soon?"

"I hope so, but I don't mind sitting with you."

"Before you go," I began, because as much as I enjoyed visiting with Gran I knew she couldn't keep this up for much longer, "do you know why all of these changes hinge on when I was kidnapped? No matter how much time passes, everything seems to want to bring me back to that point."

Gran blew out a breath. "Many things changed when you were born, Eli. I lived a long time before I had your father, and then he lived a long time before he had you. For many years there was talk of the Moore line dying out, and many wondered if a new family of seers would rise in our place... But then you were here, and the world knew the Moores would have yet another Mistress of Seers."

"Bet that irritated some people."

"Oh, it certainly did. As you know, those who can't come by their own power love to steal it from others."

"Like Amir," I said, and she nodded. "Then, for people like him, me being kidnapped was a good thing?"

"Your abduction signified another shift in power," Gran replied. "If we hadn't been able to rescue you, it would have meant the end of our line, whether or not we died out. But Alex and Tessa got to you, and my boy taught the witches a lesson they will never forget."

"In the last timeline, I'd never been kidnapped, and my life seemed better, but it was all superficial," I said. "In this one I was kidnapped, and my life is worse. Way worse. Who is benefiting the most from me not being able to interact with the dead?"

Gran kissed my forehead. "You've always had a knack for asking the right questions."

The next moment, my eyes snapped open. I was back in my body. Thank the gods, Gran had given me enough healing energy to hold off dying, at least for a little while.

I tried to sit up.

Bad idea.

Pain shot from my shoulder down my arm and I fell back, wheezing.

"You're alive," Renato said. "I didn't mean to shoot you so badly!"

"Why shoot me at all," I ground out. With my good arm, I moved the bloody towels away from the wound site. Renato had ripped open my shirt, but other than packing towels around the bullet hole, he hadn't done anything else to stop the bleeding or otherwise help me. If not for Gran's intervention, I would have bled to death. "I need an ambulance."

"It wasn't supposed to be like this," he said, tearing at his hair as he paced in front of the couch. "You were supposed to be nicer to me, and you were supposed to teach me what you know. You were supposed to help me!"

"I can't help you if I'm dead," I snapped, then I heard the back door open and close. A few moments later, Dan was standing in the parlor entrance with his gun raised and trained on Renato.

"Get away from my wife."

All That Matters

"She's not your wife," Renato snapped. "Not here!"

"Step away from Eliza," Dan ordered. "Now!" When Renato remained rooted in place, Dan continued, "I don't like killing people, but I've got no qualms about ending you to save Eli. Move!"

Renato stepped back from the couch, and Dan put himself between me and him. "Talk to me, baby."

"I'm okay. Well, not really, but I'll live."

Dan nodded, and said to Renato, "On your knees. Hands on your head." Renato did as told, then Dan cuffed him. He searched Renato and found the gun he'd shot me with. Dan confiscated Renato's gun and removed the ammunition, then he holstered his own weapon and he knelt beside me. "What happened?"

"He shot me." Dan moved the makeshift bandages aside, and frowned. "Gran's spirit was here. She saved me, otherwise I'd already be dead."

"This is all her fault," Renato began. Dan stood and kicked Renato in his shoulder, knocking him sideways so he sprawled out on the floor, then he picked me up and carried me into the kitchen while my assailant bitched about police brutality. He sat me on the counter, then he rested his forehead against mine.

"You're all right?"

"I am now."

Dan kissed me. "You know how you always say you're going to freak out, but later? Me too, this time." He shifted me forward, then he removed what was left of my shirt and looked at my back. "The bullet went clean through."

"Is that good?"

"Means I don't have to dig it out. Where's your first aid kit?"

"First cabinet in the pantry, second shelf." Dan squeezed my hip, then he went to the pantry. While he grabbed the kit, I caught my reflection in the glass solarium doors; it was dark out, so they acted as a mirror. Dried blood crusted my skin from my shoulder down my entire right side, and had soaked into my jeans. I'd never seen so much blood on one person in my life, on me or anyone.

"You all right?"

I blinked, and focused on Dan. "Yeah. Just wondering when bloody topless woman got added to my bingo card."

"You look good topless." Dan set the kit on the counted next to me. "This needs stitches."

"It probably doesn't," I said in a rush, and not just because the idea of a needle and thread pulling at the wound made my skin crawl. "Gran already did a bunch of healing."

"No stitches, then. Your grandmother's spirit was here?" he asked, and while he washed and bandaged my shoulder properly, I told him what I'd learned about this reality, who Renato was, and about my conversation with Gran.

"And that's why there aren't any spirits here," I concluded. "When Renato and the rest worked their spell, they didn't know they were supposed to include them."

"They only mentioned witches and mortals, so that's all we got," Dan said, and I nodded. "When I couldn't get a call through to you, I thought it was just a bad connection, but when Alex called me—"

"Dad called you?"

"Yeah. Him and Tessa can't leave her place just yet. Not sure why. He was trying to let you know, but neither one of them could contact you, either." Dan set down the bandages, and braced his hands on either side of my hips. "I've never been so scared in my life. When none of us could reach you..." Dan cleared his throat. "Then when I saw you lying there..."

"Hey. Hey—ow." I'd moved to put my arms around him, but my injured shoulder had other ideas. "I'm here. I'm not going anywhere." I wrapped my good arm around him. "I'm not leaving you." Dan gathered me against him, and as his body tensed against mine, I realized he was exhausted. "What time is it?"

"Not sure. Way after midnight." He shifted so we could see one another, and he smoothed back my bloody, stiffened hair. "It's like a war zone out there. If I hadn't been in a police vehicle, I don't know if I would have made it back."

I shuddered, only partly from blood loss. "We have got to get out of here. This reality is an actual nightmare."

"No arguments here." Dan stepped back, then he unbuttoned his shirt and took it off, and helped me put it on. As he fastened the buttons, he said, "Let's go deal with the asshole."

I only swayed a little bit when I hopped down from the counter. Dan steadied me, then we returned to the parlor. Which was devoid of morons.

"Looks like Renato's running around town in handcuffs." The front door was wide open, but Renato was long gone. "I hope that works out badly for him."

Dan closed and locked the front door. "When we get with Alex and Tess, our first order of business is getting home. Once we're back where we belong, I am going after him."

"Dan—"

"Eli, he almost killed you," Dan said, rounding on me. "Don't try to stop me."

"I don't want to stop you," I said. "I was going to say that since a witch must have helped them, Tessa might be able to trace the magical signature on him back to the source of whatever power boosted him."

He blew out a breath. "Okay. That's good. I didn't mean to snap at you like that."

"It's okay." I held out my good arm. "Come on. Let's get some sleep."

"Should we stay here? All the bad guys know where you live."

"I don't think they'll come by tonight, and even if they do, the house is warded. Renato only got inside because I let him in. Which, in hindsight, was not one of my better moves."

"Not your fault he had a gun. Hang on," he said, then he whipped out his phone and started typing.

"Is that about work?" I asked.

"No. I told Alex I'm with you."

"Did you tell him I'm hurt?"

"No. That's more of an in-person discussion." He slid his phone into his back pocket. "Want me to carry you upstairs?"

"I can handle it, but can you grab my backpack and jacket?"

"Sure. And you need a backpack for bed, because?"

As we went upstairs and into my room, I explained my theory of how we could bring objects with us from one reality to the next, and how my ring was proof. Once we were in bed, he kissed my hand and held it against his heart.

"Glad you like the ring," he said. "I wish I could take credit for giving it to you."

"You did give it to me," I said. "Should we go by the house? There might be some stuff there you want to get."

"Not a thing," he replied. "All I need in this or any timeline is you. I haven't even driven by our place."

"Aren't you curious?"

"In these new realities, curiosity leads to problems. Besides, none of this is real." He traced the contour of my cheek. "You're real, and I'm real, and that's all that matters to me."

Hours later, I woke up to a sore shoulder, and Dan's arms locked tight around me. It was reminiscent of a few days ago when I'd woken up at our house after our epic bout of make-up sex. Both times, Dan had thought he'd lost me.

Last time, we'd beaten the odds and come back stronger. We'll do that this time, too.

I slipped out of Dan's arms, crossed the room, and stood in front of my mirror. Even though Gran had pumped me full of healing energy, I looked like hell. My hair was stiff with dried blood, my face was pale and drawn, and Dan's blue shirt had rusty brown stains traveling down the right side. With my left hand, I unbuttoned the shirt and let it fall to the floor, then I peeled off the bandages and checked out my new scar. Since Gran had been the one in charge of my healing, the scar was a healthy pink, though it was far from fully healed. I wondered if the scar would disappear once we got back to our own reality, or if I'd be pestering my dad for a new tattoo to cover it.

It had been years since I'd gotten a new tattoo, mostly because I'd started running low on blank skin. After Dad and Tess had rescued me from the Beauclaire house, he had obsessively tattooed protection sigils on me until I resembled a walking spell book. I hadn't minded at first, because I understood that everyone processes emotions differently, and my father had almost lost his only child. Besides, after what I'd gone through, I thought having more protection was a great idea.

Eventually I told Dad I thought I had enough tattoos, and while he still occasionally tried to put a new sigil on me for the most part, he'd backed off. That had coincided with him taking me along as he visited clans and seers across the world. For almost two years, my dad and I had been inseparable. I now understood we had both been healing, and I was glad we'd gotten to spend so much time together.

I gave my reflection one last look, then I went into the bathroom and showered off the rest of the blood. I washed my hair three times, because the last thing I wanted to be reminded of was lying on the blood-soaked couch for hours, with my life slowly slipping away while Renato paced around the room and muttered to himself. I wondered what Dan was planning on doing to Renato once we returned to the correct timeline. With any luck, Renato will leave the country and never return.

After I'd toweled off, I slipped back into bed. My movements woke Dan.

"You smell good," he said, as he slid his arm around my waist and pulled me close.

"I showered."

He cracked an eyelid. "You didn't invite me?"

"You seemed like you needed the sleep." He grunted, and drew me closer. "It's really bad out there?"

"We don't do police work anymore," he began. "All we do is hunt down witches, take reports about possible witches, and put people on trial for using magic. It's like living in *The Crucible.*"

"What do you do if someone's a witch?" I asked. "What happens to them?"

"We make a report, and send the person off to Tessa's side of town." Dan rolled onto his back, and draped an arm over his eyes. "At least, that's the official explanation. Some of those folks just disappear, never to be seen again. I gotta say, Eli, I've never once been ashamed to be a cop, until yesterday."

"Like you said, none of this is real. This all came about because four idiots tried to make themselves powerful, but they didn't do any of the research needed to understand how to use that power. Working magic without first gaining knowledge is like handing out knives to toddlers. Lots will happen, and none of it will be good."

Dan grunted. "Where did they even get the idea for all of this?"

"Remember when we opened your shed, and instead of your lawn mower, we found all sorts of magical implements?"

"I still miss that lawn mower."

"I will buy you a new one. Anyway, Tessa and Dad went through most of the books. They were packed full of spells for all sorts of purposes. That, coupled with them hanging around with Amir and hearing all his half-baked ideas, is probably where they got the idea to make a new reality. Also, Mike really didn't care for Tessa, so that's probably why she was reduced to an errand girl," I added.

"Tessa's gonna kick his ass when we get home," Dan said, and I didn't disagree. "Your grandmother said a witch helped them? She have any idea who?"

"No, but it all hinges on me. Specifically, me getting kidnapped." I flopped onto my back and stared at the ceiling. "In the last reality, I was never kidnapped and my life was fantastic. In this reality, I was, and everything is awful. I get why things are awful now, because Renato's getting me back for not letting him into the paranormal club—"

"That guy is unhinged," Dan interrupted. "I can see why you dumped him."

"Before I met you, my taste in men was epically awful," I said, then I paused. "Actually, I broke it off with Renato a few days before we met, and I never went on another date afterward."

"See that? We were love at first sight. You just didn't know it right away."

"Maybe if you hadn't been stalking me, I would have had a second to realize it."

"I was not stalking you! You kept turning up at crime scenes I was assigned to investigate."

I laughed, only to wince when pain shot through my shoulder. "Anyway, like I was saying, we need to figure out why all of this relates back to my stupid kidnapping."

"And we need to know what witches these ghost clowns knew about," Dan said. "Think it's Beauclaire?"

"You know, for once I don't think he's involved," I said. "He also got what he wanted, which was Jemima alive and ruling the clan at his side, but I think if he'd been holding the wheel he would have gotten real Jemima, not a wax double."

"Good point." Dan propped himself up on his elbow, and checked out my gunshot would. "We need to get you some antibiotics. I don't want that getting infected."

"Don't need them." I pointed to a sigil near my collarbone. "This tattoo wards against infection."

"Convenient," Dan said, then he dipped his head and kissed the tattoo. "Come take a shower with me."

"I already showered."

"So take another one." He kissed a line up my neck. "You're gonna be all sweaty in a few minutes, anyway."

"I will be?"

"Definitely." He paused, and added, "I mean, if you want to. How do you feel? Do you want to sleep some more, or get something to eat?"

I smiled, because nothing was cuter than Dan when he was flustered. "I feel fine, but I bet you can make me feel even better."

The Witch And The Police Officer

After my second shower of the day, I made breakfast while Dan rooted around in my father's closet for a clean shirt. I'd already put the bread in the toaster and had started cracking eggs when Dan joined me.

"You're cooking?" he asked. "This really is a different world."

"If it's as bad as you say out there, I figure we'll need the protein." I cracked the last egg, and started whisking them one handed. The bowl almost skidded off the counter but Dan steadied it at the last minute.

"Let me do this," he said, and began beating the eggs into submission. "Do you know if there are any painkillers in the house? Your shoulder must be sore as hell."

"It is," I acknowledged, as I poured coffee and got a few plates out from the cabinet. "But we don't have any of that stuff. I don't like painkillers, and neither does Dad."

"You prefer pain?"

"No. Dad meditates to relieve pain and increase his own natural healing ability."

"And what do you do?"

"Suffer, mostly." The toast popped up, and I plated them one at a time. "I've never been very good at meditating for myself."

"For yourself?" Dan declared the eggs cooked and divided them between our plates. "What does that mean?"

"Well, if I'm meditating to reach a spirit, or to cast a spell, that's different," I replied. "That comes easily for me. But when I have to stop everything and meditate to help myself, it doesn't work so well. I feel like I'm wasting time."

"Taking care of yourself is not a waste of time." He grabbed my toast and buttered it. "After we eat, I'll check the first aid kit in the car. Probably has a few painkillers in it."

"Thank you," I said, as he handed me my now-buttered toast. The ache in my shoulder was so bad it kept me from using my right arm or hand. If popping a few painkillers would restore my arm's mobility, I was all for it. "How long do you think it will take us to get to Tessa's?"

"In the normal world, that drive would take about twenty minutes. Out there, it might take all day."

I sighed, and stabbed at my eggs. "I guess we should pack a lunch."

After we'd finished eating, we packed a cooler with sandwiches and bottled water, and loaded it, my backpack, and my leather jacket into the car. Dan was adamant that he didn't want to stop by our house for anything, but he did grab one of my dad's crossbows and quiver of bolts.

Speaking of my dad, when I turned on my phone, I found dozens of texts from him. Since I couldn't text him back one handed, I called. He answered on the first ring.

"Eli? Are you okay?"

"I'm all right now." I debated how much I should tell him over the phone, and decided to go for broke. "Do you remember me telling you about that guy I dated a few years ago, Renato?"

"Vaguely. Was he the paranormal studies major?"

"Yeah. He shot me."

"What? Where?"

"My shoulder, but it's mostly healed. Gran was here, and she helped me."

I heard him blow out a breath, and I could picture him running a hand through his hair. "How bad is the wound?"

"Dan said the bullet went straight through."

"Eli—"

"Dad. I'm all right. I mean, it's sore but I'll live."

He was quiet for a moment. "Sorry. I was nodding, then I realized you can't see me."

I laughed. "I get it. We're getting ready to leave the house and join you two. Do we need a code word to get into Tessa's?"

"I'll tell her you're coming. You won't have any problems." Dad paused, then asked, "How is Renato involved in all of this?"

I explained how Gran and I thought he and the Ghost Guys engineered not one, but two half-assed realities. "But what I can't figure out, and neither could Gran, is the identity of the witch that helped them. This clearly took a crap ton of power, and Tessa's the most powerful witch we know. She didn't have anything to do with this, so who could it have been?"

"Perhaps they were assisted my more than one witch," Dad said, which was something I hadn't even thought of. It must have been nearly impossible to convince one witch to go along with their plan. Convincing two must have been quite the feat of bullshittery. "And, Bug, Tessa is not the most powerful witch we know."

"Then, who is?"

"Your mother."

"Why so quiet?"

I glanced at Dan, and realized I hadn't said a word since we got in the car. He'd driven over to Gran's house in an armored police truck, which was great. Once we turned off of Essex Street and crossed into the mortal side of town, everything resembled an active war zone.

"Sorry. I was thinking about something my dad said, and that led me to something my mother said." He reached across the center console and took my hand.

"Want to tell me about it?"

"We were talking about who could be powerful enough to create this world, and Dad said we might be looking for more than one witch," I began. "Dad also said that my mother is more powerful than Tessa, and that really blew my mind. I mean, I knew she was powerful, but for Dad to say that..."

"Does he think Christina is involved in this?"

"He doesn't know, but when I went to see her in the last reality, she said she created this life to find happiness." I faced Dan. "I thought she meant she moved away and started over, but what if she actually created an entirely new life, not just for herself, but for all of us?"

"That would explain why you weren't kidnapped in the last timeline we got stuck in," Dan said. "She might not be a great parent, but no mother would want their child hurt that way."

"Then the last version could have been her idealized reality, but when it wasn't going well Renato redid the spell so he could have his revenge." I blinked. "Okay, I just made him sound like a comic book villain."

"If he was a comic book villain, he'd have a cooler name," Dan said, then he cut the wheel and we skidded left. "Get down!"

I ducked below the dashboard and heard bullets hit the back of the vehicle. "Why is there no gun control here?" I shrieked.

"There is." Dan checked his mirrors, then he backed down the road and onto a side street. "The people shooting at us were cops."

"But you're the chief," I said. "Aren't you?"

"Yeah." Dan swung the truck into an alleyway and onto an access road, and we drove alongside the canal.

"Then why would the cops be shooting at one of their own?"

"I didn't get to tell you much about what happened at the station yesterday. Basically, word on the street is that I've got a soft spot for a certain woman suspected of being a witch."

"Who?" Dan gave me a look. "Oh! The cops think I'm a witch?"

"Just like the last place, no one seems to know about seers. So yes, they think you're a witch. I spent a big chunk of yesterday defending myself against allegations I was helping you with whatever magical conspiracy the rest think you're involved in."

"Conspiracy," I repeated, then I realized what else he'd said. "Wait, are we together here? Meaning, I am not with Renato?"

"Not sure." He glanced at me, then continued, "The person in charge of investigating me had pictures of us meeting up together. They even had a surveillance video of us talking behind a building, as if we were trying not to be seen together."

"What were we saying?"

"There wasn't any sound." Dan entered a parking lot behind a factory, pulled between two Dumpsters, and killed the engine. "We'll hide out here for a bit. Hopefully, they'll move on, then we can get to Tessa's."

"Renato said I'm not your wife here," I muttered. "Everyone thinks I'm a traumatized recluse, but I'm actually sneaking around with you doing... what are we doing?"

"No idea, babe." He rubbed his eyes. "Your guess is as good as mine."

"Maybe we're having a clandestine love affair."

He peeked over his hand. "Clandestine? Really?"

"You know, because you're the respectable police officer and I'm the witch who swayed your mortal heart."

"Those painkillers are going to your head."

"Yeah. Maybe." I picked at the seat belt. "Your mom really didn't like me?"

"You really want to talk about this now?"

"I've got time."

Dan sighed, then he unbuckled his seat belt and turned toward me. "First of all, that wasn't my real mother. It was some alternate reality doppelgänger. You and my mother have not met."

"I know, but what if your real mother doesn't like me, either?" I glanced up, saw Dan's creased brow, and felt like an idiot. "I'm sorry. I don't mean to be so needy. It's just that I've never met anyone's parents before."

Dan leaned closer and caressed my cheek. "Don't apologize. I like that you need me."

I covered his hand with my own. "You said, first of all, we've never met. What's second?"

He sighed again. "Ma can be prickly, and sometimes she dislikes people for completely ridiculous reasons. It's a rite of passage for her to find something wrong with everyone me and the rest date."

"Did she like Charlotte?"

"No, she did not."

"Really? But you married her!"

"I did, and Ma was pissed right up until the wedding day." He tilted his head back and closed his eyes, and I suddenly felt awful.

"I don't mean to pry," I said. "You don't have to tell me any of this. It's none of my business."

Dan faced me, and said, "Of course this is your business. So, Ma had a litany of reasons why Charlotte wasn't good for me. She was a few years older than me, wasn't healthy, couldn't have kids... The list went on. Ma thought I was wasting my life on someone who couldn't give me what she thought I needed."

"It sounds like your mother loves you an awful lot, and she only wanted the best for you."

His eyes narrowed. "Already taking her side? I see how it is. You two are gonna gang up on me, probably get my sisters involved, too." I giggled, imagining family dinners with Dan and his parents and all those siblings. He smiled, and stroked his thumb across my cheek. "You got nothing to worry about, baby. Ma will act like Ma, and no matter how you two get along, I am going to keep loving you. Promise."

I kissed his palm. "You say the best things."

"I do what I can. Besides, Ma already knows about you. Alicia showed her your picture and everything."

"You sent your sister a picture of me?" I demanded, then a woman dropped onto the hood of the truck and tried to kick in the windshield.

Meet The Brute Squad

"**S**hit," Dan yelled as he started the engine.

"Where did she come from?" I demanded.

"Jumped down from the roof of the fucking building." Dan threw the truck into gear as the woman on the hood withdrew an axe from a sheath on her back.

"Why does she have an axe?" I screamed, then she started hacking at the windshield. Dan floored the gas, but another vehicle pulled in front of us and cut off our escape. Dan slammed on the brakes, causing us to jerk forward. Our attacker skidded back, but she plunged the axe into the hood and hung on. A corner of the windshield crumbled away, and I saw our attacker's face.

"Jill?" Standing on the hood of the truck wearing riot gear was Jill Sanders, who in the real world was the department's forensic scientist, and my good friend. Here, things appeared to be different.

"Don't say my name, witch," Jill snarled. She brought down the axe again, and I realized she wasn't trying to stop us. She wanted to kill us.

"Get back," I shrieked, and a wave of energy pulsed out of my hands and toward Jill. The energy took out what was left of the windshield and sent Jill flying off the hood amid a shower of broken glass.

"Do that again," Dan yelled. "Move that van out of our way!"

I focused on the armored van in front of us, and yelled, "Move!"

Another wave pushed outward from me, this one so strong I could see the waves of magic shimmer in the air. The wave knocked the police van onto its side and shoved it back far enough for Dan to get out of the alley. With tires screeching and the sharp stench of burned rubber, we made it out of the alley and away from our attackers.

"What the actual fuck." I twisted around and watched the chaos we'd left behind us through the rear window. "Is Jill the one investigating you?"

"Seat belt," Dan said. "I don't need you flying out the window."

I faced forward and grabbed the belt, but my hands were shaking so badly I couldn't fasten it. "I-I can't do it."

"What's wrong? Shoulder?"

"Adrenaline. I'm not used to moving that much power all at once." I leaned against the side window and listened to the blood pounding in my ears. My throat felt like sandpaper, so I grabbed one of the water bottles we'd packed earlier and drank. It barely helped. "Do you really think we could go out the window?"

Dan reached over and squeezed my good arm. "I got you, baby." He pulled onto the main road, and I could see Tessa's place looming over us. "We're gonna have to ditch the truck and go on foot."

I drank more water, and resisted asking him if we would be safe. Obviously, nothing in this reality was safe, least of all us. "Where can we leave it?"

"Someplace without cameras, preferably." Dan pulled into a strip mall, and parked near the back of the lot. "Let's get our stuff out from the back."

We went to the rear of the truck and grabbed what we thought we could carry. Even though it was warm, I put on my leather jacket, then I looped my backpack over my good shoulder. As for Dan, he found a duffle bag in the back and filled it with his and Renato's guns, ammunition, the first aid kit, and my dad's crossbow and bolts.

"Is it a good idea to walk around with all this weaponry?" I asked. "Doesn't exactly seem legal."

"It'll be fine as long as we don't get caught." He handed me my half empty water. "Want a sandwich?"

"I can't really eat right now," I said, leaving off how my stomach was extra queasy and I thought I might throw up.

"Hey. Come here." Dan wrapped his arms around me. "We're almost there. We just have to go a little farther, then we'll be with Tess and Alex, and the four of us will figure out how to get back home. You with me, baby?"

"Yeah." I nodded, then I stepped back and my backpack slid off my shoulder. I grabbed the strap, but my arm was so weak it was like trying to heft a boulder. "I don't think I can carry this."

Dan stashed it in the back of the truck. "We'll come back for it. You okay with that?"

I really wasn't, but Dan was already loaded down with far more important supplies. Leaving it behind was the smart thing to do. "Let's go."

Since the shortest distance between two points was a straight line, we made a beeline straight up the hill. The beginning of the walk wasn't too bad, since the ground was level and we mostly walked on paved surfaces. Also, Jill's witch hunters didn't seem to be following us.

"We're on the supernatural side of town now," Dan explained, when I mentioned the lack of pitchforks following us. "Police have no jurisdiction over witches, so they stay clear."

"Is it safe for you to be here?"

"Probably not, but you'll protect me, right?" Dan grinned at me, but it became a frown when he looked at me. "What's wrong?"

"A little of everything." The painkiller Dan had found in the cruiser's first aid kit had worn off, and my shoulder throbbed with white hot pain. Add to that my unexplained nausea coupled with the chills and my clammy, sweaty hands, and I felt like I had the flu. Only, I had protection sigils that were supposed to keep me healthy. "I think I'm going to be sick."

"Let's take a rest." Dan looked around, then he beckoned me toward a large house surrounded by a hedge. We slipped through a break in the hedge, and sat down on the far side of a garden shed.

"We're out of sight here," he said. "Let's catch our breath for a few."

"Okay," I said, then I leaned against him and everything faded away.

When I woke up, I felt like a balloon was inflating inside my chest. I looked at Dan, then I turned away and puked my guts out. Once that was over, I leaned against the shed, panting and sweating and way too exhausted to be embarrassed. Dan felt my forehead, then he started unbuttoning my shirt.

"What are you doing?"

"You're burning up," he said. "That wound might be infected after all."

I shook my head. "It's not."

"I'll be the judge of that," he said, then he bared my shoulder. "Actually, it looks pretty good."

"I feel like I have food poisoning," I said. "My stomach's all acid."

"Shit. I wonder if you're allergic to the pain pills."

"You can be allergic to those?" I asked, but Dan was rummaging through the first aid kit. He found an instruction book, and flipped through the pages.

"Okay, you don't have the symptoms of an allergic reaction," he said, then he turned another page.

"It has instructions for nausea," he announced. "It says I should give you clear liquids and feed you bland food."

"I don't really wat to eat anything."

"There's meds here for nausea," he began, but I grabbed his hand.

"I don't know if taking more medication is a good idea," I said. "My body doesn't work like a mortal's."

Dan put down the booklet, and pushed my hair back from my face. "Can you heal yourself?"

"Theoretically yes, but I don't know how." I smiled weakly. "I'm not very good at being a witch."

"Bullshit. I saw how you got us out of a jam back there. You're the best witch that ever lived. However, I don't think you should be walking any more than necessary." He pulled out his phone and started typing.

"Who are you contacting?"

"Alex. I sent him our location and told him we need a pickup."

"Why didn't we ask for a pickup earlier?" I asked, since we could have avoided being attacked by a gang of witch hating cops.

"Because any supernaturals coming into the mortal side of town can be shot on sight." Dan pocketed his phone, then he took his gun out of the duffel bag and shoved it into his belt. "Think you can walk?"

"I can try." He helped me stand, and I promptly got woozy and puked again. "Maybe I just need to get whatever it is out of me."

"That's a good plan." He slid his arm around my waist, and steadied me. My ribs ached and I must have smelled like garbage, but Dan didn't complain. "Let's see how far we can get before we need a rest."

"Aren't you taking the rest of the stuff?" I asked, because he'd left the duffel bag on the ground.

"We need to travel light. I will take the water, though." He grabbed the water bottles, then his phone beeped. He checked it, and said, "Car's going to meet us on the corner. Ready, baby?"

I looked up the hill. Due to the angle I couldn't see Tessa's house, but I could sense her power, and my father's. "Let's go."

Dan half dragged me out of the innocent person's yard—sorry about all the puke, dude—and to the nearest street corner. Less than a minute after Dan and I got to the meeting spot, a black limousine driven by LeClerc, Jacob's Allwood's amazingly competent assistant, pulled up. I hoped it was the same magically reinforced vehicle he drove in the real world. Dan loaded me into the back seat, and I promptly passed out.

When I opened my eyes, I was in an unfamiliar bed, and an unfamiliar Tessa was sitting beside me.

"What the hell are you wearing?" I croaked.

"You decide to rejoin the living after giving all of us the fright of our lives, and that's the first thing you say to me?" she countered. "And to answer your question, this version of me is quite enamored with the renaissance era."

"I can see that." Tessa was wearing a burgundy velvet gown decorated with gold embroidery on the bodice and sleeves, and a pearl and ruby choker. Her black hair was piled on top of her head, and secured by many jeweled hairpins that caught the light. "Is this the sort of outfit you wore back in the day?"

"Oh, no. This is much more comfortable, and it has a zipper! No more laces and stays. And look at this." Tessa stood, and thrust her hands into the folds of her skirts. "It has pockets!"

"It's a modern marvel," I said, and she agreed. "Where's Dan?"

"He's with Alex. I believe they're discussing the merits of using a crossbow for defense versus modern firearms." Tessa felt my forehead. "How do you feel?"

"Much better. Did you heal me?"

"I did not, but your father did. According to Alex, you were poisoned."

"Really? How?" I sat up and leaned against the headboard. "Dan thought I was having an allergic reaction to the pain medication he found in the police car, or that my gunshot wound got infected. Not that I doubt Dad," I added, because no seer in the world would doubt the marksman when it came to poisons. As I contemplated my poisoning, I noticed the utter lack of pain in my arm. "Did you fix my shoulder? It doesn't hurt anymore."

"I took a look at the wound, and it's well healed without a trace of infection," she said. "There's really not much more I can do for it. Dan said Helena helped you back at the house?"

"Yeah. After Renato fricken' Florian shot me."

Tessa's lip curled. "Do we think he's the alleged mastermind behind all of this?"

"Him, the Ghost Guys, and whatever witch or witches they convinced to go along with their plan." I looked at my hands. "What does Dad think I was poisoned with?"

"It's the coincidence of all coincidences."

"What does that mean," I began, then I figured it out. "Wolfsbane."

"Mmm hmm. Alex said he's never seen a case as bad as yours. Whatever healing energy Helena used for your shoulder also held off the worst of the poison."

"It must have been in the water bottles," I said. "I drank half a bottle of water, but Dan didn't have any. If he had, he probably wouldn't have survived long enough to get here." I rubbed my arms, suddenly chilled.

"You're correct, which means that whatever Renato's up to has moved from curiosity about the paranormal and on to attempted murder," Tessa said. "Once we're home, you will need to hold him and the others accountable."

"I will," I replied, and I meant it. Renato wasn't just screwing around with my life, but the lives of every person in the region. "Although Dan might beat me to it."

"Letting Dan have his revenge is all well and good, but as Mistress of Seers you cannot let these actions go unpunished," Tessa said. "You must stand firm against the mortals, and the witch that aided them."

"I've been thinking about the witch in question. What if it the witch didn't realize the extent of what they were doing? What if they were powerful, but untrained and inexperienced?"

"What you really mean is, what if that witch was your mother?" Tessa countered.

I shrank down against the headboard. "Yeah. We know she doesn't understand very much about how supernatural things work. What if she was involved, but they tricked her into helping them?"

"If Christina was coerced by these fools and went into this without a full understanding of the consequences, then I agree that she should not be punished as severely as the rest."

"But she does need to be punished?"

Tessa shrugged. "I suppose it depends on the extent of her involvement, if she was involved at all. Don't worry. I won't let any witch be punished without just cause, nor will I let a guilty party avoid being disciplined."

"Right, because you're the evil queen here?"

"I must say, I do enjoy having a court again." Tessa practically glowed when she mentioned her court. Or maybe that was some leftover poison causing me to have visual disturbances, who knew. "Perhaps I'll buy out the rest of the condos in my building and establish a similar estate once we return to the true reality."

I imagined Queen Tessa ruling over the local witch clans, and smiled. "I've been thinking that the witches could use a change in leadership."

"You and me both."

The Court Of Della Scala

After I took a shower and got dressed in some of Tessa's non-medieval clothing, we went to find Dan and my father. They were waiting for us in one of the over decorated parlors.

"Eli," Dan said when I entered the room. Both he and my father stood, but Dan let my dad get to me first.

"How do you feel?" Dad asked, as he felt my wrists and forehead in much the same way Tessa had.

"I think the last of the wolfsbane's out of me," I replied. "Thanks for healing me. Gran helped, too."

"So Dan told me," he murmured, as he glanced at my shoulder. "Also, we have a new rule for this timeline. Since reality is now mimicking a horror movie, we will behave as if we're characters in one and not split up for any reason."

I leaned past my father and looked at Dan. "This sounds like one of your rules."

"Damn straight," Dan said, as he approached me. "At least two of us need to be together at all times. Strength in numbers."

"Speaking of strength, I think we need to pay Mom a visit," I began, then I explained to my father how I suspected she had gotten involved in all of this. No one was thrilled about bringing her into our plans, but it looked like we didn't have a choice in the matter.

"I guess you're going to meet my mother before I meet yours," I said to Dan.

Dan wrapped his arm around me and kissed my hair. "Guess so."

Tessa set about speaking to her staff and arranging transportation out to my mother's place in Oak Grove. It was quickly decided that LeClerc would take us in his armored limo; much like in the real world, he was the only one allowed to drive it. While he got the car ready, we sat around and stared at each other as we waited to take a trip none of us wanted to embark on.

"Are you okay about going to see her?" I asked my dad. He hadn't seen my mother since before she'd abandoned me at the hospital over twenty years ago.

He smiled tightly. "I'm fine. I just hope Christina doesn't throw anything at me, magical or otherwise."

"Has she thrown things at you before?" Dan asked.

"Many times," he muttered.

"Since Alex and Eli are very polite people who see the good in everyone, I will speak the truth," Tessa said. "Christina is a bitter, unhappy woman. She always has been."

"Didn't she also get a raw deal, what with being bred by the All-woods to potentially take in Jemima's spirit, and then starting out her life in the orphanage with no one to look out for her?" Dan asked.

"She wasn't born into the best circumstances," my father said. "That much is true. However, she has been given many opportunities to improve herself and her situation, and she's rejected nearly all of them."

"Rejection is her middle name," I muttered, and my dad winced. Before I could launch into my usual tired old reassurances that none of her actions weren't his fault, LeClerc reentered the room.

"Ma'am," he said, nodding toward Tessa. "You have a visitor."

"Tell them to come back another time," Tessa said. "And how are the preparations for the car coming along? We'd like to leave for the Lind residence as soon as possible."

"Actually, that's your visitor." LeClerc stepped aside, and my mother, Christina Lind, entered the room. Even though I'd seen her just a few days ago, I was shocked at her appearance. She looked exactly the same as she had when I was a kid, from her golden blonde hair to the frown lines that creased her face. It was odd how she looked so young, and yet so world-weary.

"Christina," Dad said, as he stood. "What are you doing here?" My mother folded her arms across her stomach and glared at him.

"Alex," she snapped. "What have you two done to me?"

"No one's done anything," he began.

"Bullshit," Mom yelled, pointing her finger at him. "For the first time since I met you, I was happy. I had a life that fit me, and..." Mom glanced at me, and turned away. "Then two days ago I woke up in this hell. What did you do?"

"What did *you* do?" I countered. "When I went to see you, you said you created a new life for yourself. Mind sharing how you did that?"

"Her refusal to learn how to use her ability has finally done her in," Tessa muttered.

Mom glared at Tessa, then she asked Dad, "Why is she here?"

"This is my house," Tessa said. "Why are you here?"

"Because I want my old life back!"

"Ma'am, Tess, let's all take a breath before we say things we might regret," Dan said, as he stood in the middle of the room. "This situation is stressful for all of us, but right now we need to work together. Have a seat, Ms. Lind, and let's talk this through."

Mom pursed her lips, but she took Dan's advice as she crossed the room and sat next to me. Because I did not appreciate her turning up out of the blue and accusing my father of things she didn't understand, I got up and sat next to Tessa.

"Petty, thy name is Eli," Tess murmured.

I leaned close to Tessa's ear, and whispered. "You two don't like each other. I thought you'd only met twice before."

"Yes, and those were two memorable occasions."

My father closed his eyes, and tilted his head back against the wall. "What happened, Christina? How did you go about creating a newer, better life for yourself?"

"I was approached by friends of Eli's," Mom began. "They said I could help make things more balanced between witches and mortals, and that this new fairness would help you." She nodded toward me.

"Balanced?" I repeated. "Exactly what was unbalanced?"

"Right now, witches have all the power," she replied. "This new world was supposed to give mortals access to some power of their own."

I glanced at Dad. He still had his eyes closed. "What about seers?"

Mom blinked. "What about them?"

"Whatever mojo you and my supposed friends worked left out seers," I replied. "I'm the Mistress of Seers, but there are no spirits here for me to help."

"You are not the mistress of anything," Mom scoffed. "That's just Helena trying to make you into something you're not."

"Don't you dare insult Gran!"

"Okay," Dan said, placing himself between me and my mother. "Let's all agree to speak well of the dead. Can we do that?"

Mom blinked. "Helena died?"

"Yeah," I snapped. "Years ago."

"Oh." Mom's head drooped. "I didn't know. I had many disagreements with Helena, but she was always kind to me."

"That was Ma," Dad said. "She wielded kindness the way others wield guns, or a sword. Her kindness was her greatest asset."

"We can all agree that Helena was a great lady, and is sorely missed," Dan said. When no one argued, he asked my mother, "Ma'am, how was this new world supposed to help Eli?"

"It could help her live a normal life," she said to Dan, then she looked at me. "So many awful things have happened to you, and none of it was your fault. It was all because you live with witches instead of regular people, but if we could take all of that away, you could be happy."

"You tried to make me into a mortal?" I asked. "But, you're the reason I'm half witch! I'm a seer on Dad's side, but you can't undo the fact that you're witchborn." I watched as her gaze dropped to the floor. "You wanted to be mortal, too. That's the real reason why you did this."

"Of course I want to be normal," Mom said. "I was normal, before I met Alex."

"Normal isn't the same as mortal," I began, but she shook her head.

"For me, it is. I lived as a normal person for years, and no one batted an eye at me. Then I met Alex, and he started bringing me to all of these places with magic, and he drew out part of me that should have remained dormant."

"You're delusional," I said, but Dan held up his hand.

"Ma'am, forgive me for asking, but were your abilities really dormant?" Dan asked. "Not too long ago, Eli and I went by the orphanage where you were born. It seems that you were a resident there quite some time ago."

"And?" Mom asked, raising an eyebrow.

"Right now you look to be about thirty years old, but I know for a fact that Eli is twenty-nine," he replied. "Also, the individuals we spoke to seemed to be from the last century. Maybe even the century before." I recalled the ghosts we'd spoken to, and their decidedly nineteenth century vibe.

"That's correct," Mom allowed. "I always thought I had good skin, but I know now that witches age more slowly than mortals."

"Then your abilities were never really dormant," Dan said. "You just didn't know how to use them. Is it fair for you to blame Alex and Eli for something that was, and still is, beyond all of your control?"

"No," Mom allowed. "I suppose it isn't."

"Dan's quite good with people," Tessa said.

When Mom glared at Tess, I said, "He's the best. It's why he's such a good detective."

"You're a detective?" Mom asked Dan. "I didn't think witches lowered themselves to take on mortal jobs."

"Actually, I'm not a witch," Dan said. "I'm one hundred percent mortal."

She looked him over. "I assumed you were a wizard, or something else magical."

"No ma'am, I'm just a cop from Queens," he said. "Can you tell us how these new realities were created?"

"I don't really know," she replied. "I was approached by four men who claimed they could fix things. Those were their words, not mine. All they needed from me was power, so I gave it to them."

"Wait," Tessa said. "When you say you gave them power, do you mean *your* power? As in your ability to perform witchcraft?"

"Yes," Mom said. "It's not like I ever wanted it."

"All of it?" Tessa pressed, and Mom nodded. Tessa threw up her hands. "Your habit of giving away everything of import has finally reached its crescendo."

"What is that supposed to mean?" Mom demanded.

"You gave away your daughter, a man that loved you, and now your identity as a witch," Tessa ticked off. "No matter what beautiful and wonderful thing falls into your lap, you toss it aside."

"How dare you pretend to know me," Mom said, then Dad finally spoke.

"Tessa speaks the truth, Christina," he said quietly. "I've never known anyone to reject happiness as easily as you do. You recoil from it, as if you're afraid it will burn you." He leaned toward Mom, and continued, "We need to fix this situation, not for you or me, but for our daughter. Will you help me make this right?"

"I will," Mom said, nodding. "Alex, I swear I will."

Dad watched her for a moment, then he stood and extended a hand to Tessa. "Let's talk to some of the elders, and see if they know how Christina can get her power back. Eli, Dan, we'll return shortly." With that, Tessa and Dad left the room. Dan took the seat Tessa had vacated, and the three of us sat in awkward silence.

"Today's been fun," I murmured.

"How are you feeling?" Dan asked.

"Better," I said. Dan moved to wrap an arm around me, then he remembered my shoulder injury and put his hand on the back of my neck instead.

"Were you sick?" Mom asked.

"Yeah," I replied. "The guy you gave your power to shot me. Then he poisoned me."

"Oh, Eli," Mom said. "I'm so sorry. I never meant for any of this to happen."

"I know you didn't," I said, because this was typical Mom. She was known for ignoring a problem and hoping it somehow resolved itself, but she was never intentionally malicious.

"If you don't mind my asking, what were your intentions?" Dan asked.

"I wanted Eli to be happy," she replied.

"Newsflash, Mom. I was happy." I laced my fingers with Dan's. "We were happy."

Mom's gaze focused on our hands, and how close we were sitting to one another. "Are you two... together?"

"We are," I replied. "Mom, meet my husband, Dan Lyons."

"Nice to meet you, ma'am," Dan said.

Her eyes went round as saucers. "You're married?"

"Handfasted, really, but it's the same concept."

"I always dreamed about planning a wedding," she said. "Do you have pictures?"

"Um, no," I said; getting married in the seventeenth century had meant no photographers. "It was a small ceremony."

"It was perfect," Dan said, as he kissed my hair.

"I wish I could have been there," Mom said, and I had enough.

"Really? You didn't even want to talk to me the other day, but now you want to be all mother of the bride for me?" I demanded. "Want a list of all the things I wanted but never got?"

"Eli," Dan murmured, but Mom waved away his concern.

"She's right," Mom said, then she focused on me. "You're right. I've made a lot of mistakes. I'm sorry."

My blood was threatening to boil over. She was sorry? Now, after all this time, she was finally sorry? Before I could tell her exactly where she could stick her way overdue apology, one of Tessa's staff entered the room.

"Ms. Lind?" she said. "We've prepared a room for you."

"I get a room?" Mom asked.

"Of course," the staff member replied. "Dinner won't be served for some time. You can use this time to rest, and refresh yourself."

"Um, all right." Mom stood, but paused before she followed the servant. "Eli, I never meant for anything bad to happen to you," she said. "I hope you can believe me."

"It doesn't matter what your intentions were, not any longer," I said. "What matters now is for you to do exactly as we say, and help us fix things."

Mom nodded, and followed the staffer out of the room. I leaned my head against Dan's shoulder and sighed.

"That was exhausting," I said. "Please tell me your mother isn't exhausting."

"If anything, my mother's exhausted." Dan stood, and pulled me to my feet. "Let's get you out of this stuffy room and into the sunshine."

Cereal And Bananas

While I'd been recuperating, Dan had taken it upon himself to explore the grounds of Tessa's lavish home. Apparently he'd had a lot of time to kill while my dad and Tessa got the poison out of me, and checking out the estate had helped him take his mind off of the horrible timeline we'd stumbled into. Which meant he was more than qualified to be my tour guide.

Dan led me from the parlor we'd been in, then hand in hand we navigated the maze of corridors, and went down several sets of stairs, to an indoor courtyard with a fountain in the center. Marble benches sat on raked gravel paths, and the perimeter of the space was lined with climbing roses and orange trees heavy with fruit.

"This is a very Tessa space." I took a deep breath, enjoying the orange blossoms' sweet, citrusy scent. "When she lived in Italy, she was surrounded by orange groves."

"Was that when she ruled her clan?"

"No. It was later." I sat on the edge of the fountain, and trailed my fingers through the water. "After her second husband died, she came here. That husband was a Beauclaire, and many of them had already come over from Europe. After a while she went back to Italy—I forget why—and she met a man named Tomas. His family owned the orange groves."

"That must have been a nice life." Dan sat beside me, and took my hand. "How are you really feeling?"

"I'm okay," I replied. "My shoulder's a bit sore, but I can deal with it. I think the wolfsbane's completely out of me."

"If we come across Florian again, I might kill him."

"Go ahead. I don't appreciate how he tried to kill me, and you, and I really don't appreciate all of this." I gestured toward the courtyard, though I felt bad about including the innocent orange trees. They were rather nice. "What do you think about Mom's story?"

"That she was only trying to fix things? Something's not right. How does she go from refusing to talk to you, to wanting to be mother of the year a few days later?"

"Parenting in general is out of character for her. Her default state has always been ignoring my existence."

Dan regarded me for a moment, then said, "She's the reason you live off cereal and bananas."

"No," I said. "I love cereal, especially the healthy ones. Grape Nuts is my favorite."

"It's also a complete meal a kid can make without needing the stove," he said, and I felt myself deflate. I had no memories of my mother ever cooking a meal or even washing or chopping vegetables. It was prepackaged foods or bust in her house, and bananas were one of the few foods we had that didn't come wrapped in plastic.

"Do you have to be so good at figuring everything out?" I asked. "I assume your mother fed you all sorts of home cooked foods, unlike mine."

He laughed through his nose. "Fed ain't the half of it. Between her and my nonna, it's a wonder I fit through the door."

"You'd look cute chubby," I said, and he smiled.

"Be that as it may, it stands to reason that no matter why Christina went along with Florian's plan to make a new reality, it wasn't to benefit you." Dan kissed the back of my hand. "I'm sorry, baby."

"For what?"

"For pointing out she wasn't truthful."

"It's okay. Believe me, this isn't the first time she lied to me or Dad in order to pretend she was a good mother. What's funny is that she mostly just lies to herself. When I said she's delusional, I meant it."

"How delusional? As in, needing treatment?" Dan's brows lowered. "Do these delusions make her dangerous?"

"I'm not sure," I replied. "Dad would know better than me. Why?"

"Because she didn't come here for you," he replied. "So why is she here?"

"Especially when she didn't want to share a front step with me a few days ago," I began, then I gasped. "It's a trap."

"What's a trap?"

"Mom being here is the trap," I said. "I bet Renato sent her here. He knew we'd think she was harmless, so she's either a distraction—"

"Or a time bomb," Dan finished as he stood. "Let's find Alex and Tess. They need to know."

We found my dad and Tessa in a conference room with the rest of the witch elders, three of whom were deceased in the real timeline. I swallowed the lump in my throat, and hoped their spirits were well and safe, wherever they were. When we got back to the real world, I would need to check on each one of them.

"What happened?" Tessa asked without preamble.

"We think Renato sent my mother here," I replied. "It's the only thing that makes sense."

"And if Florian sent her, it probably wasn't for a good reason," Dan added.

Tessa turned to Ned Burroughs. "I had Christina Lind put in one of the guest rooms on the second floor. Seal off the area," she ordered. Ned left immediately. "Do we think she brought something in with her?"

"I don't know," I replied. "She seems to think removing magic is the answer to all her problems. Maybe she has a null spell on her?"

"What's a null spell?" Dan asked.

"It dampens magic," I replied. "Depending on the strength of the witch who casts it, it can last for days or even weeks." I faced Tessa, who was sitting with the rest of the clan elders. "And she's the strongest witch we know."

"Merda," Tessa muttered. "We need to get you out of here. Eli, get to the garage, take a vehicle, and go."

"I can't leave you!"

"If we can't contain her and she neutralizes us, we need someone on the outside who can counteract her. Right now, the only person strong enough to do that is you." Tessa handed me a leather wallet. "That contains alarm codes to the garage and the key cabinet, along with cash and other information. Go, and let us handle Christina."

I stared at the wallet, then I looked up at my dad. "Why am I the only one who needs to leave?"

"Because if we fail, you're the only one who will be able to help us," he replied. "It's okay. We'll contain whatever's happening here, then I'll come find you." He glanced at Dan over my head. "Take care of her."

"I will," Dan said.

I didn't like this plan, but my dad and Tessa were confident. "All right," I said. "Should we go now?"

"Yes," my dad replied. "You should go before Christina realizes what's happening." He patted my uninjured shoulder. "We'll be together again soon, Bug."

I nodded, then Dan took my hand and led me out of the room. "Garage is this way."

"What if they can't stop what's happening?" I asked. "What will happen to them?"

"You're asking the wrong guy," Dan said as we jogged down the stairs. "I didn't even know what a null was until a few minutes ago." We reached the garage door, and I handed Dan the wallet. He opened it and found the access codes, then he entered it onto a keypad. A moment later, the door slid open. We stepped inside, and he went straight to a metal cabinet on the wall.

"Let's take a sedan," he said, as he grabbed a set of keys. He clicked the key fob, and we followed the chirping alarm to a blue four-door car.

"We're leaving right now?"

"That's the plan." Dan paused, and cupped my face with his hands. "Do you want to stay? See if you can reason with Christina, or figure out what she' up to?"

I shook my head. "No. Let Tess and the rest stop whatever she's put into motion, then we'll decide what's next."

We got into the car, and Dan drove out of the garage and down the hill. I was about to ask him where we were going when an explosion rocked the car and almost sent us skidding off the road. I turned back, and screamed.

Tessa's house was gone.

THE SPARK

"**N**o!"

I twisted around in the seat and saw black smoke billowing from the crest of the hill.

There was nothing on the hill but smoke. No trees, no rocks, no house.

My father had been in that house.

My mother, too, but Dad.

Dad.

I reached toward the empty space, screaming and wailing and damn it, I did not want to be an orphan.

"Eli, get down," Dan said. "We don't know if there'll be aftershocks, or another—"

Rage and fear erupted out of me as I screamed. I spun around and yanked on the door handle, but it was locked. I struggled with the lock, then I got it open and fell out of the moving car. I stumbled against the pavement, then I got to my feet and started running toward the smoke.

"Dad," I yelled. "Dad! Tessa!"

Suddenly Dan was there, throwing his arms around me as he dragged us down to the ground.

"Eliza, baby, there's nothing left," he said, and he was right. Now that the smoke was clearing I could see the flat, vacant lot where the house had been a few moments ago. "We can't go up there. What if there's leftover booby traps from the spell?"

"They could be alive up there," I shrieked. "They were going to contain her—contain it! They could be okay!" I stared at the smoke through my haze of tears. "My dad's up there." Dan tightened his arms around me, and I bawled into his shoulder. My dad, Tessa, the clan elders, and even my mother was gone. "This reality is hell."

"This reality isn't real." Dan moved so he was in front of me, and grabbed my shoulders. "Remember, nothing here is real."

"Getting shot felt pretty fucking real."

"I can't explain that," he said. "Remember when we were lost in the time tunnels, and we saw a future where your grandmother's house was gone? Then we got back home and it was there. I think this reality is like that; stuff feels and looks real, but it's all a trick."

"Magic is tricky," I mumbled, because it was true. If you didn't understand the magic you were working with the simplest spell could blow up in your face, literally.

"It is, and that's why I believe that everyone's okay. We just have to get home to them." He pushed back my hair. "Are you with me?"

I nodded, focusing on him instead of my parents' smoldering grave. "You really think they're okay?"

"I do, and we're going to get back to them."

"What if they're not okay?" I pressed. "What if they're all really dead, and we're stuck here in this hell where I can't reach their spirits?"

Dan rested his forehead against mine. "We have to try."

I nodded, because he was right. We did have to try.

I stood up, and let Dan draw me back toward the car. He'd left it running with the doors open, but it hardly mattered. It's not like anyone was going to walk by and take the car. It's not like my father or Tessa needed a ride anywhere.

Dan put the car in gear, but I sat backwards with my chin on the headrest, staring at the billowing black smoke. No sirens wailed in the distance, and no rescue crews sped toward the devastation. Mortals really didn't care if witches died.

We rode in silence until we reached the main road. "Can you face forward for me?" Dan asked. "We don't want to attract attention, not if we can help it."

I did as asked, and sat properly. I even buckled my seat belt, not that it mattered. If I died, I would only die in this reality, right? Based on Dan's theory, I would still be around in the myriad other shitty timelines four pissy mortals had constructed as part of their lame revenge scheme.

Or maybe it wasn't a revenge scheme. Honestly, I had no idea why Renato or the Ghost Guys had done any of this. For something that must have taken a crap ton of power to pull off, there was no obvious goal or endpoint to creating these elaborate false realities. That was the lamest part of all.

Lame reality or not, we were stuck here, and we needed to fix that. Dan turned onto one of the main roads into town, which I didn't think was a good idea.

"Where are you going?" I asked.

"No idea. For now, I just want to keep moving."

"Can we go back to where you left the police truck? If it's still there, I can get my laptop and the other stuff we left behind." I turned to the window as my face crumpled in grief. "Not that a stupid laptop matters."

"It matters." Dan squeezed my forearm. "How do we get home?"

"If I knew that, I'd be there already," I snapped.

Undeterred by my outburst, he asked, "How do spirits find their way back to their loved ones?"

I blinked, and faced him. "What?"

"The spiritual plane's gotta be huge, right? But your grandmother found you when you needed her. You find spirits all the time. How?"

"I-I don't know."

"Yes, you do. It's a reflex for you, as natural as breathing. I don't have that reflex, so I need you to describe it to me."

"I follow people," I began. "It's like a fishing line. I tug on it, and it leads me to the person who needs help."

"How do you find the line?"

"I feel a bit of them, like warmth or a—" I faced Dan. "Or a spark. Dan, in the last reality, I left a spark of power at the Beauclaire cemetery!"

"Why'd you do that?"

"I left the spark in case any spirits wanted to reach out to me." It was an old seer trick, one I'd used many times. Gran always said seers were like candles in the endless spiritual darkness, offering hope for anyone in need. "That was in the last reality. Maybe, if we follow the spark back to that reality, we can find something else to lead us from that reality to home."

Dan grabbed my hand, and kissed it. "Now you're talking, baby."

The police truck remained exactly where we'd left it, which was great. What wasn't great was that to get to it, we had to venture back to the mortal side of town. That meant we had to clear out anything we wanted from the truck quick, and get the hell out of there.

"I can't believe I left this behind," I said as I grabbed my backpack. I opened the top flap and verified that everything I'd packed was inside—laptop, mementoes, it was all there. "I was definitely not thinking clearly."

"You'd already had some of the poisoned water, and your shoulder wasn't fully healed," Dan said, as he checked another gun. Being that this was a police vehicle, it was stocked with all sorts of weaponry. Dan had the truck's rear door open as he went through the stash and grabbed whatever he thought we could use. "Cut yourself some slack."

"Yeah." I put my backpack in the sedan, and rejoined Dan. "Is there anything non-lethal I can help with?"

"Want to try on a bullet-proof vest?" Dan asked. I was about to say yes, when a bullet hit the truck's frame next to his head.

"Down," he bellowed. We ducked as gunfire pelted the car like hail.

"Where's it coming from?" I demanded.

Dan threw a vest at me. "Get behind the truck," he ordered, then he raised his gun and crept forward. I pulled the vest over my head, and contemplated grabbing one of the other guns.

Dan returned fire, then the shooter stepped out from behind the building. It was Jill, who'd apparently staked out the police truck and had been waiting for us to return.

"Surrender," Jill yelled. "We can spin this, Dan. Tell everyone you were working undercover to bring the witch in. This can all work out."

"Fuck me," Dan muttered. "What am I supposed to do, shoot Jill?"

"You said none of this is real," I pointed out, then a bullet whizzed past my head. "Maybe just kneecap her."

Dan stared at me, slack jawed. "Where'd you hear about kneecapping someone?" he asked, then a bullet struck the truck's window and glass rained down onto him. Jill's next shot hit the hinge on the rear door, which ricocheted and hit Dan's face hard enough to daze him.

"Dan," I yelled. He held up a hand to tell me he was okay, while the other went to his jaw. I saw blood seeping from between his fingers, and that was the last straw.

This version of Jill was going down.

"Jill Sanders," I said as I stood. "What would Angel say about you shooting at innocent people?"

"Say my wife's name again and the next bullet goes in your head," she said.

"Shoot at my husband again and bullets will be the least of your problems!"

"He married you?" Jill screeched, then she went on about how Dan's standards were lower than mud. That was great for my self-esteem. Her tirade about my and Dan's relationship made her loosen her grip on her weapon just enough for me to magically yank the gun out of her hand. I flung it toward the other side of the parking lot, and hoped she didn't have reinforcements stationed over there.

Next to me, Dan groaned. "Stay down," I said, then I focused on Jill. She was using the corner of a brick building as cover, and she seemed to be alone. I consciously reached for my witchcraft, and asked myself what Tessa would do.

Tessa would disable the enemy in the simplest way possible. She would also make sure it hurt. I focused on the building shielding Jill, and formed a plan.

Bricks are heavy and painful if they fall on you, and the wall Jill was hiding behind was held together with mortar. Mortar was made of cement and sand, and while I didn't know much about cement, I was plenty familiar with sand. I closed my eyes, and pulled the sand out of the mortar.

For a moment, nothing happened. Then Jill leaned on the wall, and the bricks came down like a waterfall.

Jill screamed, then she was drowned out by the massive roar of the collapsing building. I opened my eyes just in time to see the bricks entomb her, while piles of sand dotted the perimeter of the parking lot like tiny desert dunes. As people filed out of the collapsing buildings and tried to figure out what was happening, I checked on Dan.

"Hey. Show me." He dropped his hand, and I saw a red mark down the length of his face from the door hitting him, along with many scratches courtesy of the broken glass. "Where's the first aid kit?"

"We took it to Tessa's," he said. "Can you drive us out of here?"

"Yeah." I helped Dan into the sedan, then I grabbed my backpack and the duffel bag Dan had filled with weapons and tossed them in the back seat. I pulled out of the parking lot just as the caravan of emergency vehicles began assembling on the opposite side of the strip mall. For the moment, we were safe.

"How do you feel?"

"Like shit." Dan's cuts had stopped bleeding, but he had an awful bruise spreading across the right side of his head. "I can't remember the last time my head hurt this much."

"Give me your hand." After he laced his fingers with mine, I asked, "When we were trying to summon our ancestors, you said Lyons... and Matarazzos?"

"Yeah," he said. "Matarazzo. My mother's family is from Sicily."

"Tell me about them."

"They're good people. Hard working, strong people. You'll meet my nonna when we go home for the holidays."

"Oh, we're doing that?"

"We sure are. They all want to meet you."

"When were you going to tell me you sent your sister a picture of me?" I asked. "And that she showed it to your mother?"

"I sent it to Alicia right before we went back to see Katherine and Monty," he replied. "She texted me, and she's always been on me to get back out there—"

"Out where?"

"You know. Dating. So she texted me, and she asked me if I was seeing anyone, so I told her about you." He took out his phone, and after a bit of searching, he held the screen toward me. "This is the picture I sent her."

Since we were on a straight stretch of road, I glanced at his phone. On it was an image of me taken right before one of our running dates at Braerton College, though I hadn't called those meetups dates at the time. Back then, we were just two people running around the same track, and I was still pretending I felt nothing for Dan. I looked forward to those dates every week.

"You sent her a picture of me in workout gear?" I asked. My hair was up in a ponytail, and I was wearing a dark green running shirt. I was twisted around and grinning at Dan over my shoulder, like I used to do when I won our races. "You must have a better picture than that."

Dan turned the phone toward him, and smiled. "Nah. You're beautiful here."

"Did you tell her you threw all of our races so you could ogle my butt as you lost?"

"I left that part out." Dan touched the side of his forehead. "Are you healing me?"

"I'm trying to." I flashed him a smile. "I can't do real healing like Tessa can. I only know how to use your ancestors' energy to strengthen you. It's why I asked you about your family."

"You're doing great. My head feels a lot better." Dan thumbed through his pictures. "We should take more pictures. I don't have any of us together."

"I do, on my phone." Since he was feeling better, I asked, "How did you know to ask me how I find spirits?"

"I couldn't think of anything else to try," he said. "Ever since I found you almost dead on the couch with that asshole standing over you, all I've been thinking about is how to get out of here. While you were resting at Tessa's, Alex and I talked."

I swallowed the lump in my throat at his mention of my father. Dad wasn't gone, not really. I had to believe that. "You did? I thought you were exploring the house."

"I was, but Alex was the one who showed me around. It was his opinion that since you were the only one who came from the real timeline with all of your memories—real memories, not the fake ones everyone else got—that makes you the only one who can lead us home."

"You kept all your memories, too," I said, but he shook his head.

"I did, but I'm not a seer," he said. "I'm just your mortal sidekick."

"You are not just a mortal. Or a sidekick!"

He leaned over and kissed my shoulder. "Thanks, baby. But the fact remains that on the magical side of things, you're in charge."

"Great." As I turned onto the access road that led to the cemetery, I thought about my father and Dan spending the day together. They'd always gotten along so well, and to be honest, that had surprised me. My father was notoriously overprotective, so much so that before Gran's death, many of his associates didn't even know my name; I'd learned that firsthand when we went to Iran, and the local coven leader, Mehrded, teased Dad about his reticence to talk about me. I understood that Dad hadn't shared many details about me to keep me safe, and I appreciated it. He'd always told me that since the day I was born I was his number one priority, and his actions proved it time and again.

But Dad had never been that way with Dan. My father had trusted Dan since the moment they met. It was no secret that my father was the most important person in my life, and I wondered if his ready acceptance of Dan had helped me admit my own feelings for him.

Dad...

I bit the inside of my cheek to keep myself from crying again. My father told Dan that I could get these realities straightened out, and if he believed in me the least I could do was believe in myself. He's sounded so confident when he told me to leave Tessa's home, and—

Oh, shit.

"Dad knew this was going to happen," I said. "Remember how him and Tess and all the elders were so insistent we leave the house immediately? They knew something was about to go down."

"Tessa even had that wallet handy," Dan said. "Why would they send only you and me out of the house, and not just evacuate the place?"

"They must have learned something." That room had held some of the oldest and most powerful witches on the planet. Before I could speculate further on what they might have discovered, we reached the entrance to the Beauclaire cemetery.

"We're here."

The Beauclaire cemetery gates appeared exactly the same in this reality as it had in the last. I'd never see it in the real world, so I didn't know if this was what they really looked like. Those Beauclaires were sneaky in every reality, which meant anything was possible. We exited the car, and Dan opened the back door and started rifling through the weapons bag.

"Do we really need guns in a cemetery?" I asked, as I slung my backpack onto my left shoulder. The right one was still a bit sore.

"Anyone comes near you I'm shooting first and asking questions later," he replied. "You have everything you want out of here?"

"Yeah." I shut the door, and Dan and I passed underneath the gates. "Jemima's tomb is this way."

"Think she's wax in this reality?"

"I am not discussing Her Waxiness again."

We followed the main path, which led us past dozens of ornately carved gravestones. When the mausoleum came into view, Dan let out a whistle.

"He built her a smaller version of the Taj Mahal," he said, and he was right. I'd never seen anything as opulent as Jemima's tomb in the New World, at least not in this reality. The tomb she'd been interred in a reality past was rather bland. I wondered if that meant she was still dead in this timeline. "Gotta say, I disagree with Beauclaire on pretty much everything, but he does treat his wife well."

"Jemima is the only person he's ever loved." We entered the mausoleum, and I led Dan to the central chamber that held Jemima's tomb. In this world the decoration was much more refined than the bland marble building I'd visited before. It was all carved and elegant stonework, accented with colorful tapestries and brightly painted details.

"I still don't understand this link you have with Beauclaire," Dan said. "I used to think it was all him, but now I think it's between you and Jemima."

"I'm not linked to either of them," I began, then I felt it. "Dan, I can feel the spark I left in the last reality."

"Can you tap into it?" he asked. "Follow it, maybe?"

"I can try." I closed my eyes, and reached toward the spark. It was easy, since it was my own energy. "Dan, take my hand."

I felt him wrap his arms around me. "Not taking any chances on losing you," he said, with his mouth against my ear. "I am never letting you go."

I turned my head toward him, but before I could say anything reality thickened around us. We were sucked down and away, but there was no sense of foreboding. It was like being drowned in honey, with the promise of a sweeter life on the other side. At the last moment, Dan covered his mouth with mine, which I found fitting. We were going out as we'd lived. Together.

Operation: Wolfsbane

When I opened my eyes, we were lying on the mausoleum's floor, but still kissing. I drew back, and asked, "Why'd you do that?"

"When the air got thick, I could barely breathe. Figured you couldn't either, so I needed to help you."

I stroked the side of his face, which had been battered and bloodied yet again, all for me. "Do you take care of everyone as well as you take care of me?"

"Nah. I like you best." He looked around, and said, "This is different."

I looked around the mausoleum, which was the ornate yet bland tomb I had visited with Tessa. "We're in the last reality. I'm sure of it."

"That means we're one step closer to home. I like that." Dan got to his feet, and I followed suit. "Let's get out there and see what's happening."

We exited the tomb, and followed the path through the cemetery to the main gates. On the way, I verified that I still couldn't sense a single spirit in this reality, not even Jemima. Once we got outside the gates, I saw something even stranger.

"How is the car here?" The blue sedan we'd driven out of Tessa's estate was waiting for us, right where we'd left it in the last reality. "It being here doesn't make any sense."

"Maybe these timeline's are finally working with us instead of against us." We reached the car, saw the keys in the ignition where I'd left them. "I'll drive."

My nascent healing abilities must have been on the right track, since Dan had no problems driving us out of the cemetery and back to town. As we traveled, I saw that the roads were well maintained, and I didn't see any of the burnt-out buildings or fallout shelters than had littered the mortal side of town in the last timeline. I let myself feel the barest glimmer of hope.

"Where are we going?" I asked.

"Good question. Where do we think these clowns are operating from?"

I remembered the people in my old building that had quite obviously been spying on me and Dan. "My apartment?"

"Bingo." Dan took a left into the main downtown parking area. "I figure they're either at your old place, or at Valley Burger."

"That was the worst burger I've ever had."

"Agreed." Dan pulled into the downtown parking lot. "Think this car will be here when we get back?"

"I'm not taking any chances." I took my backpack with me when I got out of the car. No way was I chancing losing my laptop again. "Want to try my apartment first?"

"Lead the way."

I didn't want to go first, but one of us had to. Since I was the seer, this was definitely my territory, rather than Dan's. We followed the alleyway down to Main Street, and quickly learned that this version of reality hadn't held up so well after all.

"Before, everything looked like a movie set," I said. "Now it's more like a school play." Storefronts I'd walked past dozens of times now appeared to be made of painted cardboard instead of brick and mortar. The newsstand, which had stocked only one title the last time we walked by it, now had stacks of blank papers for sale. Weirdly, people were still buying them. It made me wonder what they could see, that was hidden from me and Dan.

"Think they diverted a bunch of energy to that second reality, at the expense of this one?" Dan asked.

"That's a good theory." We approached the crosswalk, and waited for the light to change. At least the traffic controls appeared to be functional. "Why are some things working, and some not?"

"Let's just be glad the ground's solid." The light changed, and we crossed. At the next corner stood my old apartment building; or rather, a poor facsimile of it.

When Tessa and I had scoped out the building, the first thing we noticed—aside from the fact that it was intact—was that the walls were glitching in and out of reality, like a show played on an old television set. Now the entire building wavered, as if it was an image being played by a very old film projector.

"I don't know if we should go in there," I said.

"Come around to the side," Dan said. "I want to see if it looks like anyone else is up there."

I followed Dan to the western side of the building, and checked out the windows and balconies. Sure enough, there were people moving inside my apartment.

"There's our answer." I hiked my bag up on my arm. "Let's go."

We entered the building through the coffee shop, and I led Dan up the back stairs. Even though the walls and floors flashed in and out of view, they were solid, and we didn't stumble or fall. When we got to the kitchen entrance, I swung my bag around, grabbed my lock picks, and went to work on the door.

"Just like old times, huh?"

I glanced up at Dan, saw his grin. "You know it. And, we're in."

"Me first." Dan raised his gun, then he pushed the door open and stepped inside. The back door led into the kitchen, which was empty. We crept past the sink and around the table, and found all three of the Ghost Guys sitting on the waiting room couch, guzzling soda and eating chips.

These were my mighty adversaries, three glorified couch potatoes.

"Police! Hands up," Dan ordered. They hadn't heard us enter, and Dan's booming voice scared the crap out of them. Mike screamed, Gary dropped the bowl of chips, and James—who turned out to be the waiter from Valley Burger—grabbed his chest as if he was having a heart attack.

"Are we being arrested?" Mike asked.

"You deserve to be put away for life," I said, as I stepped out from behind Dan. "What the hell is wrong with all of you?"

"Hey, Eliza," Mike said. "How have you been?"

"How have I been? Seriously?" I clenched my fists. "You are going to tell us, very slowly and with extreme attention to detail, exactly what you did to cause this mess."

Because he was an idiot, Mike grinned. "Operation Wolfsbane is pretty impressive, huh?"

I blinked. "Operation, what now?"

After Mike, Gary, and James had calmed down, and cleaned up the mess around my couch, they explained exactly how these alternate timelines came about. Dan stood over them, scowling, the entire time. We learned that Renato was indeed the mastermind behind Operation Wolfsbane, which wasn't shocking. Since I was amazed the Ghost Guys managed to tie their shoes, I knew they hadn't come up with this plan on their own.

After we'd beaten Amir's bone army, Renato had tracked down the Ghost Guys and bailed them out of jail. Since Amir was incapacitated, Renato became their new leader, and with the help of a few old grimoires, they began piecing together a spell that would alter reality.

"This had nothing to do with the nexus?" I asked, since reality had first altered when Dan and I came home through the portal.

"We timed the new reality to coincide with your birthday, but no one mentioned anything about a nexus," Mike replied. "Happy birthday, by the way."

"Thanks," I muttered. "So, you four managed a spell of this magnitude in a week?" Dan and I had returned from our visit with Katherine and Monty exactly nine days after Amir had been hauled off to the hospital in a comatose state.

"Oh, no, it took way longer," Mike said. "Renato had been planning this adventure for years. He had everything all worked out, but what he didn't have was a power source."

"Why did he want to do this in the first place?" Dan asked. "Exactly what is his endgame?"

"Paranormal studies, of course," Mike replied, as if it was obvious. "He had his doctoral thesis all lined up, and he was going to leverage his degree into speaking engagements, book deals, the whole nine yards."

"Talk shows, too," Gary added. "He put together a killer press kit."

"Renato was setting himself up to be a celebrity," I said, and Mike and Gary nodded. James just sat on the far end of the couch, frowning. "You said he was going to leverage his degree. What went wrong?"

Mike cleared his throat. "Ah, you did, Eliza."

"Me?" I turned to Dan, but he only shrugged. "What did I do?"

"The way he tells it, he was all set to have you teach him about spirits," Mike began. "He even submitted some preliminary work to his advisors about how he had a person on the inside who was ready to share some secret information. And then, um, you changed your mind."

"That is not what happened," I snapped. "He lied to me about what he was studying and tried to date me under false pretenses!"

Mike shrugged. "Well, whatever happened, you really wrecked him. When he wasn't able to submit his thesis on time, he got kicked out of the program. He's still pretty upset about it."

"Hold up," Dan said. "You mean to tell me that Florian didn't get his degree in spooky shit, so he took it upon himself to learn how to make an entire new reality as part of some lame revenge plot?"

"We thought it was nuts, too," Gary said. "We only went along with him because he bailed us out, you know? We owed him after that. I was shocked as hell when he pulled this off."

"But he didn't make one new reality," I said. "He made two."

"The first one didn't really go the way he planned, and he couldn't figure out what went wrong," Mike said. "Renato said everyone was too happy."

I remembered that version of reality, where I'd lived a happy life and had never been harassed by my enemies, Beauclaire or otherwise. "So you re-did everything, with the intention of making us miserable?"

"That wasn't the entire plan," Mike began, but James finally spoke up.

"Yes, it was," James said. "Renato redid the spell with the intention of isolating you, Eliza. He thought that if you were lonely and unhappy, it would be easier for him to gain your trust."

"And then what?" I demanded when he paused. "What was the plan for after he magically gaslighted me?"

"Then he'd convince you to tell him everything," James finished. "About spirits, the paranormal, the whole nine yards."

"This is some of the creepiest shit I've ever heard," Dan said. "You three just went along with this asshole? Did you ever stop to wonder what he was going to do with Eli after he learned everything she was willing to teach him?"

"We didn't have much of a choice," Mike said.

"Everyone has a choice," I said. "If my choices were either gaslight someone until she trusted me or go to jail, I would get myself into a cell in a heartbeat." When Mike tried to argue, I held up a hand. "Just so you know, he shot me. That's what Renato did when the second false reality didn't go as planned. He shot me, and I almost died. Oh, and then he poisoned me and I almost died *again*."

"Shit, Eliza," Mike said. "We never wanted anyone to get hurt."

"I told you we shouldn't have listened to him," James said. "He was shady from the beginning."

"Here's what you can do to help us fix things," Dan said. "We know Florian needed power to pull this off, and we're pretty sure we know where he got it. Blonde woman, goes by Christina?"

"That's her," Mike said. "The one thing we had that Renato needed was the lineages. Amir stole them from some magical librarian, and Renato used them to find witches who might be willing to help him."

"What else did he use for power?" I asked. When they stared blankly at me, I continued, "My mother is powerful, but there's no way she manifested an entire reality. What else did he use?"

"Christina's your mother?" Mike asked.

"What. Else," I repeated.

"It's something in the restaurant," Gary said. "It's Valley Burger here, but in the real world it's a Chinese place. Renato said there was a rift there that led to a magical place. We don't know what kind of a magical place," he added.

Dan and I shared a glance. "We've got an idea about that. So he grabbed power from my mother, went to the back room of a Chinese restaurant, and here we are?"

"He also had some bones," James said. "Said they were from a powerful witch."

"Got a name for this witch?" Dan asked.

James shook his head. "He never said her name."

"But this is a bone from a woman?" Dan pressed.

James shrugged. "I guess. Renato seemed to think so."

Dan turned away from the Ghost Guys, and said, "Didn't Sarah Allwood's bones go missing a while back?"

"And she's rotten to the core, so of course none of these spells would turn out as intended," I said. "She might even be the reason Jemima has a form."

"What, as a punishment to Beauclaire?" Dan asked me. I shrugged, then he turned back to the rest. "Where are these bones now?"

"The skull is in the kitchen at Valley Burger," Mike replied.

"That's disgusting," I said. "No wonder the food there is so vile."

"You should have tried the gravy," James said.

"You shouldn't have gotten between me and Eli that time we stopped for lunch, and then tried to make me look like an abusive husband," Dan said, and the three of them shrank back against the cushions. "Mark my words, once we get back to the real world all of you are going to be held accountable."

"What are you going to do, arrest us?" Mike asked. "On what charges?"

"I will hold you accountable," I said. "I am the Mistress of Seers, and you've pissed off me and every powerful witch in the area. If you can think of anything else that will help us, and possibly make me look at you in a more favorable light, now's the time to come clean."

"We never thought it would go this far," Gary said; he was clearly the brains of this operation. "When Renato got us out of jail we were grateful, so we agreed to help him. When he started hauling out grimoires and bones, we thought that was a little weird, but it would also be great content for our podcast."

"Or a show on one of those streaming platforms," Mike said. "I've always wanted to do television."

"Gary's right," James said, as he shot Mike a quelling glance. "We thought Renato was full of it, and we got in over our heads."

"You sure did," Dan said. "You three stay here. We're going to check out the restaurant."

"Are we under house arrest?" Mike asked.

"Yes," Dan replied. "Don't leave this apartment without my say so. Got it?"

After a resounding chorus of affirmations, Dan and I left through the main door and took the stairs down to the street level.

"Operation Wolfsbane," Dan said. "Now we know why that plant was popping up all over the place. These plants really do speak to you, in their own way."

"I guess they do," I said. "I need to pay more attention."

"Let's start now." Dan pointed at the sidewalk. Growing up through the cracks was a stand of bright blue wolfsbane.

Katherine's Bones

"This is weird," I said.

"Babe, everything in our lives is weird."

"I mean, something is weird about the wolfsbane. This is not its usual habitat." I crouched down to get a closer look at the plants. Even though their stalks were growing out of a crack in the sun baked sidewalk, the plants seemed healthy. "They prefer cooler alpine regions, but they're thriving here."

"There's more across the street," Dan said. "Want to follow them, see where they lead us?"

"Might as well."

We followed the bright blue flowers, and they led us straight to Valley Burger. The restaurant was closed, which wasn't surprising seeing as how the place's sole employees were back at my apartment under house arrest. I followed the wolfsbane around to the back, and tried the delivery door.

"Unlocked," I said.

"Maybe your flower friends unlocked it for you," Dan said.

"That's just silly," I said, and we entered the back storage area of the restaurant. "When Tessa and I came here, there was an entity in the kitchen," I said. We hadn't known it at the time, but Amir had transported the cook's consciousness to an alternate plane, and let a demon inhabit his body for about twenty-four hours. It was a test run for when he had Dan possessed the next day. "It made the stove's burners spit out columns of fire, and it rained knives near the prep table."

"The fun never ends with that guy." Dan flipped on the lights. Everything in the kitchen was pristine, as if it was brand new and had never been used. It made me wonder where the food we'd eaten actually came from. "Where do we think this rift might be?"

"Not sure." I turned in a complete circle. "Anything here seem off to you?"

"No, but," Dan approached the walk-in refrigerator, "when the cook was returned and we got called here, he kept going in the cooler."

"Was he prepping food for the day?"

"No, he just kept walking back to it, over and over." Dan opened the cooler door, then he beckoned me over. "Found it."

"Found what?" I peeked inside the cooler, and saw a human skull sitting on the shelf. Next to it was a carved wooden box, which I was betting was the repository for whatever power my mother had gifted to Renato. I approached the skull, and looked into her vacant orbits.

"I don't think this is Sarah Allwood."

"Really?" Dan stood beside me. "Why not?"

"She feels familiar." Tentatively, I touched the skull. Then I passed out.

Blackness faded to red, then white. I raised my hand to shade my eyes against the bright sunlight. I sat up, and realized I was lying on the lawn behind Gran's house. Only, the house was the wrong color, the rose gardens were gone, and there were several unfamiliar outbuildings scattered around the property. Then I heard a little girl's laugh, and understood.

I was at Gran's house, but it wasn't Gran's yet. I'd gone back to when Katherine owned it in the seventeenth century.

Laughter floated toward me again. I turned, and saw Katherine's daughter, Elizabeth, running through the tall grasses on the side of the house. Watching her from the shaded porch was Katherine herself. She was sitting in a rocking chair with a bundle of blankets on her lap.

I approached Katherine, and sat on the porch railing next to her. "Is this a dream?" I asked.

"It certainly isn't reality." She glanced at my jeans. "Eliza, you must not dress so strangely when you're here. Mortals will talk, and nothing good will come of it."

"Sorry," I mumbled, as I wondered why I needed to wear period appropriate clothing in a dream sequence. "Why isn't this real?"

"I'm not sure. You were here, then you came back, and after you left the second time everything changed." Katherine angled the bundle on her lap toward me, and I saw a sleeping baby nestled within the blankets.

"Is this Daniel?"

"He surely is." Katherine beamed at the baby. "He isn't real, but I love him just the same."

"What if you stayed in this reality?" I asked. "Then he could stay."

Katherine shook her head. "It isn't right." She faced me, and instead of a flesh and blood woman, I saw her skull. "Someone has taken everything that's real from me."

I reached toward Katherine, but the world went sideways. A moment later I was falling inside the walk in cooler, and Dan caught me.

"You okay?" He eased me down to the floor, then he sat and pulled me into his arms. "What happened?"

"The skull is Katherine's," I replied. "I saw her. Dan, she's trapped in a false reality, too."

"Shit," he muttered. "Is she okay?"

"She's like we were. On the surface, everything is fine, but she knows things aren't right." I gripped his forearm. "I saw her baby. Daniel."

Dan drew me closer, and kissed the top of my head. "He's not real. Just like your cousins, it's all a trick."

"I know," I said, nodding. "But now that I saw him, it's hard to let him go."

"That's probably the plan." He held me for another moment, then he got to his feet and grabbed the power receptacle. "Let's get out of here."

"Where are we going?"

"Back to the apartment. I'd like to know when and how these clowns acquired Katherine's skull."

"We used a dowsing rod," Mike said.

I glanced at Dan. He shrugged, and asked me, "Are dowsing rods a real thing?"

"No." I pinched the bridge of my nose. "They're in the same category as magic eight balls." Dan and I had brought Katherine's skull back to the apartment along with the power receptacle, where they now sat on the kitchen table. When we asked the Ghost Guys how they came to be in possession of my great-great-grandmother's skull, I hadn't expected them to reply with pseudoscience.

"But it worked," Mike said, pointing at the skull. "Renato gave us a special dowsing rod, and told us to look for the most powerful grave in the Moore cemetery. Once we found it, we dug her up."

"I think I'm going to be sick," I muttered, as I rubbed my stomach. "You mean to tell me you three tramped around my family's burial grounds, and dug up my great-great-grandmother's skull?"

"Not just the skull," Gary said. "We took the whole coffin."

"I can't believe this." I walked away from the table so I wouldn't murder those morons. "Isn't grave robbing a crime?"

"It is," Dan said. "As is unlawful possession of human remains. You guys really don't think before you act, do you?"

"The cemetery was really old," James said. "We figured no one would miss one body."

"You short sighted, stupid, imbecile!" I lunged toward James, but Dan grabbed my waist.

"They will get theirs," he said. "In the meantime, I've got an idea." Dan released me, and said to the others, "Bring me the rest of the skeleton. Now!"

They scrambled into the bedroom, and returned with a large wooden box; someone had had the foresight to transfer Katherine's bones out of her coffin and into a smaller, more discreet container. Even though Katherine had suffered the indignity of being dug up from her grave, at least her skeleton had been treated with a modicum of care. The interior of the box was lined with silk, and her bones were carefully arranged inside.

"Why did you take her entire skeleton out of her grave, but only bring her skull to Valley Burger?" I asked.

"Renato only wanted her skull, but it didn't seem right to separate her head from her body," Gary replied. "So we took all of her, and kept her as safe as we could."

"Thank you," I murmured. Dan placed the skull inside the box, and after ordering the Ghost Guys to remain in the apartment on house arrest, we left.

"About my idea," he said, as we walked to the car. Dan was carrying the crate with Katherine's bones, while I carried the wooden box. "Everyone keeps saying the nexus had nothing to do with this mess. I don't believe that."

"Why not?"

"Everything's lining up a little too neatly. We used the nexus to go back and see Katherine, and these guys just happened to use a magic stick to find her grave at the exact same time?"

"That story is not the full truth," I said. "Mike and the other two seem to think it is, but they're stupid. Besides, if they were really looking for my most powerful ancestor in the cemetery, they would have found my grandmother."

"But, what powerful witches were contemporary with Katherine?"

"Nathaniel and Jemima," I said. "You've thought they were the key all along."

"One or both of them is pulling Florian's strings. How much you want to bet when Beauclaire came out with a wax version of Jemima, he put the wheels in motion to make that second reality?"

"One where Jemima might be a real girl," I said. "Assuming you're correct, how will we undo this?"

"Not sure, but I think Jemima is the key. Can you think of any way we can talk to her without Beauclaire hovering nearby?"

I was about to say that was unlikely, when I remembered a talent of mine I hardly ever used. "What if I astral projected to Jemima? Then we could talk on the spiritual plane, just the two of us."

"Is that safe?" Dan asked.

"As safe as anything we do ever is."

"I'm serious." Dan grabbed my arm, halting me. "If it's not safe, we'll find another way. I'm not risking you."

"We have to take risks," I said. "Fixing the timeline is more important than our personal safety."

"No, it's not." He put down the crate, and pulled me closer. "Nothing is more important to me than you." Once again, I saw myself reflected in his eyes. In them I looked small and fragile, and I felt much the same. Despite all of that, Dan didn't see me as someone who needed to be protected. He did protect me, but that wasn't because he thought I was weak. He protected me because he loved me. And because I loved him, I would fix this reality, so we had a chance at happiness in the real world.

"I've astral projected before," I said. "Gran taught me how when I was a kid. I projected all the time back then, and nothing bad ever came of it."

"Why don't you project anymore?"

"From when I was seventeen up until about twenty, I didn't want to be a seer," I replied; I didn't add that after I'd been kidnapped, I rejected all forms of the supernatural. Dan already knew that part. "I stopped doing a lot of things; projecting, talking to the dead, all of it. I did my best to hide and... and I became a recluse, just like I'd been in Renato's version of reality."

"What snapped you out of that mode?"

"My dad." My voice caught, so I began again. "He started taking me with him on his trips around the world, and we visited all sorts of seers and witches. They were all good, strong people, and after a while I began to trust magic again. He saw how hurt I was, and he knew exactly what I needed." I dashed my hand across my eyes. "I wasn't expecting to have such a soul baring conversation in an alley. Warn me next time?"

"Come here." Dan wrapped his arms around me, and I let myself feel the sense of safety only he could give me. "We're going to get Alex and Tess back. Promise. But I need to make sure I won't lose you in the process."

"You won't," I said. "That's my promise to you."

HOME

Since making my body comfortable would help my spirit ascend to the astral plane, we went to the one place that was always relaxing for both of us: home. The house was in the same state as we'd left it before we ended up in the second false reality, which was great. What wasn't great was the pared down garden was still full of petunias and impatiens, and not the baneful herbs I wanted to work with.

"Want to swing by your grandmother's house?" Dan asked, as I scowled at the raised bed. "Plenty of poisons in her solarium."

"No. I suspect this is a false reality problem, not a plant problem." I linked my fingers behind my neck, leaned back, and stared at the sky. "The purpose behind the herbs is to relax myself. The more comfortable and relaxed my body is, the easier it is for my spirit to slip free."

"How free?"

I peeked at Dan, saw his brows knit together. "Not that free. Besides, no matter where my spirit flies, I'll know where you are. You will lead me home, almost like a trail of breadcrumbs."

"I will?"

"Yes. Even if I can't find my way back to myself, I'll always be able to find my way back to you. It's like I'm tethered to you." While he thought on that, I turned toward the house, and spied the yellow and blue curtain in the bathroom window. "I'm going to take a bubble bath."

"That'll be plenty relaxing," he said, then he picked a few stalks of wolfsbane.

"Why'd you do that?"

"I don't know," he said. "But these plants want to talk to you, so I figure the least we can do is listen."

We went inside, and while Dan put the wolfsbane in a vase, I ran a bath. The water was so hot the entire room steamed up, and the candles imparted a golden glow. By the time Dan joined me, the bathroom looked positively otherworldly. We undressed, and after I put up my hair and Dan kissed the scar on my shoulder, we got into the tub.

"This is nice," he said.

"Yes, it is." I leaned back, and let the hot water unwind the knots of stress lodged in my back and legs.

"I'm your tether?"

I cracked an eyelid. "Yeah. You've been thinking about that since we were out back, haven't you?"

"It's a concept that deserves thought," he replied. "Have I always been your tether, or is this a side effect of the handfasting?"

I opened my mouth, closed it, and thought a bit. "I was going to say it's because of the handfasting, but I'm not so sure," I said at last.

"Remember when we were in the Allwood basement, and I called your spirit back into your body? I did the same thing after you were possessed. Both times, I reached out and grabbed your spirit. I knew exactly where you were. Even though I couldn't see you, I could feel you."

He reached for me, and I moved through the water and into his arms. "Why can't I feel you that way?"

"I think you're supposed to take care of our bodies, while I take care of our spirits."

"Like the witches say, a circle unbroken."

I laid my head on his shoulder, with my torso against his chest and my butt on his thigh. "A circle unbroken" was a witch term for soulmates, but it went deeper than that. As much as Dan and I cared for each other, we also replenished each other, and lent each other strength when and where we needed it.

Dan kissed my forehead. "I'm scared."

"Of what?"

"What if you send you spirit out, and something happens? What if something keeps you from coming back?"

"I'll always come back. Unless my body dies, my spirit will have no choice but to return, eventually."

"Hassan trapped Jemima's spirit," he began, but I shook my head.

"Jemima's body was already dead. It wouldn't have worked, otherwise."

He tightened his arms around me, pressing his forehead against the top of my head. "I've almost lost you twice in a week. I don't know if I can handle a third time."

I moved so I was facing him. "Astral projection is no big deal. Promise. In fact, if we were anywhere but this nightmare reality, I would teach you how to project so you could see how safe it is."

"Why won't you teach me here?"

"I need you to watch my body, just in case. I don't trust anything in this world, except you."

"Same, baby." His hands glided down my back and under my hips, then he moved my legs apart so I was straddling him. "It's always gonna be you and me against the world."

"You know it," I said, then I kissed him. Dan positioned his cock against me and pushed upward. My body convulsed around him as my foresight sparked at the base of my skull.

All of a sudden, Dan pulled back. "What was that?" he demanded. I was about to ask when he meant, when I realized his hand was against the nape of my neck.

"My foresight," I replied. "You felt that?"

"Felt like an electric shock." He rubbed my neck. "Does it hurt?"

"No. Never has." I rolled my shoulders. "That feels good."

"Yeah?" Since I was obviously okay, he began moving his hips again. "What did you see?"

"Us," I replied. "Together, like this, but in the future. In the real world."

"I love these visions."

After we dried off, I put on a tank top and sweats and sat cross-legged in the center of our bed. Normally, I preferred being naked after a hot bath to give my skin time to cool down, but my astral form always took on whatever clothing I was wearing. I didn't think Jemima would appreciate me invading her private space in the altogether.

I recalled her wax form, and shuddered. I hoped she would be dressed, too.

"You cold?" Dan asked.

"I'm good."

He'd also put on some sweatpants, but his upper body was bare. I liked that, but I wasn't going to give him the satisfaction of admitting it. I was still recovering from when he found out Tess and I used to call him Officer Muscleman. Besides, this time we had a thoroughly innocent reason as to why he was half dressed.

The plan was that after I went out, Dan would set a timer. If I didn't return to my body in ten minutes, his job would be to sit behind me with my back against his chest. Hopefully, skin to skin contact with him would draw me home. If that didn't work within two minutes, he would put me in an ice cold shower and shock my spirit back into my body. I really hoped it didn't come to that.

I wound my damp hair up into a messy bun, and shook out my hands. "I'm ready if you are."

He started the timer. "Ten minutes. Be safe, baby."

"I will. Promise," I said, then I closed my eyes.

Astral projection is pretty simple, once you get the hang of it. I recited a mantra Gran had taught me long ago, and sighed as my spirit loosened itself from my corporeal form. I looked down, and saw Dan pacing in front of the bed as he watched over me. Since he and my body were safe, for now, I went in search of Jemima.

Being that Jemima was the only spirit in this false reality, she was easy to find. Her soul was a bright golden glow against this staid world, like the only firefly to be found on a hot summer night. She was in the Beauclaire house that incongruously existed in this world, even though my father had destroyed the real one.

I paused, and laughed to myself. How could I have not realized that the Beauclaire house's existence more than proved that Nathaniel and Jemima were instrumental in the creation of this false reality? Dan was right. Everything around us had been engineered to destroy our focus, and keep us from noticing the clues that were all around us in plain sight.

I found Jemima in what I assumed was her bedroom. She was sitting at a vanity, staring at the many creams and oils laid out before her. "Jemima," I said. "Can we talk?"

She glanced at the mirror, and met my reflection's gaze. "Hello, Eliza. I was wondering when you would come back. In fact, I was surprised you left as quickly as you did the last time."

"What can I say. This version of reality has me a bit off my game." I moved to the side of her, so she could see me directly. "Have you been wax for the last three hundred years?"

"No. This situation is all new to me." She turned toward me, and I saw a bouquet behind her on the vanity. Among the white carnations and roses were bright blue sprigs of wolfsbane. Dan was right, these plants wanted to talk to me. "After you ventured to the past, the present-day version of my Nathaniel killed the older version of himself, and brought the bottle with my spirit inside it here to the present day. I've only been trapped in this wax form since the reality spell was cast."

"Oh," I said, horrified that Nathaniel actually killed his past self, and that his actions apparently hadn't affected the future. The more

I learned about time travel, the more I understood why it was forbidden.

"Do his actions shock you?" Jemima asked. "His every deed has been done out of love."

"I don't doubt that, not for a moment." Pleased with my answer, Jemima preened a bit.

"Dan thinks you and I are linked," I said, leaning a bit further into Dan's theories. "At first I didn't buy it, but everything significant that's happened to me since I was eight years old tracks back to you."

"Yes. I've noticed that as well." Jemima rubbed her finger against the vanity, leaving streaks of wax in her wake. "My memories of you are so clear, even though we first met so long ago."

"Do you remember both realities?" I asked, and she nodded.

"I remember being trapped in that bottle, and then when I was finally free, my mother snared me in a trap of her own me before I could move on," she began. "She used me as the prize to force Nathaniel to do her bidding."

"But when you made the new reality, she was already gone," I deduced. "That's how you ended up like this."

"Nathaniel kept his promise, and didn't place me in another's body." She grimaced, but I didn't ask her what it felt like to be made of wax. Obviously, it was awful. "My mother isn't gone."

"But the fruit rotted in the orchard," I began. Jemima held up her hand.

"That her bones and apples needed to be cared for was a ruse she put forth centuries ago," Jemima said. "My mother excels at lies and misdirection. The truth is that she's slipped back into a body she once inhabited, and this time you won't be able to exorcise her."

"Why not?"

"Because the body was near death when she arrived," Jemima replied. "The soul slipped out at the very moment Mother slipped in."

"And to remove her spirit now would be murder," I said, and Jemima nodded. I watched her for a moment, the daughter of the queen of lies, and wondered why she was telling me this. "Why do you want me to think about your mother instead of you?"

"I-I thought you should know." Jemima's hand fluttered over her breast. "Isn't she your true enemy?"

"Not really. If anything, she's your and Nathaniel's enemy." I felt something cool on my left hand, then warmth against my back. "Has it been ten minutes?"

Jemima glanced at the clock. "Not nearly. Have you an appointment?"

"Yes, and I can't be late." Since Dan was apparently gearing up to bring me back early, I drew on my foresight for guidance. "What does my mother have to do with all of this?"

"She also wants the other witch clans to be eradicated," Jemima replied. "Christina seeks vengeance against those who, and these are her words, bred her like a dog."

I sucked in a breath. My bitter, grudge-holding mother was smack in the center of this tornado. "Thank you, Jemima. That was the clue I needed." My astral form began to fade, when Jemima stood.

"Wait," she called, reaching toward me. "What will you do to me?"

"You haven't done anything wrong," I said. "In fact, you've always helped me. I won't forget that."

"And what about Nathaniel?"

"I won't lie to you. My actions against him will depend on what he's done, and who he's hurt. I swear to you that I won't administer any punishment or censure until I have all of the information."

She nodded. "That is as much as I could ask for. Thank you, Eliza. You have always been good to me."

I faded away from Jemima, and settled back into my body. Dan had positioned himself behind me on the bed with my back against his chest, and his legs were stretched out on either side of me.

"Hey," I said. "I'm back."

He slid his arms around my waist, and kissed the curve where my neck met my shoulder. "I didn't mean to pull you back so quick like that. I was just getting us ready, and you were here."

"It's okay. Jemima told me what I needed to know." I turned face him. "This time around, my mother really is the big bad witch," I began, and explained her role in everything.

"That's why she went to Tessa's in the other reality," Dan said. "She wanted the elders together so she could take them out all at once."

"All of them, and my dad," I began, then I realized who hadn't been there. "All of them, except Nathaniel."

Dan shook his head. "His absence proves that at least some of Jemima's story is true."

"Do you think they'll try something like that in the real world?"

"No idea. I feel our best bet is to get home, and see what's happening there." Dan tucked a stray piece of hair behind my ear, and I saw something flash on his left hand.

"What's on your hand?" I asked. He showed me his hand. On his ring finger was the white gold band that he'd found in the closet, packed away in a velvet jewelry box along with two rings sized for me. Remembering the sensation of cool metal on my own hand, I looked at mine. I was wearing the matching ring. "You put these on us?"

"I thought it would strengthen the tether." He nestled me closer, and said, "I know you said astral projection is safe, and I believe you. I swear I do, but I wanted a little extra insurance."

I laid my head on Dan's shoulder, and laced the fingers of my left hand with his. "People are going to ask us about these rings."

"Let them."

Back To Reality

"**I**f we go to your grandmother's, think Alex will be there?"

I set down the box of cereal, and thought for a moment. After I'd reassured Dan that my astral visit to Jemima left me none the worse for wear, we went downstairs to find something to eat. Luckily none of the food had gone bad while we were in the second false reality. Perhaps supernatural preservatives were in play. "I'm not sure, but I don't want to go there."

"Then we won't go. However, that leaves us with a problem."

"How so?"

"According to everyone in the know, some sort of conduit is needed to slide from one reality to the next. If we're not going to your grandmother's, that means we aren't using the nexus."

"I don't think we need it. We traveled through time that way, but however the rest managed all of this," I twirled my spoon, encompassing this entire false reality, "they didn't do it with the nexus."

"Good point. The cats wouldn't have let them near it, anyway."

My lower lip trembled when Dan mentioned the cats. I missed those little furry guardians almost as much as I missed Dad and Tess. Seeking to change the subject, I said, "I wonder if Sarah Allwood knows."

"I thought she was gone for good."

"Jemima told me she possessed a body that had just died and she's been walking around town like that."

"Great. Here, or in the real world?"

"I didn't ask. I figured Jemima was trying to distract me from what was really going on with stories about her mother."

"Wonder what else she was trying to distract you from." Dan poured himself a glass of orange juice, and stood in front of the kitchen window surveying the backyard. "I've got it."

"Got what?"

"I know where we can move to the real world."

"Really? Where?"

"My shed."

We took our time eating lunch, and then getting ready for this latest bout of inter-reality travel. After all, if we were moving through time, it's not like we would be late, right?

As we stood in front of the garden shed, me with my backpack slung across my good shoulder while Dan had a pack of his own holding weapons and first aid supplies, I couldn't believe we were doing this again.

I couldn't believe that this had become my life.

For eleven years I rejected my destiny, and did everything I could to avoid becoming the Mistress of Seers, and now here I was about to cross realities in a desperate attempt to find out if my father and Tessa were still alive. Yes, there were other reasons why we were doing this, and a lot of other people who were counting on us, but right then nothing mattered to me more than saving Dad and Tess.

No matter how much they mattered, or how much I loved them, I needed to live my own life.

"This is it," I said.

"What's it?" Dan asked; he knew I wasn't referring to the shed.

"This is my last act as Mistress of Seers." I glanced at the house, and continued, "I never wanted this life. On the run from witches and demons, having to cross false realities just to keep my family safe, getting shot and harassed and... and..." I swallowed, and began again.

"I don't want to do this anymore." I faced Dan. "I want the life we have here, but in the real world. I want a life with you."

Dan watched me for a moment while my mind raced with all the things he might say. That I can't leave behind my destiny, I'll never be free of people hunting me, that I wasn't meant to have a simple life with a family and a house and maybe even a dog. He didn't say any of that. Instead, he wrapped his arms around me, and held me as if I was cherished.

"You know I'll support you in anything you want to do," he said.

"Really?"

"Of course I will." He kissed the side of my head, then he stepped back and put his hand on the shed door. "Let's get this situation taken care of, then we can talk about the future. Deal?"

I smiled. "Deal."

He grinned, then he opened the shed. "Shit."

"What's wrong?" I asked, then I got closer and peered inside the shed. Back in the real world, Amir had linked Dan's shed to the time tunnels, so he could harvest the poisonous herbs Charlotte grew in her greenhouse. When we'd investigated the shed, Tessa broke the concealment spell, and revealed a plethora of herbalist supplies and handwritten spell books. In this reality, the shed held an assortment of garden tools and dusty clay pots.

"Found your lawn mower," I said.

"This blows a few holes in my theory," Dan said.

"Maybe not." I approached the doorframe, and touched the hinges. "There might be another concealment spell in play."

While I investigated the doorframe, Dan crossed his arms over his chest and scowled at the long forgotten tools and planters. "I can see why you'd rather leave magic behind. Gotta say, I won't miss it." He paused, then asked, "Can you leave it behind? Is that something a seer can do?"

"You'd be surprised at how many witches and seers pass themselves off as mortal," I replied. "Many just don't want to deal with the political hierarchy of supernatural communities, so they relocate, get a low profile job, and blend in. Here it is." The spell was hidden under one of the screws in the center hinge. "Got a screwdriver?"

"Phillips or flat head?"

"Flat."

Dan rummaged around the work bench, and found the tool I needed. "Which one?"

I pointed at the screw in question. He set to work, and in less than a minute he had it loose. "Now what?" he asked.

"Now, we need to remove that which doesn't belong." I placed my palm over the hinge, and sent my awareness into the newly revealed hole. My senses poked and prodded at the old, dry wood, and then I found it. The spell was reminiscent of Amir's magic, but there was a thread of something different wound in with the rest. Something very, very powerful.

"Get out," I whispered, and I pulled the spell out of the door as if I was unwinding a ball of cursed black twine. The length of the spell piled up at my feet, where the tendrils wiggled around my ankles, seeking things to latch onto.

"Not today, creepy snakes," Dan said as he smothered the tendrils with a plastic garbage bag. I dropped the last spell thread onto the ground, faced the hole, and wondered how we would ever fit through that.

"Bigger," I murmured. "Be the doorway we need to go home."

The portal enlarged until it covered the open doorway. On the other side was the backyard identical to the one we'd just walked across, but I knew the image in the portal was our real yard in the real timeline. I could see the belladonna growing in the raised bed.

"That's it?" Dan asked.

"It is." We linked hands. "Let's go home."

Dan squeezed my fingers, then we stepped out of the false reality and into the real one. I took a deep breath, trying to fill my lungs with the real air of home, and divest myself of air that was the byproduct of a lame spell. Then something crashed behind us, and I almost choked.

"You all right?" Dan asked, as he patted my back.

"Yeah." I turned around and peered into the shed. "Something fell in there."

"Everything looks okay," Dan said. "Maybe it was that other reality crashing to bits."

"If only." I approached the raised garden bed. In it was the usual belladonna, foxglove, and stray bleeding hearts, but a few clumps of bright blue wolfsbane were dotted among the usual plants. "How can we know if we're really home? I mean, it feels like home, but we've been tricked before."

"I know a way." Dan walked through the side yard and around to the front of the house. Intrigued, I followed, and found him standing near the front door. Before I could ask him how standing in the yard proved anything, I heard a familiar screech.

"Dan, is that you?" called Gretchen, also known as the world's most annoying neighbor. "Where have you been?"

"Hey, Gretchen," Dan said. "We took a little trip."

"Another one?" She shook her head. "You weren't even here when they replaced your garage door."

"The insurance company said we didn't need to be," Dan said, but I remembered something else that would prove we were in the correct world. I opened the garage's side door, and went to the pile of boxes in the back. Lying on top of the boxes was the sign Dan had gotten me for my business, Nine Lives Investigations.

"Dan," I yelled. "It's here!"

He joined me in the garage, and grinned when he saw the sign. "We're home, baby."

"That's a nice sign," Gretchen said, because of course she'd followed us into the garage. "Are you two going into business together?"

"Yeah." I traced the lettering on the sign. "I think we might."

We shooed Gretchen out of the garage, then we hopped into Dan's car and we sped toward Gran's house. When we got there, my car was in the driveway, which was exactly where I'd left it before all of this madness began. I leapt out of the car and raced up the back steps, yelling for my father.

"Dad!" The mudroom door banged against the wall, but the interior of the house was silent. "Dad! Dad?" More silence. "Daddy?"

I fell to my knees, but before I could cry or scream or do anything I heard the thunder of twelve tiny paws. A moment later, the Feline Federation—Pumpkin, Smokey, and Muffuletta—erupted into the room.

"Hey, guys. I'm so glad to see you." I scooped all three of the cats into my arms and squeezed them. "I missed you so much."

"Hey, kitties." Dan knelt beside me, and Smokey and Muffuletta wiggled free so they could say hello to him. Pumpkin stayed with me.

"Is Dad okay?" I asked. She put her paw on my cheek, and tilted her head to the side in a feline version of a nod. "What about Tessa?" Pumpkin rubbed her head against my shoulder and purred. She'd always liked Tessa. I gave myself a moment to breathe and truly enjoy the feeling of relief, then I moved so Pumpkin and I were facing each other.

"Fluff, Dan and I have been stuck in a false reality. When we came back through the nexus something snatched us away. I'm not sure if it happened while we were in the nexus, or right after we arrived here."

Pumpkin slid out of my arms, and with a twitch of her tail she beckoned the other two to follow her. They disappeared up the stairs, and I assumed they were headed up to the nexus to find out what had happened, and fix anything that had been broken.

"Pumpkin says Dad and Tess are okay," I said. "They did not explain where they are, though."

"Last time we saw them they were at Evil Tess's house on the hill, which was where the Allwood Compound is here," Dan said. "Want to go pay your friend Jacob a visit?"

"That's a great idea."

It only took us about twenty minutes to reach the Allwood Compound. It sat at the highest point in town, looming over the mortals in much the same way Tessa's black palace had loomed over the town in the false reality. Of course, the Allwood Compound was nothing like alternate reality Tessa's foreboding home. The Allwoods' home was filled with light, and happiness, even though the clan elder was a spirit. Even so, Jacob didn't let his death keep him from running the family business as effectively as ever.

The guards admitted us without a problem, which wasn't surprising. Dan and I had been on the Allwoods' permanent guest list ever since we'd freed Jacob's spirit from a barrel of apple seeds in the barn at Sarah Allwood's ratty old orchard. What was unusual was when Jacob himself met us just inside the home's main entrance.

"I had a feeling you'd be by," he said without preamble. "About an hour ago, your father and Tessa appeared in my conference room, and cannot seem to explain how they got there."

"My dad's here?" I demanded. "Where?"

Jacob stepped aside, and I saw my father standing behind him in the corridor. I ran into his arms so fast I almost knocked him over, but he didn't complain. He just hugged me back.

"Hey, Bug," he said. "I don't suppose you know how we ended up here?"

I peeked over his shoulder, and saw my best friend. "Hey, Tessa."

"Hey, yourself." She looked from me to Dan. "Let me guess, we have something dire to deal with?"

I stepped back from my dad, and said, "Dan and I have been trapped in a false reality ever since we returned from the past. In that other reality, my mother and Nathaniel Beauclaire tried to murder all the clan elders."

"And Jemima Beauclaire is made of wax," Dan added, because of course he did.

Jacob shook his head. "Time travel always has its consequences, and they're never good. To my office, all of you."

We filed into Jacob's office, and the six of us—me, Dan, my father, Tessa, Jacob, and Jacob's assistant, LeClerc—stood there staring at each other.

"I feel like Dorothy at the end of *The Wizard of Oz*," Dan said, breaking the silence. "We were in another world, and you were there, and you and you and you."

Tessa raised an eyebrow. "Were there flying monkeys?"

"No, but you were an evil queen in a black castle," I replied.

Jacob smiled at Tess. "Just like the good old days, my dear?"

"I'm more concerned about Christina working with the Beau-claires," my father said. "How did they attempt to murder the elders?"

"I don't really know," I admitted. "Tessa was the most powerful witch in the community, and all of the elders were at her castle. Then Mom showed up, you and Tessa made Dan and me leave, and before we got to the bottom of the hill, the house blew up."

"You're certain everyone perished in the explosion?" Jacob asked.

I faced him. "There was nothing left."

"That all happened in the second fake reality," Dan said. "In the first one we went to, Eli had never been kidnapped, Nathaniel was the head of his clan, and Tessa was the Beauclaire's secretary."

"Secretary," she hissed. "They couldn't afford me."

"I don't think they paid you," I said. Tessa harrumphed.

"The indignity of free labor aside, what part do we think Nathaniel played in all of this?" Jacob asked. "I don't want to discount Christina's role in the plot, but I'm sure you understand why I'm warier of him."

"I'm not really sure what either of them did," I said. "In the first fake timeline, everything was set up to be perfect, and Nathaniel had Jemima with him, sort of."

"He placed her spirit into a poppet," Tessa said. "It's a simple enough spell, though engineering a life-sized wax form must have taken some effort."

"Not only that, a waxen wife must have been rather unsatisfying," my father said. "My guess—and this is only a guess—is that Nathaniel became involved with the engineering of these realities after you visited him. He must have realized that things had been altered, and he sought out those responsible."

"We were thinking that too. The one thing everyone agrees on is the Ghost Guys' involvement, and that Renato Florian is the leader." I paused, and looked around the room. "What should we do first? Round up the mortals?"

"Them, and Beauclaire," Dan said.

"Holding Nathaniel accountable will require finesse," Jacob said. "If we approach him with accusations, he will consider it an attack, and I'd rather not risk him going on the offensive. No, if we're to bring in Nathaniel we will need an iron-clad case, and the full support of the rest of the elders."

"What if we go to him seeking help?" I asked. "We can tell him everything that happened, and tell him we need a powerful ally to keep reality safe from people like Renato."

"We could also approach him on the pretext of looking out for him," LeClerc offered. When we all stared at him like he'd grown an extra head, he continued, "Hear me out. You two just left a reality where Jemima was alive, albeit not in an ideal condition. Once you share that information with Nathaniel, I'm betting he will move heaven and earth to figure out how that happened."

"We really don't want him recreating the false reality," I said, as images of Nathaniel and an army of waxen Jemimas dancing in my head.

"What if we hit him with a null spell?" Dan asked. "That way he can do the research, but he won't be able to pull it off."

"That could work," Tessa said. "Who's been teaching you about null spells?"

"I learned about them at your place back when you were the big bad witch," Dan replied, to which Tessa nodded approvingly.

"All right, here's what we're going to do," I began. "We need to round up the Ghost Guys and Renato, and we need to create a null spell that's powerful enough to dampen Nathaniel, but soft enough for him not to notice it."

"I can retrieve the mortals," LeClerc said, then he slipped out of the office.

"He's like Batman, but with magic," Dan said.

"He is," Jacob agreed. "My dear Tessa, would you do me the honor of crafting a null spell with me?"

"I'd love nothing more," Tessa said, and they approached Jacob's spell cabinet. That left me, Dan, and my father standing in the center of the room.

"I guess that leaves three of us to deal with Mom," I said.

"I can go to her alone," my dad began, but I wasn't having that.

"Absolutely not," I said. "She's apparently got this major beef with you and all witches, including herself, and she was in on a plot to kill you. No way am I letting you near her."

"Why don't we just make a double batch of that null spell, and use half on Christina?" Dan suggested.

How I adored my brilliant husband. "That is a great idea."

Jada, Jemima, and Suffolk Street

A few hours later, Dan and I drove toward the town where my mother lived while my father, Tess, and Jacob stayed behind. The plan was for those three to wait for LeClerc to return with the mortals, while Dan and me cased out Mom's neighborhood in the hopes of running into her. If we saw her out at the market, or maybe casting evil spells in the local bus station, we were going to act like we had no memories of the alternate realities, and somehow make casual conversation with her. That would be tough. Tougher still would be dousing her with the null spell Jacob and Tessa had brewed up.

"Tough, but doable," Dan said. "You can always use introducing me to her as your cover."

"Shit," I said. "We never told Dad we're married. Handfasted. Whatever."

Dan took my hand. "Want to turn around?"

"No. Let's get this over with."

As we approached my mother's place, one thing became perfectly clear. This was not a nice, quiet suburb like her fictional home in Oak Grove. If anything, this neighborhood resembled the mortal side of town from the third extra evil reality.

"This neighborhood's a little rough," Dan said, in the understatement of the day.

"Why does she live in a place like this?" We passed yet another boarded up home. This one had an overgrown yard filled with trash, and I could see people huddled around something in the open garage.

"Maybe she doesn't have the means to move anyplace else," Dan suggested. "Do you know what she does for work?"

"I don't remember her ever working. She was always home, hanging out in her room or watching television."

"Did she go to school? College, maybe?"

"Not that I know of. Now that I think about it, I don't remember ever seeing her read a book, either." We stopped at a red light. I looked out the side window, and saw what I was pretty sure was a drug sale take place on the corner. "Do you think when the Ghost Guys approached her, they took advantage of her situation? I mean, if she lives out here, she's obviously poor. Maybe they told her she could have a better, easier life."

"That's a strong possibility," Dan said. "She wouldn't be the first person to do something morally questionable in the hopes of it leading her to a better life." He pulled over and parked in front of a red brick apartment building. "We're here."

I looked up at the building. It seemed to be in better shape than most of the houses we'd driven past, which I guess was nice. According to Bennet, she lived on the second floor. "Want to go inside?"

"I think it will be better if we walk around the neighborhood, see if we can find her in a neutral location," Dan replied. "Unless you think she's home? Can you, uh, sense her?"

"I don't really want to use magic around her. Even though she's a witch, she doesn't trust anything remotely magical, including me. The last thing I want to do is put her on the defensive."

"Then it looks like we're walking."

We got out of the car and started walking, but not toward the sketchy park. That was good. When we stopped at an intersection, and waited for our chance to cross, Dan took my hand.

"You know, this is the first sort of normal thing we've done in the real world since we came back." He rubbed his thumb against the gem in my ring. "Think we should have a party?"

"What, a handfasting hullabaloo?" I asked, and he smiled. "I don't really feel like partying. Ask me again after all of this is over with."

"I can do that." The light changed, and we crossed. "Since I'm currently unemployed, I was thinking about getting a private investigator's license. Know anyone who'll hire me?"

"Are you really not going back to the police force?" I countered.

"I don't think so. I was pretty much over it after Chief got possessed and I got suspended. After what I saw in the last timeline, I need to take a step back from the force. I know none of that was real, but it left a mark."

"Was it really that bad?"

"It was a lot worse than I've told you," he began, then he paused. "Is that Jada?"

"Jada? Here?" I followed his gaze, and saw Jada Morales walking out of the corner market. "Should we say hello?"

No sooner had I said the words than Jada saw us, turned around and speed walked in the opposite direction. "That was odd."

"Was it?" Dan countered. "She's probably still trying to put her life back together. Kid just needs some space."

"Did you just call Jada a kid? She and I are the same age." Before Dan could attempt to defend himself, my phone pinged. I withdrew it, and gasped when I read the screen.

"What is it?" Dan asked.

"I just got a text from Nathaniel fricken' Beauclaire," I said. "He wants us to stop by his place. Says he's got some weird memories he thinks I'm responsible for. And let's face it, I probably am. Or rather, we are."

Dan sighed. "Great. Want to go now?"

I glanced at the building my mother lived in. Part of me wanted to get my confrontation with her done and over with, but most of me was glad to put it off for now. "We were going to confront him, anyway. Might as well."

The sense of relief I felt as we drove away from my mother's sketchy neighborhood was amazing. I had no idea how or why my mother lived in such a dump, and I honestly didn't care if it was due to her circumstances or flat out stubbornness. I just knew I never wanted to go back there. As we drove back to town, I realized that now knew beyond a shadow of a doubt I would rather spend time with Nathaniel Beauclaire than my own mother. That was just crazy.

But, there was one thing nagging at me.

"You really don't think Jada's behavior was weird?" I asked Dan.

"Nah. She's been through a lot, and everyone processes grief and trauma differently. She probably just wants to leave it all behind and start fresh."

"I'd like to start fresh, too," I muttered.

"Then that's what we'll do," Dan said. "We'll finish this, and once everything's done, we'll figure out what happens next. Sound good?"

"Yeah. But Jada—"

"What's really bothering you?" Dan interjected. "You deal with people acting strangely all the time, but you never circle back like this. What's up?"

I took a breath; he was not going to like this. "When I astral projected to Jemima, she told me her mother is out here somewhere living in a recently deceased body."

"That was a fake reality," Dan began, but I shook my head.

"Jemima was the only spirit that made it to that new reality. That means it was real Jemima telling me about real Sarah inhabiting a real body in the here and now."

Dan glanced at me. "And you think she's possessing Jada again?"

"After Jada fell off that roof, you saw her and thought she was dead," I said. "Jemima said her mother slipped inside a dying body as its soul was leaving." Dan frowned, but otherwise didn't react. "You think I'm crazy, don't you?"

"I think I very much hate magic," Dan said. "I know you're steeped in magic, and I love you, but if all this magic disappears tomorrow I won't miss is."

"Neither will I."

The rest of the ride to Nathaniel's was quiet, but at least it was short. Since this was the real world, we didn't have to go two hours outside of town to the gothic manor that was the Beauclaire Estate. That monstrosity was still nothing but a burnt out cellar hole, and Nathaniel still lived in a townhouse a few blocks away from my grandmother's place.

"I don't like this guy living so close to us," Dan said, as he parked. "Can you cast a spell on him so he moves?"

"I thought you hated all magic, but now you want me to cast relocation spells?"

"I would make an exception for this." He took my hand, and we walked to the townhouse's front door. "The last time we were here, we got tied up in the basement."

"I told Tessa and Dad where we are. We'll be fine."

"Glad I've got my gun, and you've got that null spell." I gasped, because the spell wasn't properly warded for Nathaniel, then Dan raised his hand to knock on the door. Nathaniel threw it open before I had a chance to either put the spell back in the car, or tell Dan we couldn't use it.

"Thank you both for coming." Nathaniel stepped aside so we could enter.

"Wait," I said, and both Nathaniel and Dan paused. "Before we enter, I need you to know that I am carrying a null spell. It wasn't crafted for you, and I won't use it on you."

Nathaniel nodded sharply. "Thank you for your candor. Why tell me at all?"

"Because if you somehow detect the spell, you might assume that me carrying it is an act of aggression." I held my hands out, with my palms facing him. "It's not."

"I believe you, Miss Moore. Please, come inside." We did, and Nathaniel shut the door behind us. "Null spells aside, do you know where these new memories of mine came from?"

"How would I know what you do or don't remember?" I countered.

"Don't play innocent with me," Nathaniel warned. "The last time we saw each other, you had just assisted Jemima's ascension to the spiritual plane. Now my mind is filled with memories of her and I existing together in modern times. We both know that is not a coincidence."

"You're wrong," I said. "The last time we saw each other was when you followed us into the past. Did you really kill your past self, and steal Jemima's spirit?"

"It was not theft," Nathaniel said. "She is my wife, and Hassan convinced her to drink poison. I rescued her!"

"As I recall, past you was in cahoots with Hassan, but we can debate that another time," Dan said. "You really don't know what happened?"

"I do not," Nathaniel ground out.

"That blows another one of our theories out of the water," Dan said. "What happened is a few mortals and one disillusioned witch cast a whopper of a spell, and it created a false reality. That's why you have extra memories."

Nathaniel stared at Dan, then he said, "You must think me a fool."

"It's true," I said. "We thought you played some part in the spell, since Jemima was the only spirit that existed in the false reality."

"Why was she the only spirit present?" he asked.

"Because you had her trapped in the spirit bottle, she made the transition. No one else did."

"But she wasn't ethereal. She had a form," Nathaniel said.

"The form you remember was wax," Dan said. "She wasn't a person."

Nathaniel closed his eyes. "I waited almost four hundred years to hold her again. To you she was wax, but to me she was perfect."

My heart clenched. For all that Nathaniel was morally gray on his best day, he truly loved Jemima. "Is she here? In the bottle, that is."

"She is." He beckoned us down the hall, and we followed him into a modern office. On a shelf surrounded by candles and fresh flowers was the spirit bottle Amir had trapped Jemima in all those years ago.

I stood on my toes to get a better look at the bottle's contents. There was a bit of a powdery substance in the bottom, and that was it. "She's still in there?"

"She is. Go on, touch the bottle."

Tentatively, I touched the antique glass. Instantly, I was flooded with Jemima's warm, loving presence. "She's there, and she's... she's happy."

"She is," Nathaniel said again. "But how do I get her out?"

"Into a person?" I countered. "You know Jemima didn't want that."

"I doubt she wants this, either." Nathaniel wiped his hand down his face, and stared at the bottle. "What am I to do?"

Dan slid his hand against mine. "Let's give him a moment," he said, and we retreated to the hallway. Once we were outside of the office, Dan lowered his voice, and said, "You do realize that our real reality is officially altered, by time travel and otherwise."

"He's got memories of when Jemima was in the poppet," I said. "As in, memories from the fake timeline. What if other people have memories, too?"

"We should ask if he's been in contact with Jada," Dan began, then both of our phones rang at the same time. Dan checked his phone, and said, "I got Tessa."

"Dad's calling me." I accepted the call. "What happened?"

"LeClerc found the Ghost Guys," Dad replied. "They're all dead."

We left Sad Nathaniel and Bottled Jemima behind, and went to the address where LeClerc had found the Ghost Guys. In the coincidence of coincidences, it was fifty-four Suffolk Street.

As in, the exact house where Jacob Allwood's dead body had been found, surrounded by oleander.

"And the crazy just went up a notch," Dan said, as he parked behind LeClerc's all black limousine. "What are the odds?"

"There are no odds here," I said as I exited the car and stalked up the front path. "Whoever did this is sending us a message."

"Agreed." Dan got to the door first, then he whipped out a handkerchief and used it to shield his hand when he opened the door. "Don't want to contaminate the scene."

I nodded, since that was a smart move. We went inside the tidy home, and found LeClerc sitting at the kitchen table. I opened my mouth to tell him that was the chair we found Jacob in, but Dan grabbed my wrist. Yeah, best to skip that fact for now.

"Where are they?" I asked.

LeClerc stood. "I'll show you," he said, and led us into the living room. Laid out on the bland beige carpet were Mike Delacorte, Gary Williams, and James Roberts.

"No visible wounds, no blood," Dan said, as he crouched down for a closer look. "I'm guessing no fingerprints, either."

"There's not one speck of evidence," LeClerc said. "It's as if they decided to get down on the floor, and simultaneously expired of natural causes." He looked at me. "What's your take?"

"Someone's trying to frame us," I said, the words just falling out of my mouth. "We screwed up their plans, and this is the beginning of their revenge."

Dan frowned. "Is that your foresight talking?"

I heard cars pull up, and looked out the front window. "Yeah, and it's spot on. The cops are here."

SUPERNATURAL MUSE

This is the story of how Dan and I got arrested. Again.

"At least this time we're being held by modern day police officers," I said, since the last time we'd gotten arrested, it had been by officers that had been plucked from thirty years in the past. They had also been wearing riot gear, which just added to the confusion.

"Also, unlike last time, they found us alone with three dead bodies," Dan pointed out. "That's not good, babe."

"But we didn't do anything wrong! LeClerc said—"

Dan gave me a sharp look, and I stopped talking. LeClerc had slipped away as the police pulled up, and was therefore not associated with the Ghost Guys' deaths. We needed to keep it that way.

"We're not actually arrested, either," Dan continued. "Not yet, anyway. We're cooperating with the investigation and going in for questioning. It's good to cooperate."

I shrank down in my seat. "I don't feel good."

When we go to the station, we were escorted from the cruiser to the interrogation room, and let me tell you, that was a fun walk. All of Dan's former coworkers stopped what they were doing and gaped at us as if we were the prime suspects in a murder investigation. Which, in a way, we were. Then we took our seats in the interrogation room, and Chief Renault entered.

"Is this why you never called me back about returning to work?" Chief asked as he slammed the door shut. "Got yourself a new career as a hitman?"

"No, sir," Dan said. "I was sorting through some personal stuff. I'm sorry I didn't call."

Chief watched Dan for a moment, then he said, "I really could have used your help with the fallout from the Morales girl."

"What happened with Jada?" I asked. Chief glanced at Dan, who didn't offer up any clues.

"I'm sure you remember the incident on my roof," Chief began. "In fact, I believe that was the last time we were all together."

"That's true," Dan said, in his patented give nothing away detective voice. "I recall she had you in a compromising situation, and somehow she ended up moving from the roof to the parking lot. Rather quickly."

"Officially, you were never there," Renault said. "Sanders said she went to check on me alone, and no one has ever disputed her account. Jill is quite the loyal friend."

"She is a very good person," Dan said, and I officially had it with all their fake politeness.

"Cut the shit, you two," I snapped. "Why did you want us around for Jada?"

Chief ran a hand over what was left of his hair. "You know, at first they thought I pushed her off the roof. Even though I was the one tied up and bleeding, they thought I did it. They even thought I set her up in the motel she was staying at, like a kept woman."

"We know you weren't responsible," I began. "Amir Hassan—"

"Is still in a coma," Chief finished. "There's talk he might not come out of it. As you can see, he's not such a good witness here. If Morales hadn't recovered, I would probably be fighting a murder charge."

"Yet here you sit, still the chief," Dan said. "How'd that shake out?"

"Even though she took a flying leap off a four story roof, Morales made a complete and miraculous recovery," Chief replied. "Physically and mentally. As soon as she was able to, she gave a full statement taking all the responsibility for kidnapping me. That, coupled with Jill's statement, saved my ass."

"What was her motive?" I asked. "Kidnapping the chief of police is pretty random."

"She blamed it on a psychotic break, and the court appointed doctors agreed," he replied.

"That doesn't make sense," I said. "There is no way Jada could have survived that fall."

"What, you want to add to your body count?" Chief countered. "I know you had a history with the three men who turned up dead, and the house they were found in. In fact, I've got a report about Lyons bringing you to a crime scene at that same address as a consultant."

"Yeah? And?" I demanded, in my lamest comeback ever.

"Seems like history is repeating itself," Chief said. "Want to tell me what happened back there?"

"We need a lawyer," I said. "Shouldn't we get a lawyer?"

"Are you guilty?" Chief demanded.

"Are we under arrest?" Dan countered. "For anything?"

"Not yet."

"Then we really have no reason to be here."

We stood to leave, and Chief said, "Are you at least going to tell me how Morales brainwashed me and got away with it?"

I faced Chief. "Jada didn't do anything to you. You were put under a compulsion spell by Amir Hassan. Working with Amir were the three men we found dead earlier today. They ran a podcast about ghosts." I paused, and added, "Renato Florian was also working with Amir."

"To what end?" Chief demanded. "What's Florian's end game?"

"I'm honestly not sure," I replied. "He used to want to study the supernatural. Now I think it's all about revenge."

"Did he want you to be his supernatural muse?" Chief asked, and I shuddered.

"That's just creepy," I said. "Good luck with your investigation."

"I didn't say you could leave."

"You have no authority over me, or Dan." I flicked a spell toward Chief. It was just a few harmless lights, since I couldn't manage anything interesting on the fly, but it did the trick. Chief stayed glued to his chair as Dan and I walked out of the interrogation room, and left the station.

"That was dramatic," Dan said, once we were in the parking lot. "So much for cooperation."

"This was a waste of time," I said. "We have bigger problems."

"Agreed," he said, then he pointed to the far side of the lot. LeClerc was waiting for us in his vehicle with the engine idling. "There's our ride."

"Good," I said, as we walked toward him. "We need LeClerc to track down three more people."

"Florian, your mother, and Beauclaire?"

"Yes to the first two, but not Nathaniel. Jada Morales. I think she really did die in the fall, and Sarah Allwood's been possessing her since then."

Bacon Trees?

LeClerc was down for searching out a few more people, and he understood that time was of the essence. Therefore, Dan and I went on the hunt with him.

"We should go get the car," Dan said. "We left it on Suffolk Street."

"It's been taken care of," LeClerc said. He had lowered the barrier between the driver's seat and the rear passenger area so we could talk. "I went back for it after the police departed. It's currently sitting in your driveway."

"Thank you," Dan said. "Is there anything you can't do?"

"So far, no." LeClerc glanced over his shoulder. "I do enjoy a challenge."

"What do you think the odds are of Sarah Allwood possessing Jada's corpse?" I asked.

"I think it's a possibility," LeClerc said. "However, if she did possess Jada, that would bring its own set of problems."

"Such as?" Dan prompted.

"If Jada's spirit moved on, her body is dead. As in rotting. Sarah won't be able to hide that for very long."

"I had not thought of that," I said, because who assumes they'll run into a corpse out running errands or going for a walk? No one, that's who. "How long could the body stay, um, fresh?"

"Unsure. Sarah's very powerful, so she could hold off decay for a few weeks, or perhaps a few months."

"Then what would happen?" Dan asked.

"The body will eventually decompose, at which time I imagine Sarah will search for a new host."

I flopped back against the seat. "And she can rinse and repeat for as long as she wants," I muttered. While I wondered how we would ever contain Sarah—and if we even should—I remembered that we were in the real world again. I'd gotten so used to not contacting spirits I almost forgot about them.

"Prudence?" I called out to my best ghost friend. "Pru? You'll be shocked to hear this, but I need your help."

"Eliza, the only thing shocking about you is your wardrobe," Prudence said, as she materialized on the seat across from me. When she saw Dan, her entire mood changed. "Hello, Mr. Lyons."

"Nice to see you again, ma'am," Dan replied.

"Remember when we asked you for help about the young woman in the motel?" I asked. "Her name is Jada. She may have died, and her body may be inhabited by an interloping spirit."

"That is an abomination of the natural way of things," Prudence declared. "Why can't you seek out this child's spirit yourself?"

"I don't know if she'll be willing to talk to me," I admitted. "The last time I saw Jada, she was pretty mad. I don't want to upset her by barging into her afterlife."

Pru patted my hand with her ghostly one. "You always were sensitive to others' feelings, Eliza. I shall have a look around and see what I can learn."

"Thank you, Pru." She nodded and dissipated from view. Once she was gone, Dan extended his arm. I snuggled up against his side.

"Have faith in Prudence," Dan said. "She's never let you down."

"I know. This is all so messed up." I looked up at Dan. "I have no idea how to fix this."

"It might not be fixable," LeClerc said. "Some things cannot be undone, no matter how much power you amass. Take Sarah, for example. She's been trying to undo her death for centuries, but at best she's a powerful spirit. She'll never be alive again."

"And neither will the Ghost Guys," I murmured, then I asked, "Are you saying that Renato might have permanently altered things?"

"If he murdered those three men, he already has," LeClerc replied.

"And who knows what else he's done." I laid my head on Dan's shoulder. "How would he have located my mother? I didn't even know where she was."

"But he had the lineages that were stolen from Bennet's office," Dan reminded me. "He probably got her name and did an old-fashioned search."

"Or maybe he asked the right people the right questions," I said. "Even if he read my mother's name, and saw that she was witchborn, he wouldn't know anything about her power levels. That's not something that's recorded, at least not on the lineages. That means he went around asking about unusually strong witches, and someone pointed him toward Mom."

"That in itself doesn't make sense," LeClerc said. "The Allwoods didn't even know your mother existed until recently. Only Cecily was aware of your relationship."

"Did Florian visit her in prison?" Dan asked.

"No," LeClerc replied. "I keep pretty close tabs on Cecily. The last visitors she had were you two."

"Then there was no reason for Renato to go to my mother for power," I said. "He brought her in on his plan as revenge against me."

"Maybe, but that doesn't explain where he did get the magic and knowledge to pull this off not once, but twice," Dan said.

We passed a fruit stand, all decked out with cornstalks and pumpkins and baskets of apples... and it all made sense. "The apples rotted in the orchard," I said. "He figured out how to siphon off Sarah's power. That's probably why she ended up possessing Jada again."

"All right." LeClerc pulled into the turning lane. "Let's pay the orchard a visit."

The moment we pulled up to Stone Creek Orchard, despair settled into my gut. "I think I'm going to be sick."

"That's not surprising," LeClerc said as he turned off the engine and pocketed the keys. "We're surrounded by death."

We got out of the car, and immediately covered out mouths and noses. The apples that had been so red and shiny a few weeks ago were now piles of brown sludge heaped up around the tree trunks. The stench was nauseating, but it didn't remind me of rotten fruit.

"This stinks like an abattoir, not an orchard," Dan said. I approached one of the apple trees, grabbed a fallen stick, and poked at a few of the apples.

"These apples aren't apples," I said. "They look more like... pork."

"Pork?" Dan repeated. "As in, we have an orchard full of bacon trees?"

I shrugged. "All I know is that this looks more like flesh that fruit."

LeClerc approached one of the trees and scrutinized the smelly globs. "I don't know if Sarah's responsible for this, but it's definitely black magic."

"How can you tell?" Dan asked. "Is there an aura around the trees, something like that?"

"Rotten heart, rotten magic," LeClerc replied.

"Jacob always says that magic works with your intent and emotion," I murmured, and LeClerc nodded.

"Even if you're pretending to do the right thing, magic can't be fooled." He looked past the rotting fruit toward the barn. Since the leaves and fruit had fallen from the trees, it was clearly visible. "Is that where you found the bones?"

"Yeah, bobbing in a cider vat," I replied, as we headed toward the barn. "The farm store is where we found Jacob's spirit."

"He told me," LeClerc said, then quickened his pace. Once he was a few steps ahead of us, Dan wrapped his arm around my shoulders.

"Didn't he have something with Jacob?" Dan murmured against my ear. His warm breath made my neck tingle, and I scrunched up my shoulder. "This can't be easy for him."

"I'm sure it isn't." I watched LeClerc's back as he stalked toward the barn, and wondered what it was like to be around your significant other all the time, but unable to have any physical contact with them. "Like Nathaniel and Jemima. Always close, but always apart."

"When Nathaniel said Wax Jemima was perfect, even I felt bad for the guy," Dan said.

"I need you to work with more magic," I blurted out.

"Why's that?"

"Your life span increases based on how much magic you use. Just look at my dad, and Tess."

"I cannot believe Alex is over one hundred years old," Dan said. "Exactly how old is Tessa?"

"I'm not sure." Tessa was quite evasive when it came to stating her actual age. Personally, I thought she forgot how old she was a long time ago. "She remembers when tobacco was first brought to Europe."

"That was in the early sixteenth century," Dan said, then he shook his head. "So you're planning on keeping me around for five hundred years? You could always stick me in a wax doll."

"That's not funny," I said, then we were at the barn's entrance. The wooden vats were still present, though everything else had been cleared out.

Dan pointed at the center vat. "There," he said. "All the energy is coming from that one."

LeClerc raised an eyebrow, no doubt wondering how the mortal could sense magic's origin point. But he didn't ask any questions, and we didn't offer any information. Instead, he stepped aside and let Dan lead the way up the ladder and down the catwalk toward the central vat. Then, he held up an arm and blocked our way.

"Stay back," he said, once he could see into the vat.

"What is it?" I asked, as I peeked under his arm. Whatever was happening in the vat glowed purple, and threw crazy shadows against the interior walls. "Is it more of the apples?"

"It's Florian."

The scene inside the cider vat was the stuff of nightmares. Or as Dan put it, an alien abduction horror movie.

Renato was standing inside the empty vat, and some sort of webbing bound his legs to the floor. The same webbing covered his arms and held them outstretched from his body and attached to the sides of the vat. His skin was mottled with old purple and green bruises, and his head dangled limply to the side. While his eyes were closed, his mouth gaped wide open. The worst part was how Renato's chest rose and fell. He was alive in there.

"One thing is certain," LeClerc said. "Florian is definitely not the mastermind of this operation."

"No, he is not," I murmured. Based on the way he was trussed up in the cider vat, he was either being used as a power conduit against his will, or he was being punished for a rather large infraction.

"Should we call an ambulance?" I asked.

Dan shook his head. "I really don't know what a paramedic could do for this guy."

"What is this stuff?" LeClerc crouched at the edge of the vat, and used a pencil to poke at the webbing. When he raised the pen, the webbing came away in a long, gloopy strand. "It's viscous, and it's not affecting the vat or my pencil."

"But it's hurting him," I said. "He looks like he passed out screaming in pain."

Dan frowned, and rubbed his chin. "I've got a thought, but it's a long shot."

"I'm sure it's better than the nothing we have right now," I said.

"Remember when that demon slug possessed me?" he continued, as if I could forget the time a demon attacked us from above. Dan shot it, making its body disintegrate into a thick, sticky mess. "You said it covered us in some kind of slime that burned when it touched us."

"It did." I looked at the webbing covering Renato, and frowned. "I guess this could be the same stuff."

"How would we know if this substance is demonic in origin?" LeClerc asked.

"One easy way to find out." Dan leaned over and touched the slime where it had oozed up to the edge of the vat, and immediately snatched his hand away. "Yeah, that stings," he said, as he shook out his hand.

"Does it still hurt?" I asked.

"Nah. It only burned when I touched it." I glanced at Dan's skin; it was unmarked, just like we had been after we washed off the slime.

"All right, we have possible evidence of demons. Are you saying that you think Renato's been possessed?" I asked.

"Maybe not possessed, but he's definitely being tortured," Dan said. "Or punished."

"Who would be punishing him?" LeClerc asked. "If this really is demonic, there's a pretty short list of people who could be responsible."

"Why's that?" Dan asked. "Is working with demons forbidden, like time travel?"

"It's not forbidden," LeClerc replied. "It's stupid. Only a fool, or someone truly desperate, would attempt any kind of magic involving a demon. You'd end up double crossed, cursed, or dead."

"Or maybe all three," I muttered; I only knew of one person who regularly worked with demons, and he was currently in a hospital hooked up to a room full of machines. "LeClerc, can you find out about Amir Hassan's current medical status? Specifically, I want to know if he's in a permanent vegetative state."

Without a word, LeClerc withdrew his phone and stepped away to make a call. Dan turned to me, and asked, "Is LeClerc his first or last name?"

"Add that to the list of things I don't know." I couldn't stop staring at Renato, trapped in a vat and restrained with demonic slime. I wrapped my arms around my stomach, and said, "I know how my mother got involved."

"Tell me."

"Amir," I said softly. "I told him all about my mother, my childhood, everything. He knew exactly where she was, and how to find her. When he read the lineages and found out she's witch, it was just a bonus for him."

"But he's in a coma," Dan said.

"If he's brain dead, his soul has left his body," I began. "And Jada died near one of the time tunnels he used. I think he's the one possessing Jada."

Dan ran a hand over his hair. "You know what this means?"

"Yeah. We need to find my mother and figure out if she's an accomplice or a victim."

Axe Murderer Jill

When LeClerc returned, we learned two things. His first name was Jacques, and Amir had been declared brain dead a week ago.

"The hospital is currently trying to locate his next of kin," LeClerc continued. "The protocol states that they must keep him on life support until a family member or a judge says otherwise."

"Which means that unless someone pulls the plug, Amir's soul will always have a place to go back to," I said. "He's not really a ghost, but since his own body isn't functional, his spirit can hop into any other body he wants. If he wears it out, he can just go home until he finds a new one."

"Great," Dan said. "Let's table Ghostly Houdini for now. How are we getting Florian out of the vat?"

"I thought you wanted him to die a thousand painful deaths," I said.

"He shot Eli in one of the other realities," Dan explained to LeClerc.

"He poisoned my water, too," I added. "With wolfsbane."

LeClerc grunted, then he returned his attention to Renato. "Perhaps he's where he belongs."

"Normally, I would agree with you," Dan said. "However, in light of all of this, maybe none of that was his fault. What if Hassan possessed him, and that was how he ended up getting involved in the first place?"

"Good point," I said, leaving off how Renato had always seemed rather weak minded and therefore prone to suggestion. It wasn't polite to insult someone who was already being tortured. "If this slime is similar to the demonic gunk we got doused with, it should wash right off."

We found some rags and buckets in the corner of the barn, and while Dan and I visited the water pump LeClerc got Renato out of the vat. How he managed that I had no idea, but when we returned with our full buckets, Renato was laid out on the catwalk. After we poured the water over Renato, and got the bulk of the slime off of him, he blinked his eyes open.

"Am I dead?" he rasped. "Why is the pain gone?"

"We washed the slime off of you," I said. Renato looked toward the sound of my voice, and his eyes widened when he recognized me. "Surprised I didn't bleed to death? Or that the poison didn't get me?"

"Eliza, I was under duress at the time," Renato began, then Dan entered his field of vision.

"Remember me?" Dan demanded. "When all of this is done, you and me are going to have a talk."

"What do you mean, when this is done?" Renato asked. "It's never going to be done. Amir's not going to let Eliza rest, not until she's dead. He's finally more powerful that you are," Renato added.

"Doubtful," Leclerc said. "Besides, no matter how much power Hassan amasses Mistress Eliza can more than meet him. Her allies won't let her fall, and Hassan doesn't have any allies left, save for you."

"What do you mean, no allies?" Renato demanded. "He's got a whole team working in this timeline, and others."

"Would this crack team happen to be Mike and his podcast friends?" I asked. When Renato's face betrayed his shock at me making that connection, I continued, "They're dead."

Renato's shoulders slumped as his resolved melted away. "They are? All of them?"

"We saw the bodies ourselves." Since Renato's mind was obviously blown, I asked LeClerc, "Is there any place we can stash him for now?"

"Stash me?" Renato huffed. "I'm not luggage."

"We have some enchanted safe rooms at the compound," LeClerc replied, as he effectively ignored Renato. "He'll have to ride in the back of the limo with you, though."

I took in Renato's slimy, wet, naked state. "Can we at least wrap him up in a blanket?"

LeClerc stocked blankets, towels, and spare clothes in his car, because of course he did. He claimed that he liked to be prepared. I was just glad we didn't have to ride back to the Allwood Compound with an unclothed Renato sitting across from us. As for our prisoner, during the trip he was uncharacteristically quiet.

"I figured he would have told us his life story by now," I murmured to Dan. I didn't know if Renato was deliberately ignoring us, or if he was so wrapped up in his thoughts, he wasn't paying attention to anything we said.

"Might be in shock," Dan said. We were turned toward each other with our faces close together while we discussed what to do next. "You believe him?"

"The problem isn't believing what he said, it's verifying any of it." I replayed seeing Jada walking out of the market over and over in my head. "If Amir is possessing Jada, that means he's been in there for a few weeks already. Wouldn't the body be a little worse for wear by now?"

"We didn't get that close," Dan said. "Although, she moved like a regular person. Would a possessed corpse still move around the same as a living body?"

"I wouldn't think so," I said. "Unless Amir really is that powerful."

Dan brought my hand to his mouth and kissed my knuckles. "Don't worry, Mrs. Lyons. We'll figure it out."

"I never said anything about taking your name."

"You're not supposed to be with him," Renato muttered. I'd almost forgotten he was in the car with us.

"Well, I am," I said. Renato frowned, then he resumed staring out the window.

"The trick is olive oil," Renato said. "At least, according to Amir, it is. Other oils can work in a pinch, but only olive oil can be used to preserve a body for an untold length of time. Some sort of compound in the oil staves off decay."

"Do you rub it on the body's skin?" I asked.

"That, and ingest it. If you can get enough to fill a bathtub, you can soak in it."

"Now we know what Jada was picking up at the market," Dan said. "Probably her weekly olive oil run."

"Olive oil." I imagined a tub full of greasy, gross oil. "That's got to get expensive. Where is she getting the money to keep up her oil habit?"

"Hassan had resources. I can," Dan began, then he blew out a breath. "I was going to say I can run a trace on his credit cards, but I can't do that anymore."

"Not the chief of police here?" Renato sneered. We ignored him.

"You can't, but Jill can. Think she'll talk to us?"

Dan pulled out his phone. "Only one way to find out."

Jill agreed to talk to us, but only on the condition that we meet at her place. LeClerc dropped us off at the Sanders residence, then he went on to the Allwood home to stick Renato in a safe room and hopefully throw away the key. Dan knocked on the front door, while I tried to calm my racing pulse.

"It's not the same Jill from the last reality," Dan said. "This one's good."

"Does this one own an axe?" I muttered. "I bet she has a bone saw."

"It's probably in her lab," Dan said, then Jill opened the door. She looked just the same, with her blonde hair pulled back in a bun, and wearing her usual outfit of a fitted black tee and khakis.

"You two go no contact for weeks, then you show up for five minutes and turn the station on its ear," she said, and she beckoned us inside. "Again."

"Hello to you, too," Dan said. "I take it you talked to Chief?"

"Chief claims you told him he was under a spell?" Jill demanded.

I shrugged. "It's the truth. Also, we went no contact because we were trapped in an alternate reality and you tried to kill me with an axe."

"Eli," Dan warned.

"Might as well get it out in the open," I said. "So if I act a little weird, it's because I'm still freaked out over Axe Murderer Jill."

"Great. I get a code name. Come on, I'll make some tea."

Dan and I sat at the kitchen table, while Jill set about making tea. I was used to having tea with Bennet, which involved delicate porcelain teacups and his amazing caramel shortbreads. At Jill's house, tea was served in mismatched mugs, and the snacks were Oreos, but everything was just as good.

"An alternate reality," Jill said. "That's wild, even for you two."

"Wild is not the word I would use," I said. "Awful, confusing, messed up. Those are better words."

Jill pushed a cookie around on her plate. "And how do you think I can help with any of this?"

"We think Jada died when she fell off Renault's roof," I began. "Amir Hassan might be animating her body."

"You have got to let go of your guilt over how Jada's life turned out," Jill said. "She didn't fall off the roof. She ran at you and tripped, then she went over the edge. If she'd gotten her hands on you, she would have taken you down with her, literally."

"Yeah, well." I blew on my tea. "She didn't take me with her, and she ended up dead all the same."

"Besides, after she recovered from the fall, she gave a statement exonerating Chief," Jill continued. "If she was possessed by Hassan, could she have done that? And fool all of her doctors at the same time?"

"After what I've seen, I'll vouch that Hassan is more than capable of putting one over on a few doctors," Dan said. "Hell, he can probably pull a fast one over the entire medical establishment. However, while Eli and I believe this to be true, we still require proof."

"Which is why you're here," Jill concluded. "What do you want me to do? Test Jada for... I don't know, something?"

"We were thinking more along the lines of a money trail," I said. "Amir had access to considerable wealth. I want to know if Jada has somehow tapped into that."

"I get why you're coming at it this way, but if I start poking around in Hassan's finances without cause, that's going to raise some eyebrows," Jill said.

"What about Jada's finances?" I asked. "Maybe we could do a background check, something low key?"

Jill frowned, but she retrieved her work laptop from the next room and started plugging in numbers. "Any idea when Jada was born?"

"March twenty-fifth," I replied. "I remember going to a birthday party at her place when we were kids." Jill looked like she wanted to continue her lecture about my ongoing guilt over Jada. Instead, she input the information and waited for the results.

"Based on this information, Jada is not wealthy," Jill said. "She's on welfare, and lives in state housing. She doesn't even have her own place. According to her social worker, she's sharing an apartment with..." Jill paused. "Eli, Jada's sharing an apartment with your mother."

"What?" Jill turned her laptop toward me. Right there on the screen was Jada's address, which was in the same red brick building Dan and I had parked in front of earlier that day. Also listed were her known associates, including her roommate, Christina Lind. "This can't be a coincidence."

"I'm sure it isn't," Dan said. "They're both on assistance?"

"How do they even know each other?" I started at the screen, wondering if this was the proof I'd needed all along, and my mother was involved in a plot to create a false world. "And if they're so poor, how does Jada afford all of her olive oil?"

"Why would she need a lot of olive oil?" Jill asked. "Does she cook often?"

"It preserves dead bodies." I leaned back and rubbed my eyes. "I officially have no idea what's going on here, but I do know one thing. No way is Amir living like a pauper. Whatever's going on with Jada, I don't think Amir's possessing her."

"Then we did learn something," Dan said. "Not something great, but we've got another piece of the puzzle."

Jill pushed a notebook toward me. "Do me a favor and write down everything you know about Hassan. I can pick away at him from the edges inward, and see what I can learn that way."

"Sure." I began listing things I knew about Amir, such as how his family was from London, how his favorite food was an absolutely vile British concoction involving sausages and mushy peas, and how he abhorred driving. As I listed these anecdotes, I was struck by all the things I didn't know about him. We'd been a couple for almost two years, and I never even knew his birthdate.

"He kept those details from you for a reason," Dan said. "Even before you were a PI, you were smart as hell. He didn't want to give you too much information, in case you ever needed to track him down."

"Dan's right," Jill said. "Hassan went out of his way to be a ghost in your life. This guy has an agenda we can only begin to speculate on."

"We know his agenda," I said. "He wants to run things. As in, all the things." I sketched out the glass bottle Jemima's spirit called home. "What I still don't understand is how the Beauclaires fit into all of this. I was so certain Nathaniel had a hand in things, what with Jemima having a body again, but after we saw him earlier, I'm not so sure."

"I hate to say it, but I'm also doubting Beauclaire's involvement," Dan said. "Earlier he did not present as man who had a handle on things. He was as confused as we are, maybe more so."

"Then let's take him off the list," Jill said. "Eli, you claim Hassan wants power. What kind? Wealth, influence, physical strength?"

"He wants to be in charge," I replied. "A king, or an emperor, even. It's why he wanted to take control of the seers from me. Amir wants the entire magical community to be under his control."

"And he failed, because here you are," Jill said. "But he's a sneaky bastard, so what would he do next?"

"Would he try to take over one of the witch clans?" Dan asked.

"Doubtful. His pride's been wounded, so he'll want revenge. If fact, he would probably take revenge over power at this point. He's a bitter, spiteful—" I paused, as the random bits of information clicked into place. "Like my mother."

"And Christina took out all of the clan elders in the fake timeline," Dan said. "Jill, can you run a check on Renato Florian?"

"Um, sure." Jill began typing. "Why am I doing this?"

"Just humor me."

Jill gave Dan some side eye, then she glanced at me. I shrugged, since I didn't know what Dan wanted to find on Renato, either, but I was curious. Jill sighed, and started looking into Renato's life.

"He's an easy search, since the department already has a file on him," Jill said.

"Why's that?" I asked. "Does he have a record?"

"No. Well, maybe," she amended. "Chief thought it was odd when he showed up out of the blue and bailed out the Ghost Guys, so he had us look into him. Just the basics, but..." Her voice trailed off, and she frowned at her screen.

"But, what?" I prompted.

"Hospital record hit," she said. "He went into the ER with cardiac arrest two days after Hassan was admitted. The next day Florian was discharged, and Hassan was declared brain dead."

"Shit," I said. "Amir's possessing Renato, not Jada!"

Dan frowned. "And we sent him right into the Allwood Compound."

MISTRESS OF SEERS

While Dan and Jill argued over who would drive to the Allwood house, I called my father.

"Dad," I yelled as soon as he picked up. "Amir possessed Renato!"

"Where is he now?" Dad asked.

"The last time we saw him, LeClerc was bringing him to the Allwoods'," I replied. "He's going to put him in some kind of a safe room."

"Good, then we can contain him."

"No! Not good," I shrieked. "You and Tessa need to get everyone out of that house now! Tell Jacob you need to evacuate all the way down to the city!"

"Bug, if he's being put in a safe room—"

"Do not call me Bug! Listen to me, and get the fuck out of that house!"

I paused, shaking so badly I almost dropped the phone. Never once had I cursed at my father, not even in a joking way. I loved and respected him too much to ever do that. But I had also watched a house explode with him inside of it in an alternate timeline, and there was no way I was letting that happen again.

"Dad, please," I said. "It's not safe in there, not for you or anyone."

"All right," he said, his clipped tone telling me he was walking. "I see Jacob now. Tessa and I will meet you at the bottom of the hill."

"Thank you."

I ended the call, and turned toward Jill's car. Dan was standing next to the driver's side door, keys in hand. "Alex and Tess are getting out?"

I nodded. "They're going to empty the house."

"Let's go," he said, and we got in the car.

"Jill's letting you take her car?"

"Yeah. She's going to call Angel, and find out whatever she can about Hassan and Florian." Dan backed onto the street, then he threw it in drive and floored it. "What's the plan, babe?"

"Right now, I just want to make sure no one else dies."

Dan squeezed my knee. "Then that's what we'll do."

As we drove toward the Allwood Compound, all I could hear was the blood pounding in my ears. There wasn't a direct route from Jill's place to the Allwoods', and Dan had to drive like a maniac as he navigated through dozens of side streets. Normally, I would be worried he would hit another car or even get a ticket. Right then, I only wanted him to drive faster.

Finally, he turned onto the street that led up the hill to the mansion. Dozens of people were gathered in front of the gates, and I dared to hope my dad and Tess had gotten out. Then I saw my father's shaggy black hair, and jumped out of the car as soon as it stopped moving.

"I'm sorry I swore at you," I said as I hugged my dad. He laughed as he squeezed me back.

"Don't worry about it," he said. "I'm sorry I didn't listen to you immediately."

"What do we think Amir's planning?" Tessa asked.

I drew back from my dad, and said, "I'm really not sure. I just didn't want anyone else to get hurt." I glanced at the dozens of people standing around at the entrance. "Maybe I freaked out a bit."

"Better caution than bravado," Dad said. "When was LeClerc supposed to arrive?"

I went still. "You mean he's not here?" Before he could reply, I saw Jacob.

"Where's LeClerc?" I demanded, as I jogged toward Jacob. "He should have gotten here by now!"

"I'm not sure," Jacob said. "He was supposed to check in once he arrived, but he hasn't yet." Jacob looked toward the house. "It is not like LeClerc to not check in."

"Where are the safe rooms?" Dan asked as he approached us. "Can we see into them from out here?"

"No," Jacob replied. "They're in the center of the house, window-less, and warded. They're the safest places in the entire city."

Someone shouted, and people pointed toward the house. I craned my neck to see what was happening; since I'm short, I was usually the last to know things. Based on what people were saying, a man was standing on a window ledge and in imminent danger of falling. While I tried to see the man in question, I felt a hand on my arm. LeClerc was standing next to me.

"When did you get back," I began, then I noticed the blood on his collar, and that his glasses were missing. I was talking to LeClerc's ghost. "What can I do for you?"

"No offense, Eliza, but I think I'm beyond your help," he replied. "And I don't want to move on, not just yet. There's still work to do."

"You sound like Jacob," I said. "You and he are quite the pair."

LeClerc blushed. "Can you call him over? I couldn't get his attention."

"You'll figure out how to do that soon enough." I tugged on Jacob's spirit. He approached us a moment later, then his face fell when he saw LeClerc's spirit standing with me.

"Jacques," Jacob said. "I wanted you with me, but not yet."

"Here I am all the same," LeClerc said. "Hassan has definitely possessed Florian. He's seeking to ward the entire house against witches."

"What will that accomplish?" I asked.

"His plan is to keep us out long enough to siphon off our strength," LeClerc replied. "Hassan's unhinged. I don't know if he's got an actual plan to use whatever power he steals, or if this is just gluttony at this point."

"Either way, there's a lot of power here for him to steal," I murmured. "Jacob, can you round up your ancestors and get them someplace safe? LeClerc, do you think you can help him?"

"Of course I can," LeClerc said, as he slid his palm against Jacob's. "We've shielded them before. We know how to keep them safe."

"We certainly do," Jacob said. "Be safe, Eli."

I watched as they dissipated from view, then I approached Dan. "Amir-possessed Renato killed LeClerc," I said.

"Shit," Dan said. "What do we do?"

"I'm going to get Renato's spirit and put him back in his body," I said. "Of course, I'm going to have to find his spirit first, and yank out Amir."

"Does this mean Hassan will go back to his own body?"

"Most likely." When Dan frowned, I continued. "I've never done anything like this before."

He nodded. "What do you need from me?"

"I need a safe spot for my body, and I need you to watch over me," I said. "After I go out, tell Dad and Tess what I'm doing. Oh, and tell them that Jacob's getting his ancestors to safety."

"Let's get you in the car." Dan put his arm around me, and we returned to Jill's car. He opened the back door, and said, "I'll call Jill and tell her to keep an eye on Hassan's body in the hospital."

"Thank you." I kissed him. "I love you."

"Love you too, baby. Come back to me."

"I always will."

After another kiss, I laid down on the back seat with my hands resting on my stomach. Dan shut the car door, and I let my eyes close. In less than a minute, my spirit was free of my body. I took a moment to let my spirit float, and enjoy the utter freedom that came with astral projection. Then I saw Dan standing guard next to Jill's car, and my father and Tessa's worried faces as he told them my admittedly half-assed plan. Out of the blue Tessa got into Jill's car and sat in the passenger seat. A moment later, her spirit was floating beside me.

"Did you really think I would let you have all the fun?" she asked.

"I don't know how much fun this will be." I turned toward the house. "We need to find Renato's spirit, then I'm going to pull Amir out and put Renato back where he belongs."

Tessa arched an eyebrow, but didn't comment on what a long shot this plan was. That much was obvious. "Since Renato was forced out of his body, rather than experiencing a natural death, his spirit should be nearby."

"Here's hoping." I moved closer to the house. Beyond the main structure, I sensed Jacob and LeClerc herding the Allwood ancestors away from the burial ground and somewhere safer. As soon as they had the benefit of distance, I sent up a flare with Renato's name on it.

"Are you here to help me?" Renato's spirit demanded as he materialized in front of me.

"Depends," I replied. "Are you the one that shot me?"

"Shot you?" he demanded, as he pulled at his hair. "I've never even held a gun!"

"It would seem that Amir Hassan has been pulling your strings for some time," Tessa said. "Do you recall bailing three bland podcasters out of jail?"

"What? No!" Renato looked around, panicked. "The last thing I remember is my chest going so tight I couldn't breathe, then everything went black. Now I'm this disembodied soul, but I can't find my body, and I can't find the light."

"Go into the light, Carol Anne," Tessa muttered.

"Amir must be magically cloaking your body from you," I said, as I ignored Tessa's movie reference, although Dan would have enjoyed that. "He's been driving your body around and generally being a jerk to everyone he encounters. I'm going to pull him out so you can return to your natural form."

"What if I can't return?" he asked. "What if I really am dead?"

"Then I will help you move on." When Renato gasped, I added, "You're in my world now. This is what I do. Just follow my lead, and everything's going to work out."

"Everything, except I might be dead," he muttered.

"I can't control who lives or dies," I said. "No one can. But I can keep you safe. Do you trust me?"

"I don't really have much of a choice, do I?"

That was good enough for me. "Tess, can you lead us to the safe rooms?"

"I can and I will," she replied. "Stay close."

Tessa's spirit moved toward to the estate and melted through the walls. No matter how many times I'd astral projected, that aspect always freaked me out. Renato and I followed Tess through the maze of hallways until I had no idea where we were, or what floor we were on. Then we turned a corner, and Renato's body, powered by Amir's spirit, was standing in front of a door.

"That's me," Renato said. "Does it—me?—know we're here?"

"He hasn't tried killing us, so I'm guessing no," I replied. "Tess, what's in that room?"

"I'm not sure," she said. "It's some sort of an archive. Records, perhaps? Regardless, if Amir wants access to this room, I'm of a mind to keep him out of there."

"Agreed." Since Amir hadn't noticed us yet, I figured surprise was our strongest tool. "I'm going to pull Amir's spirit toward me. Renato, once he's out, you should naturally return to your body. Tess, I'm going to need you to keep an eye on Renato, and get him help if he needs it."

"Understood," she said. "What about you?"

"I'm going to put Amir back where he belongs, in his own body."

Tessa gave me a sharp look, but didn't argue with me. Since Amir's body had been declared brain dead, I would be sending his spirit back to a dying form; however, that was his body, and where his spirit should have been all along. No seer or witch can control who lives or dies. If it's Amir's time to pass on, that was beyond my control.

Or was it?

I shoved that thought aside; I would deal with the ethics and morality of being a seer at some other time. Now, I drew on every memory I had of Amir, from our first meeting in Iran, when he'd dazzled me with his kind smile and heartfelt words, to when we used to sit alongside the Seine and acted like lovers, to when he sent an army of stolen bones after me in the past and the present. As those memories coalesced in my mind, I reached forward, grabbed Amir's shoulders, and pulled.

His spirit flew out of Renato's body so fast he crashed into my astral form.

"Ellie," Amir said; only he had ever referred to me by that hated name. "I was wondering when you'd be by."

"You're going back to your own body," I said, in an attempt to buy Tessa enough time to get Renato into his body, and out of Amir's reach. "You've caused enough trouble."

His hand fluttered above his breast. "Me? A troublemaker?"

"Why did you have to kill LeClerc?" I demanded. "And Mike and his friends? Were they just more victory notches for you?"

"Like you were a notch on my bedpost?" Amir countered. "You've never gotten over me. Admit it."

"You're the one following me around." Out of the corner of my eye, I saw Tessa's spirit dissipate. That meant Renato was safe, and I didn't need to talk to this loser any longer. "You're going back, now."

Suddenly, his hands were around my neck. "I. Am. Not," he said, as he forced me to my knees. "I am more powerful than you are, Ellie. Always have been. And now that you've sent all your ancestors away, you can't draw on them for help."

Shit, had I done what he'd wanted? I didn't have time to worry about that. I also knew he was wrong. I grabbed his wrists, and pushed him up and off my spirit.

"You're not stronger than me or anyone," I said as I stood. "All you are is a liar."

"I am strong, and I will—"

I clasped my hand in the air, stealing his voice. It was an old witch trick Tessa had taught me years ago. "You're nothing but a bag of wind, and you're going back where you belong."

Amir bowed his head, and I foolishly thought I'd won. Then he lunged toward me and roared, as all of his spiritual energy rushed out of his mouth and pummeled me like a thousand sharp pebbles. The pain was almost unbearable, and I felt myself unraveling down to the core of my being.

I couldn't let him defeat me, not even if it meant my own death. Seers hold the line between life and death, and Amir had betrayed all of us. As Mistress of Seers, punishment was mine to bestow.

I knelt, and Amir—ever the arrogant one—paused in his onslaught to laugh. "Poor, weak Ellie," he began, then I threw every bit of my power at him.

Every. Single. Bit.

The world went gold, then orange, and finally black spots danced across my field of vision. I remembered those spots from when I'd been bleeding out after being shot. Assuming this was the end, I waited for my grandmother to appear, and guide me to whatever happens next.

It was over. I was finally done being the Mistress of Seers.

My Eliza

Watching over Eli's motionless, barely breathing body as she lay on the back seat of Jill's car was one of the most unsettling things I'd ever done.

It wasn't that I didn't trust her, or think she couldn't handle herself against Hassan. Eli had proven time and again that she was the smartest and toughest person I'd ever met, and I trusted her with my life. Still, I did not like seeing her like this.

Even worse, Tessa sat in the front seat, slumped over like a corpse. She'd made the split second decision to follow Eli, and was astral projecting toward Hassan alongside her, and before I realized what was happening, her spirit was out. Eli's father, Alex, stood next to

Tessa with his arms crossed over his chest. Based on Alex's frown, he didn't like it when these two projected, either.

"How do we know if they're okay?" I asked Alex.

"We really don't," he replied. "What we do know is that Eli is highly skilled, and intelligent enough to retreat if she needs to. She will come back to us."

"And Tess?"

"Tessa won't retreat, but she'll follow Eli's plan." Alex set his hand on my shoulder. "She won't let anything happen to Eli."

Tessa gasped herself awake, and Alex crouched beside her. I went to check on Eli, but she was still out.

"Isa," Alex murmured. "What happened?"

"Eli returned Renato's spirit to his body," Tessa said, albeit groggily. "We have to get him out of the mansion and away from Amir."

"Where's Eli?" I demanded.

Tessa faced me. "She's dealing with Amir."

"You left her alone?" I demanded. "What if she needs backup?"

"Dan." Tessa turned around in her seat, and placed her hand on my arm. "Right now, we need to help a living man, while Eli deals with the spirit of a rogue seer. She's exactly where she's supposed to be."

I nodded, because while I did not like Eli facing Hassan alone, I trusted Tessa almost as much as I trusted Eli. "All right. You do what you need to do for Florian. I'll stay here with Eli."

Tess and Alex went off to coordinate a rescue. I wasn't too concerned, since a few dozen witches were more than capable of getting one mortal man to safety. Since my job was to protect Eli's body, I sat in the back seat and drew her head onto my lap.

"Eliza, Eliza," I murmured. "My Eliza." I brushed her hair back from her forehead, marveling yet again that this amazing woman wanted anything to do with me. I would never get used to sharing my life with her, and I vowed to never take her for granted. Eli was everything to me. She looked so young with her eyes closed, as if she'd never dealt with all the awful things that had happened in her life. Ironically, when we were in the timeline where those things hadn't happened, she'd looked more stressed out than I'd ever seen her. I guessed that was proof that we were shaped by our experiences, and we needed the bad to balance the good.

I would do anything to keep anything bad from happening to her ever again.

Eli stirred, and I let myself relax a bit. Her moving around had to be a good sign, right? Then she began thrashing around, like she was running away from something. Before I could calm her down, she sat up and screamed.

"Eli, it's okay," I said. Her eyes were wild and panicked, and in the space of five seconds she'd gone from almost comatose to shaking and drenched in sweat. "Eli, baby, what happened?"

"I-I killed him," she whispered. "Amir. He's gone."

I felt my phone buzz. I checked the screen, and saw a text from Jill. "Yeah, Jill says his body just flatlined."

"No, I didn't kill his body. I killed his soul." Eli wrapped her arms around her stomach and rocked back and forth. "I obliterated him."

"Hey, hey," I said as I pulled her into my arms. "It's okay. You did what you had to do to protect people."

"But he's gone," she wailed against my chest. "He'll never move on. I destroyed his soul."

I tilted her chin up. "How many people did he hurt? And how many people did you just save by stopping him?"

"I'm not supposed to choose who lives or dies," she said, then she was taken over by sobs.

"You didn't choose," I said. "Hassan's actions dictated his fate."

Eli bawled against me as I held her, and stroked her hair. I never knew a soul could be destroyed, and I wasn't too broken up over Hassan being gone, but I'm selfish. If he had to go in order for Eli to live, I accepted that. As the woman I loved cried in my arms, I only hoped I could convince her she wasn't a murderer.

An Ending, And A Beginning

After I removed Amir from both the mortal and spiritual planes, everyone treated me like a hero. Too bad they were all wrong.

No one judged me, gave me side eye, or said boo about me destroying Amir's soul. In fact, lots of people contacted me to express how happy they were that I'd spiritually murdered a man. How anyone could be happy about such a horrid act was beyond me.

Those first weeks after Amir's death were incredibly busy. First, we rushed Renato to the hospital, where he was admitted to the cardiac wing. He ended up getting discharged a few days later with a clean bill of health. That was nice.

We also had a week of funerals. LeClerc was buried first, and even though he wasn't an Allwood by blood, he was interred in the family burial ground next to Jacob's body. As for his spirit, he didn't move on, but stayed to help Jacob run the family empire. At least they got to be together again.

The Ghost Guys were buried next, one by one until it seemed like I'd be wearing black for the rest of my life. When the funerals were finally behind us, Chief Renault closed the book on the Ghost Guys' deaths, and Dan and I were officially removed from the list of suspects. I had no idea how Chief made that happen, and I didn't ask for details.

No one went to Amir's funeral.

Slowly, we got back to the business of living as best we could. Jacob still ran his family's business with LeClerc at his side, and the ancestors had allowed me to funnel enough energy into him, so he also became a robust spirit. While LeClerc could do almost anything a corporeal man could do, the clan still had to hire a new driver. The new guy was not allowed to touch LeClerc's armored limousine, and ended up driving a battle ready Jeep. As for the limo's fate, LeClerc is determined to drive it again someday.

Pru found Jada's spirit, and confirmed that she had moved on as she was supposed to. I didn't ask if Jada was holding a grudge against me, and Pru didn't mention anything either way. Jada's spirit was safe. That was all that mattered.

The Feline Federation kept watch over Gran's house, but they made sure to check on the nexus a few times per day. Tessa had all but moved in to Dad's suite, and watching her and my father rekindle their relationship was one of the few joys I still had. My other great joy was my new, quieter life with Dan.

He was adamant that his time on the police force was over, which didn't go over well with Chief Renault or Jill. That was too bad for them, since Dan's mind was made up, and he was currently figuring out what he wanted to do with the rest of his life. We did have that nice sign for Nine Lives Investigations gathering dust in the garage, and we'd talked about going into business together. I had to admit, I liked that idea, almost as much as I liked not being the Mistress of Seers.

When I told my father I wanted to walk away from it all, I expected him to argue with me, tell me being the Mistress was my birthright, or dredge up any of the usual tired old reasons. Instead, he gave me his full support. Dad reviving his relationship with Tessa had softened him, and I wondered if he also wanted to walk away from his life as the seers' marksman. Perhaps it was time for both of us to leave the supernatural side of life, at least for a little while.

But first, I had something to do.

Three weeks after Amir's demise, Dan and I pulled up in front of the red brick apartment building my mother lived in. "So, this is it?"

"This is it." Doling out her punishment would be my final act as Mistress of Seers.

"You sure you don't need me up there?" he asked.

"I'll be fine," I replied. "Besides, if it's just me, we'll be out of here faster."

"Can't argue with that." He brought my hand to his mouth and kissed my knuckles. "Be careful, baby."

"Always."

I went up to the second floor, and knocked on my mother's door. When she opened it, her eyes nearly fell out of her head.

"Eliza," she said. "I've been meaning to reach out to you."

"I'm sure you have." I looked past her, and spotted Jada. Or rather, Sarah Allwood in Jada's body. "I'd like to talk to Sarah."

My mother was taken aback, but not Sarah. She stood, and motioned for me to enter. "Lovely to see you again, Eliza," she said. "Let's go out to the balcony."

I left my mother standing by the door, and followed Sarah out to the small concrete patio. There was a table and two chairs set out, but Sarah didn't offer me a seat. That was fine, since I wouldn't be staying for long.

"Much has changed since we last spoke," Sarah began, and I agreed with her. "When did you figure it out?"

"At first, I thought Amir was possessing Jada," I replied. "We knew she died in the fall. Honestly, I'm glad it's you instead of Amir." I eyed the visible skin on her hands, neck, and face. All of it was unmarred and appeared to be healthy. "Does olive oil really help?"

"It does," she said. "I've a few other tricks, as well. Why are you here, Eliza?"

"I've come with a peace offering," I said. "I'm content to stay out of your way, as long as you stay out of mine."

She nodded. "I can agree to that."

"Are you aware that Nathaniel has Jemima's spirit trapped in a bottle?"

"I am, and I am not pleased about it," Sarah said. "Whether or not I do anything about it remains to be seen." She watched me for a moment. "Was that bit of information your peace offering?"

"No. I'm going to cast a null spell on my mother." I looked inside the apartment, and saw Mom standing in the kitchen, staring at us and wringing her hands. "She got herself involved in a plot that hurt many people, and damn near broke the natural laws of time and death. I cannot let that go unpunished."

"I understand," Sarah said. "I wonder if Christina will ever realize how much trouble she caused."

"I'm sure she won't. I'm also not going to ask how you two wound up sharing an apartment, but regardless of how that happened, I don't want her punishment to be yours. Please, shield yourself."

"I will. Thank you for the warning, Eliza. I won't forget it."

Having struck a fragile truce with Sarah, I asked, "Do you know anything about the receptacle my mother used to give Amir her witch-craft?"

Sarah blinked slowly, like an owl. "Perhaps."

"If it's here, and you were able to secure it, you might be able to house a soul in there. Not that I'm saying you should, but such a thing might be possible."

"I understand," Sarah said. "Be well, Eliza."

"You, too." I reentered the apartment and shut the sliding glass door behind me. Even though Sarah seemed confident that she could shield herself from the spell, I didn't want to risk harming her. Enough people had been harmed already.

"Eliza," Mom began, but I held up my hand.

"I already know what you've done," I said. "You worked with one of the most despicable people I've ever known. You gave him power, and he harmed me. He harmed many people—people I love—but the worst part is that you, my own mother, worked with someone who almost killed me." My voice caught, so I swallowed my grief and continued, "I've come to understand that I am your biggest regret. The day I was born was also the worst day of your life."

"Eliza, no—"

"And I can live with that, but what you didn't just hurt me," I continued. "You caused a catastrophe. An actual catastrophe."

"Eliza, please," she said. "Let me explain."

"Your explanations don't matter. The actions were yours, and now you will face the consequences." I withdrew the glass vial that held the null spell Tess and Jacob had crafted together, and threw it at my mother's feet.

"That's a null spell," I said, as the spell's tendrils wound around Mom's legs and arms. "It will bind your powers. Congratulations, you're a mortal now."

"You can't do this," Mom shrieked. "You can't take away an entire part of me, not now when I've finally learned how to use it!"

I glanced at Sarah on the balcony. She shrugged. Maybe I did want to know how they'd ended up sharing an apartment, but that would have to wait for another time.

"I can do this," I said. "Seers hold the line between life and death. Through your actions that line was blurred. As Mistress of Seers, I hold you accountable."

"What is making me powerless supposed to accomplish?"

"It's not supposed to accomplish anything. This is a punishment," I said. "Be glad your witchcraft is all you're losing."

As my mother tried to wipe the spell off of her, I left the apartment. Saying goodbye felt unnecessary, since all Mom had ever wanted was to be rid of me. How ironic that her punishment for dabbling with life and death and time would lead to her heart's desire: true mortality.

I got into the car, and let Dan gather me against him. "How was it?"

"Awful, but a bearable awful." I pulled back, and placed my hand on his cheek. He hadn't shaved earlier, and I liked the feel of his prickly whiskers against my palm. "I would like to request that we do something not awful now. A lot of not awful, if you don't mind."

"I can do that." He started the car, and pulled away from the building. "While you were inside, I got a text from Alicia. She's still working out the details, but everyone's excited to meet you."

I smiled, and stared straight ahead. Even though I was leaving my life as Mistress of Seers behind, one more terrifying act loomed on the horizon.

Dan was taking me home to meet his family.

Eli's next task—meeting Dan's family—might be her hardest yet. Read all about it in their next adventure, Mistletoe. Keep scrolling for a sneak peek at chapter one!

Mistletoe: Chapter One

"We have been driving forever," I whined.

"We have not." Dan didn't take his eyes off the road, which was smart. We were about halfway through our trip to Queens, and this leg involved driving on a historic stretch of road in Connecticut. This historically significant road was extremely narrow, packed with twists and turns, and had a bazillion on ramps so other cars were constantly being fired at us like the silver orbs in a pinball game.

"We'll be there soon," Dan continued. "Hour, hour and a half, maybe. Two hours, tops."

He reached over and set his hand on my knee, and I did my best to keep my grumbling to myself. The entire reason we were heading to Queens was so Dan could introduce me to his family. It was also the first time he'd gone home in a few years, so that made this trip stressful for both of us.

As if that wasn't enough, this was Christmas week, and Dan's family was all about the holidays. Word on the street was his father might dress up as Santa.

"How long has it been since you went back home for Christmas?" I asked.

"Four—no, five years," he replied. "It was just too much, what with everyone else getting married and having kids. Don't get me wrong, I was happy for all of them, but I needed to find my own place in the world."

"I get it." My life had quite literally been laid out for me from the day I was born. As the scion of the Moore line, my destiny was to become Mistress of Seers. I finally accepted the position a few months ago, but after some time traveling and reality altering situations that escalated from annoying to awful, I walked away from my birthright. That meant no one was leading the seers, but you know what? They're all grownups. They can figure it out.

As for me, now I'm figuring out my new life with Dan. He also recently left his career as a police officer, and we'd gone into business together in my newly reformed private detective agency, Nine Lives Investigations. So far, all of our cases had been boring, and I liked that. We'd already had enough excitement to last us the rest of our lives.

There was also the fact that we were sort of, kind of married, and as far as I knew Dan had yet to share that detail with his parents.

"Have you warned anyone about our handfasting?" I asked. "Or are we just going to walk in wearing matching rings and see how long it takes them to notice?"

"They know."

I did an actual double take. "They do? Since when?"

"I told Alicia," he began, "and she told Ma. Once you tell my mother something everyone knows, and the fastest way to get news to Ma is to tell Alicia."

Alicia was the youngest sibling, and the one Dan talked to the most often, probably because he was the second youngest. Solidarity against the older kids and all. "Have you talked to your parents directly?"

"About us?"

"About anything."

"No."

If he hadn't been driving, I would have smacked him. "Dan. You talk to your mother all the time, but you never mentioned a fricken' serious relationship? What the hell are we walking into?"

"Ma doesn't like to learn things over the phone," he said. "She likes to get news in person. That's why we tell Alicia stuff, so she can deliver it to Ma. And my dad doesn't use the phone."

"What? How does he communicate?"

Dan shrugged. "He's old school."

"The telephone was invented in the eighteen seventies, and I'm pretty sure your father was born afterward!"

His gaze slid toward me, then back to the road. "Was yours?"

"Actually, yes." My father was only one hundred and seventeen years old, of which Dan was quite aware. "Seriously, will they be okay with us dropping all of this on them at once?"

"They will be," Dan said. "It really doesn't matter what they've already heard. My parents aren't going to form an opinion about you one way or the other until they meet you in person, and see how you react."

"React to what?"

"Everything."

Almost three hours later, we pulled up in front of Dan's grandmother's house in Queens. It was a split-level ranch, and according to Dan, this was where his entire extended family congregated over the holidays. The family was so big the house had two kitchens, one on the first floor where his mother cooked, and one in the basement for his grandmother.

"If it's your gran's house, why does she get stuck cooking in the basement?" I asked, as we got out of the car.

"The downstairs kitchen is the better one," Dan replied. "Nonna holds court down there like an empress. You'll see."

I gazed up at the house. It was nowhere near as old or as big as the place I grew up in, but it was imposing in its own way. "I can't wait."

"Come on, babe." Dan took my hand. "They're gonna love you. Promise."

We left our luggage in the car, since we'd gotten a hotel room instead of staying in the family home. According to Dan he'd already spent plenty of years fighting his brothers for equal time in the bathroom, and he was ready to move on. I wondered if him coming here was almost too much for him to handle, and he'd booked the hotel as a way for him to duck out when he needed to.

Dan opened the front door, and yelled, "Ma, Dad? Nonna? We're here!"

I expected a crowded room packed with unfamiliar faces. Instead, the house was dead quiet. "Is anyone home?" I asked.

"Someone's always here," he replied, then we heard footsteps on the stairs. A few moments later, a petite brunette woman burst into the front room and leapt into Dan's arms.

"I missed you so much, Danny," she said. "You got here just in the nick of time!"

"What happened?" Dan asked, then he remembered me. "Alicia, this is Eliza. Eli, this is my younger sister."

"Youngest sister," Alicia amended, then she extricated herself from Dan and faced me. She clasped her hands over her heart and grinned. "Eliza, I am so happy to finally meet you! Danny's told me all about you!"

"Has he?" I asked, wondering just how well informed his family was.

"You know how Danny's a chatterbox," Alicia said, "but he didn't mention how beautiful you are."

"I said she's gorgeous," Dan said.

"Not this gorgeous," Alicia shot back, then she pulled me into the biggest bear hug. "Aww, I'm so happy you're here!"

"I'm happy too." I patted Alicia's back, while Dan grinned at us. "You said we got here in the nick of time?"

Alicia stepped back, and said, "Oh, it's awful. Ma and Nonna got in a fight, and Carmelo and Joey took all the kids to the park, and I don't know what's going to happen."

Dan crossed his arms over his chest. "What's the fight about?"

"Nonna wants to make fried calamari tonight, but Ma wants to have it on Christmas Eve."

"You can't have calamari on both days?" I asked, emphasis on the you. There was no way I was eating fried squid bits for dinner. Dan and Alicia both looked at me like I'd grown a new head.

"Both days?" Alicia shook her head. "That won't work."

"Will it be a calamari catastrophe?" I asked, and Alicia giggled.

"Danny, I like her. Come on, I need you to smooth things over with Ma while I show Eliza the wine cabinet."

Before I could protest, Alicia looped her arm with mine and led me deeper into the house. As we passed the stairs, I heard a scream come from the floor above. Since Alicia didn't react, I assumed it was a spirit, and kept a straight face. Dan, however, heard it too.

"What was that?" Dan demanded. "Who's upstairs?"

"No one," Alicia replied. "Everyone's in the dining room."

Dan nodded, then he looked at me. If he and I both heard the scream, but no one else did, that confirmed it was a spirit. I sighed, and realized my seer abilities were needed right here in his Nonna's house.

Merry Christmas to me.

Mistletoe will be available everywhere December 1, 2024.

About The Author

Jennifer Allis Provost is a native New Englander who lives in a sprawling colonial along with her beautiful and precocious twins, a dog that thinks she's a kangaroo, a parrot, a junkyard cat, and a wonderful husband who never forgets to buy ice cream. As a child, she read anything and everything she could get her hands on, including a set of encyclopedias, but fantasy was always her favorite. She spends her days drinking vast amounts of coffee, arguing with her computer, and avoiding any and all domestic behavior.

Find Jenn on the web here: http://authorjenniferallisprovost.com/

For up to the minute sale notifications, follow her on Bookbub here: https://www.bookbub.com/profile/jennifer-allis-provost
   For exclusive content, follow her on Patreon: https://www.patreon.com/jenniferallisprovost/
   Friend her on Facebook: http://www.facebook.com/jennallis
   Follow her on Instagram: @jenniferaprovost
   Happy reading!

ALSO BY JENNIFER ALLIS PROVOST

The Chronicles of Parthalan, a six volume epic fantasy (and one short story collection)

Heir to the Sun

The Virgin Queen

Rise of the Deva'shi

Pieces of Parthalan: Six All-New Stories From The Land Of Parthalan

Golem

Elfsong

Sunfall

The Copper Legacy, a four book urban fantasy

Copper Girl

Copper Ravens

Copper Veins

Copper Princess

A duology based in the Copper world:

Redemption

Salvation

Poison Garden, an urban fantasy filled with seers, witches, and one seriously hot detective:

Belladonna

Oleander

Bleeding Hearts

Thornapple

Wolfsbane

Mistletoe

Mandrake

Gallowglass, an urban fantasy set in Scotland and New York

Gallowglass

Walker

Homecoming

Winter's Queen, an urban fantasy set in Scotland and Elphame

Touch of Frost

Giant's Daughter

Elphame's Queen

Merrowkin, an urban fantasy set in Ireland above and below

Merrowkin

Death's Door

Manannán's Pearl

Changes, a contemporary romance

Changing Teams

Changing Scenes

Changing Fate

Changing Dates